TIBOR: WINTER'S RAGE

A BYRON TIBOR NOVEL

SEAN BLACK
STEVEN SAVILE

SBD

ABOUT THE BOOK

Still hunted by the government he fought for, Special Forces veteran Byron Tibor has taken refuge in the remote Appalachian town of Winter's Rage.

But Byron's peaceful existence is about to be shattered by the arrival of a troubled young woman on the run from a violent drug cartel.

Three killers are looking for revenge. But they haven't reckoned with running into Byron Tibor.

As a snow storm cuts off the small town from the rest of the world, the scene is set for a bloody confrontation.

1

It was the last house on the left at the end of a lonely dirt track. Tar-paper shingles flapped in the wind where they'd torn free of their nails, exposing the rotten wood underneath. The slats on the shutters had slipped, leaving strips of shadow across the sun-blistered paint. A long-abandoned climbing frame lay on its side in the overgrown yard, gently rusting in the thick air.

At the other end of the track, an old Cadillac Deville rolled slowly forward, its tires churning up the muddy surface. The air-conditioning was broken. It blew hot air into the car. The leather seats burned where they came into contact with bare skin. A C90 cassette jammed in the tape deck offered an endless loop of chart hits from the late 1980s.

Inside the Caddy sat Caleb, Dale and Henry. Blood brothers, but not in the way most people understood the term.

Henry, the guy in the backseat, leaned forward. "You ever hear about the Fukarwi tribe?"

The driver, Caleb, grunted something inaudible.

"Turn that shit down and listen. You might just learn something," said Henry.

Caleb reached over and twisted the volume dial. The music fell away to a buzz.

Henry scooted forward a few more inches. "They're out wandering the wilderness, see, looking for a land to call their own. Day and night. Always looking. Across mountains and valleys and endless plains. Through forests and across oceans. Always looking for a place to call their own." He lowered his voice. "If you're quiet enough, you can hear 'em, shouting out miserably, 'We're the Fukarwi.'"

The two men riding up front, Caleb and Dale, looked at each other, nonplussed, as Henry laughed at his own poor excuse for a joke. "You don't get it? We're the Fukarwi? *Where the fuck are we?*"

"That's hilarious, Henry," said Dale, his expression deadpan.

Caleb braked abruptly. The Caddy lurched to a halt. "This is the place."

Henry was first out, walking up the weed-raddled block-paved path to the screen door. The mesh was torn in three places. He pulled open the screen and banged on the white wood. "Little pig, little pig," he yelled, lips close to the door. "You know what comes next, Eddie."

Dale and Caleb headed to the back, ready to put an end to any thoughts of escape the home-owner might have. Henry heard movement inside. He listened until he was sure it wasn't someone coming to open the door.

"We aren't selling anything today, Eddie. No Bibles, no Mary Kay," he shouted. "This is just a friendly visit. Why don't you do yourself a favor and open up?"

More movement. Frantic. Scrabbling around.

"I just wanna talk to you, Eddie. I'm looking for an old friend. We've been told you're good with finding people who don't want to be found. That's all. Nothing to get your panties in a bunch over. So why don't you come on out, and let's talk?"

Henry heard glass breaking at the back. Either Dale or Caleb was helping things along. They were never the most patient people. Henry shrugged, world weary.

Stepping back, he rocked on his heels, planted a foot on the stoop and, using his body for leverage, kicked the door open. The wood around the lock splintered beneath the impact and the whole thing buckled as the metal tongue tore free of the hasp and the door burst inward. It bounced back on its hinges, almost cannoning into his face.

He stepped inside. In front of him, the silhouette of a man, presumably Eddie, was making a break for the back door. Behind Eddie the larger-than-life silhouette of Dale, backlit in the rear doorway.

"You might want to stay where you are," said Henry. There was no need to shout anymore.

Eddie did as he was told. He turned around, shoulders slumped, body language screaming, *Don't hurt me*. Pitiful.

"You know who we are, Eddie?"

"No," Eddie said, shaking his head. The darkness of the interior did little to hide his panic. He couldn't go forward, he couldn't go back, but the fight-or-flight instinct was still hammering at his brain, yelling at him to run.

Henry took another step forward. "That's probably for the best, if we're being honest with each other. We can be honest, right? I feel like we're old friends. I've been looking for you for a long time, Eddie. Dale started to call you a unicorn last week, he was so sure you didn't exist, see. But I knew you were out here. And I knew that eventually I'd find the road that'd bring me to your door. Nice place you've got yourself."

The kitchen was a mess of unwashed dishes, open cans and boxes of ready-meals. The most valuable thing in there was a coffee-maker that belonged in a much nicer kitchen. It was thick with a scum of grounds. All of the cups lined up on the shelf above, with kitsch gift-shop messages, like *World's Number One Dad* and *I Hate Mondays, Tuesdays, Wednesdays, Thursdays and Fridays*, were cracked and browned. "Boy or girl?" Henry asked, nodding at the mugs.

"Girls. Two."

"Nice. I like girls," he said.

There was something in the way he spoke that caused Eddie to say, "They live with their mom."

"Lucky for them, I'd say, given the state of this place, Eddie. Come on, let's go through to the living room, be civilized about this. Sit down, have a talk, man to man. You wanna do that?"

"Do I have a choice?" said Eddie, already walking toward the front room.

Henry followed him through. The furniture was arranged around a big old television set. The walls were painted brothel red, and fairy lights hung above nicotine-yellow curtains—no doubt his kids' idea of decorating. There was an ashtray overflowing with cigarette butts and a half-empty bottle of bourbon beside it.

"Take a seat," said Henry. "Now, this friend of mine," he fished a creased-up photograph out of his pocket and held it in front of Eddie's face, "you'd tell me if you'd seen her, right?"

Eddie nodded, clearly doing his best to appear eager to help.

"That you telling me you've seen her? Or that you'd tell me if you had? It's mighty confusing when you don't use your words, Eddie. Help me out here."

"I'd tell you," Eddie said.

"But you know and you're not telling me. So that right there's a lie."

Dale and Caleb came into the room. Caleb stayed by the door.

Dale, a stick-insect of a man, sank into a battered leather La-Z-Boy chair that swallowed him whole, crossed his hands behind his head and kicked out the foot rest. "You really wanna do what Henry says. Otherwise this ain't gonna end well for you, friend. He's been in a shitty mood all day, looking for someone to take it out on."

"Shut up, Dale."

"See what I mean?" said Dale.

"Take a good look at the photo, Eddie. Really rack your brain to remember her face and where you might have seen it before. We called her Elspeth, but turns out that ain't her real name. Take your time."

Eddie stared at the photograph.

"You see, Eddie," continued Henry, "Elspeth here, she screwed our employer, and not in a good way. Now, we intend to have words.

Nothing physical. We're not monsters. I know you know what her real name is, and I know you know where she is. I also know that you're gonna tell me. It's only a matter of time. Thing is, there's something you should know. I really don't mind if you get hurt between my asking and your answering. In fact, if I'm being honest with you, I'd probably rather it went down with a little blood. There's something immensely satisfying about that. So, how about we try this one last time, before the bleeding starts? Who is she, Eddie, and more to the point of the matter, where is she?"

"I don't know."

"Oh, Eddie, Eddie, Eddie. This is so unnecessary."

"I ain't lying. I don't know."

Henry suddenly brightened. "Hey, mind if I ask you something else, Eddie?"

Eddie didn't. He was glad to be off the current subject. "No. Go right ahead."

"You have a toolbox around here?" said Henry. He already knew the answer. He had spied it earlier.

"What?"

"A toolbox. You know, it's a box you put your tools in. Hammers, pliers, that sort of stuff. You have one?"

"Why?"

"The door I busted. You don't think I'm going to leave it like that, do you? What kind of man you take me for?"

Eddie didn't like this, but he answered, "It's through in the hall."

Henry turned to the man in the doorway. "Fetch it for me, Caleb."

"Gotcha," Caleb said, and disappeared.

"Who is she, Eddie?" Henry asked again, picking up from where he had left off.

"I don't know who she is, man—I swear to you. I swear. I don't know."

This time Henry didn't respond.

Caleb returned a minute later with a rusty old toolbox. Inside were all manner of neglected items. He picked out the hammer.

"Get out of the chair, Eddie," instructed Henry. "Kneel on the floor at my feet like a dog."

"Thought you said you were going to fix my door," said Eddie, although he hadn't been dumb enough to believe it.

"I lied," said Henry. "Now, get down there for me, boy."

His eyes never leaving Henry, his hands trembling, Eddie did as he was told, getting down on all fours.

Henry stood over him, slowly shaking his head. "I suppose if I told you to bark like a dog you'd do it, too, wouldn't you?"

Eddie nodded.

"But you still won't tell me her name?"

"I don't know who she is, I swear to God. I'd tell you if I knew."

"I want to believe you, Eddie. I really do. Problem is, I know you're a liar, so let's see if we can't help you make friends with the truth, shall we? Caleb, Dale, come over here and hold Eddie's hands for me."

Caleb and Dale crouched beside Eddie, each grabbing hold of one of his wrists while Henry rooted through the toolbox. When he found his prize, a couple of rusty six-inch nails, he hunkered down in front of Eddie. He rested the point of the nail against the ridge of bone that ran down the back of Eddie's right hand from the middle finger to the wrist. "Her name, Eddie."

Snot bubbles blew from Eddie's nose as he whimpered and begged, tears streaming down his face. He didn't answer.

Henry drove the nail through his outstretched hand, hammering the head again and again until five inches of rust red metal were buried in the floorboards, fixing Eddie's hand to the floor.

Eddie's screams were awful.

"What's her name, Eddie?"

Now Eddie couldn't talk even if he'd wanted to. He gasped and blubbered and choked, trying to form words where none would come.

Caleb and Dale struggled to keep him still as Henry hammered the second nail through his other hand. It took six blows to drive it deep into the floorboards. There was a surprising amount of blood.

"Rae—" Eddie couldn't finish the word. He choked on air, tried to swallow.

"Spit it out, Eddie. What's her name? Last time I'm asking nicely," he said.

The kneeling man looked up at him. "Raelynn," he finally managed. The name came out in a strangled rush. "Raelynn Cardiman."

"See? That wasn't so hard, was it, Eddie? Now where do we find the lovely Raelynn?"

"I don't know. I swear to God I don't know. I've told you everything. Please. Please. Believe me."

"I do believe you, Eddie," Henry said.

He reached around for the man's belt and started unbuckling it.

"Dale, you wanna do him first?"

"Oh, please, God," said Eddie.

"Fine," Henry said, standing straight again. He breathed deeply, just the once, steeling himself before swinging the hammer in a brutal arc. The flathead shattered the bones in Eddie's face. Henry swung again and again, smashing the hammer into his teeth and temple and kept on swinging until there was no resistance. It took less than ten seconds to end the man's life.

Done, gasping from the exertion, Henry wiped his bangs out of his eyes and looked down at the body. "Who said torture don't work?"

2

Winter's Rage, West Virginia
   Population: one more than last month

THE ONE BEING ME: actual name Byron Tibor, but to the people here, Mike Roberts, a burned-out computer programmer fleeing the relentless grind of Silicon Valley. A man looking for somewhere peaceful and off the beaten track to gather himself.

As with all good assumed identities, the core of it was true. Mike and I were both looking to escape the wider world. The difference was that I needed to be somewhere out of the way because the state wanted me dead. The same state for which I had spent the best part of my life fighting, killing and bleeding.

After a mental breakdown had left me unable to continue my duties as a special-forces-trained lone operative, the government had doubled down on their investment. Using cutting-edge neuroscience to tackle my PTSD (post-traumatic stress disorder), they had left me in a ghost world between humanity and technology. In their language, I was 'augmented', but the enhanced abilities had come with a price.

Unable to control what they had created, they'd decided to cut their losses and eliminate me. I'd had other ideas. Now I was here. Up on a cabin roof in West Virginia, hammering six-inch nails into two-by-fours, securing them before the structure's gable beam could be rolled into place.

It was backbreaking work. But it was good, honest, backbreaking work. I'd missed it.

As I drove the last nail home, Wayne, my septuagenarian boss, clambered up the ladder to join me. We leaned back against the huge cylindrical crossbeam that would form the gable and looked up at the clear blue sky. It was hard to believe that in less than a month this place would be buried under a thick blanket of snow. He handed me a cold beer. I cracked the bottle top off against the edge of one of the timbers beside me and swallowed deeply. There was nothing in the world as good as cold beer on a warm day.

"Sure beats all day in the office hunched over a computer, eh?" the old man said.

I nodded my agreement and we chatted easily for a couple of minutes, Wayne pointing out a Loggerhead Shrike's nest in a red cedar across the way, before we returned to the task at hand, rolling the huge wooden beam into place.

My hands were slick with sweat and the condensation from the bottle. The maneuver was precarious at best, the timber beam easily five times our combined weight, but I wanted it done before we called it quits for the day. We needed to keep pace if we were going to stand any chance of beating the weather.

Despite his age, Wayne was in pretty good shape. He had the wiry muscles of someone used to making his own way in the world, growing his own food, keeping his own livestock and now building his own cabin. As far as lives went, there was plenty to envy about Wayne Cardiman's, even if he didn't know it.

I concentrated all of my attention on the next big push, hoping it'd be enough to drop the beam into place. Because of that, I *almost* missed the sharp crack of betrayal as the wood beneath Wayne's right foot sheared free of the nails holding it in place. A burned-out computer programmer from Silicon Valley would have mistaken it for some natural sound out in the trees. Luckily for him, I was a liar.

I had a split second to process what had happened and react.

I saw Wayne's head turn bright yellow, fear overwhelming him. It was instinctive. His body reacted to the danger before his mind had finished processing it. That was what saved him. It gave me half a second's advantage that a normal man wouldn't have had.

I couldn't get to him and keep hold of the huge beam. It was physically impossible.

If I let go of the beam it would roll back, potentially crushing him, and if I didn't, the unfinished roof would give way beneath his feet and he'd have to take his chances with mortality. It wasn't a long way down, but it was far enough, and for a seventy-year-old man, falling backwards, the odds weren't exactly stacked in his favor. Damned if I did, most certainly damned if I didn't.

I couldn't let myself think. Thinking led to indecision. Throwing every ounce of strength that I could muster into the move, I drove the beam up and up, straining as it rose toward the tipping point where it finally fell into the recess carved into the joints at the roof's apex, and pivoted, reaching out with my right hand to grab at Wayne even as the roof gave way beneath his feet.

He fell backwards, arms windmilling comically as he lost his balance. And then he was falling. My hand clamped around his wrist and locked hard.

There was a moment, a long, sliding second between one heartbeat and the next, when his momentum and gravity combined, and I thought I'd go over the edge with him, but I was stronger than that. A lot stronger. Government-issue strong. I kept my footing, and the old man hung there, falling without falling, sheer terror in his eyes as he stared back at me, sure he was dead, just waiting for the impact to turn the lights out, then gratitude and disbelief as I hauled him back onto solid timbers.

His foot caught my empty bottle and sent it tumbling over the edge where the broken timbers had been. It shattered on impact.

"You okay?" I asked.

Wayne nodded, but the way he looked at me had changed. "I'll live," he said.

3

Maeve Cruikshank's was the single restaurant in Winter's Rage, and that was only if you considered "restaurant" a fluid term. We walked the mile and a half from the cabin in companionable silence. That's one of the things that's hardest to learn about life: sometimes it's as good to share the silences as it is to share the words that fill them. We could have taken Wayne's pick-up truck, but sometimes it's better to walk and clear the head.

Wayne didn't walk like an old man. He wasn't taking in the scenery as he shuffled along. He moved with purpose—but, then, food was waiting at the other end and we'd worked up a fierce appetite.

Way, way off in the distance loomed the spectral white peaks. The mountains were always there, wherever you looked, calling you home. The sun set redly behind them. There were no streetlights, so once it was gone we were walking in the dark and the transition from day to full night was fast, shockingly so. Less than twenty minutes from full light of day to full dark of night. Birds perched on the wires strung across the road; they made a change from the sneakers that decorated so many other telephone wires in bigger cities.

We reached the town limits, crossing the road. There was no sidewalk here, but that didn't matter much when you considered that there was little foot traffic either. The twin chimneys of an old plant dominated the horizon, once proud, now beaten into submission.

Winter's Rage was laid out in a familiar geometric pattern of Main Street with four parallel smaller roads, two on either side, the rich to the right, the poor to the left where they lived in the shadow of the plant, with the factory and its yards the natural balance to the crystal blue lake on the other side of Main. Nature and industry in delicate balance. All aspects of life were here. Or had been once upon a time.

Main Street itself consisted of less than a dozen store fronts. There was a grocery, a hardware and animal-feed place, two bars, one at either end of the strip, Maeve's diner, a couple of clothes shops, one catering only for women, the other unisex, a beauty salon and the sheriff's office. There was enough to get by, but if any serious supplies were needed there was a Walmart thirty miles away where most people did their shopping.

A middle-aged couple emerged from Maeve's, waved to Wayne, then wandered off in the direction of the school house. There were only thirty kids of school age in Winter's Rage and they shared two teachers between them. When they hit thirteen the bus rounded them up and ferried them two towns over to the local high school. Like I said, this place was a backwater, but it was just what I needed for a while.

A little bell chimed over our heads as we went into Maeve's. Inside there were seven tables, booths with red leather seats, and four stools against the counter. It was rush-hour: there were eight other diners.

"Evening, sugar," the matronly Maeve said, bustling toward us with her laminated menus. They had photos of the kitchen's various staples, which was never a good sign, but after a month in Winter's Rage I'd eaten my way through most of the dishes, and they were better than anything I'd have rustled up in my own kitchen, had I had the inclination, and that was good enough for me.

"What can I get you, boys?"

"Coffee, as black and as strong as you've got," I said, taking my seat at one of the empty booths.

"I'll have an ice tea, plenty sweet," the old man said.

She didn't need to ask—we'd been having the same combination of drinks every night for the last few weeks. "You got it," she said, with a smile.

I liked Maeve. She reminded me of better days. Simpler times. She had a kitchen cloth draped over her belt, red check that had never seen a dish, and wore soft-soled shoes because she was on her feet all day. Her hair was cut shoulder-length, dirty blond with a touch of dye to keep it looking fresh, thanks to the beauty salon down the street. She was maybe twenty years older than me, so right there at that table in her little restaurant we pretty much represented three stages of life. The booth over by the window had two kids, both pre-teen, and their parents so between us every age of man was present and correct.

"What's good today?" I asked.

"Everything, honey. You know that," she said. "We just got in some nice juicy cuts of prime rib. Or I could get Benny to rustle you up a couple of bloody steaks."

"Sounds perfect, medium rare," I said.

"Coming right up. Wayne?"

"I think I'll have a salad. Something nice and green."

Maeve chuckled. "Two steaks it is, be right back with your drinks." With that she was gone.

The coffee hit the spot. Other diners came and went. Outside it got darker than dark.

Wayne talked a bit about his life. He had good stories. He hadn't always been some reclusive hermit living out in the wilds of West Virginia. Once upon a time he'd had more of a city life, the nine-to-five grind schlepping into an office, saying, yes, sir, no, sir, three bags full, sir. Now, he joked, he'd come home to die.

4

At another diner, on the road between Florida and West Virginia, Raelynn Cardiman sat with her two kids and their not-so-happy meal. They had a plate of fries between them. It was all Raelynn could afford.

Her skin itched. She twitched. It felt like everyone was looking at her, judging her for failing her kids. She wiped the back of a hand across her nose. She hadn't showered in two days. They'd been running. She didn't have enough for a motel room, so they'd been sleeping rough. Now the money had run out.

She'd thought about ordering decent meals, filling their bellies, then just telling the waitress she couldn't pay, but that was short-term thinking. That would bring the cops. And then she'd be in deep trouble.

She looked around the diner. There was no one she could turn to for help. Not that she was thinking of begging.

"Eat up," she told the kids. Anna, the older of the two, pecked like a bird at the plate. One fry at a time. Nibbled to draw out the meal as long as possible, sipping at the plastic beaker of tap water to wash each bite down.

Chase, her seven-year-old son, had a stubborn cowlick that

wouldn't flatten down no matter how much spit she used. He squirmed in his chair, wanting to play with the little plastic toy that came with the kid's meal that she couldn't afford to buy him. He didn't understand. It wasn't his fault. He was too young to grasp just how much trouble they were in.

Through the window she saw a big rig roll into the truck stop.

It was three days since she'd scored. The itch was getting worse. The skin along her forearms burned. She dragged her fingernails across them, then saw the disapproving look the short-order cook sent her way. She bit back on the urge to ask him what the hell he was looking at. The last thing they needed was her smart mouth getting them thrown out into the night. It was cold out there, and getting colder.

A few minutes later a new truck pulled past the window. The driver came in and ordered himself a breakfast, extra grits, eggs over easy. He was wearing a ball cap, a grimy polo shirt, and jeans. Rolls of belly fat folded over his belt. He hadn't shaved for a week and he smelled like he lived in his cab.

He was perfect.

She watched him eat.

He mopped up the egg yolk with chunks of bread. He saw her looking at him and offered a lascivious grin as the yellow dribbled down his chin into his beard.

She nodded, her eyes darting to the door.

He seemed not to understand, and she couldn't exactly spell it out.

"Stay here, look after your brother," Raelynn told Anna.

"Where are you going?" Anna asked.

"Never mind that now. Just be a good girl and keep an eye on Chase until I come back."

She nodded. "Okay, Mama."

Raelynn eased herself out of the booth and walked over toward the door. She looked back over her shoulder. The trucker was staring at her ass. She nodded, smiled, and pushed the door open. When she was outside, she crooked a finger and beckoned him to follow her out into the night air.

He didn't need asking twice.

He wiped off his chin, screwed his napkin up and dropped it on the table, put a handful of notes beside his half-empty plate, and headed out.

They didn't say anything as they walked to his cab. He helped her inside.

"A hundred," she said.

"Fifty," he said.

"Eighty."

"Seventy."

"Okay," she said, because beggars couldn't be choosers, and a couple of minutes later he was inside her, and less than ten minutes after that she was back in the diner, smelling of him and hating herself as she ordered the first decent meal her kids had had since they'd started running.

She had enough change in her pocket for a room tonight and breakfast. That had to be chalked up as a win.

"You okay, Mama?" Anna asked, as the waitress put a greasy burger in front of her.

Chase had his plastic toy. A colorful superhero with a plastic cape. He was a bit old for it, but that didn't seem to bother him. He made the little action figure fly over his plate half a dozen times before he took the first bite.

"I'm fine, baby," Raelynn said.

It was getting harder to ignore the cravings deep in her belly. It was like a tumble-drier in there, everything she'd eaten churning over and over. All she wanted to do was score her next fix, to forget about what it had felt like with that fat trucker on top of her, but she couldn't do that, not to the kids. They needed her, and she was damned if she was going to let them down again. They were the only good thing in her life.

"Eat up. We're going home."

5

The call came before we'd finished eating.

Wayne made his apologies and picked up. He dabbed at his lips with a napkin a couple of times, said, "Uh-huh . . . Uh-huh, uh-huh," and "When?"

It wasn't the most in-depth conversation, but he smiled with every grunt. It took less than a minute to change everything.

"That was Rae," he said. Raelynn, his daughter. "She's coming home."

I nodded. It wasn't new information. Raelynn was why we were breaking our backs to get the cabin done before the weather turned. She was going to need a roof over her head. Somewhere for her and the kids.

My understanding was that Wayne had had her late in life. His wife had been almost forty at the time, and he'd been older. The oldest dad in Lamaze, the oldest dad at preschool, the oldest dad pretty much everywhere they went. It hadn't been an easy pregnancy. These weren't the kinds of things guys talked about, but when you worked together all day conversations took some strange turns, and he wanted to talk. So I let him. We traded life stories, his real, mine invented.

"No," he said. "She's already on the road. She'll be here in a couple of days."

"We're not going to have the place ready in time," I said, stating the obvious.

"We can do anything we put our minds to," he said.

"What were you before you retired? A motivational speaker?"

He grinned and winked at me. I really did like the old man. That was going to make things harder down the line. Caring about people always did.

"You know me, Mike. I'm an optimist."

"Well, don't go getting any ideas about working through. I've got my eye on a slice of Maeve's apple pie, then a couple of brews over at Drew's before I call it a night."

"You youngsters sure know how to live the high life," the old man said.

"If only you knew," I said, thinking of all the places across the world I'd drowned mine or someone else's sorrows. "Maeve," I called over to the counter, where the woman was pretending she wasn't listening, "how about a slice of that delicious pie you've got, and some more coffee?"

"Coming right up, handsome."

"I think she's taken a shine to you." The old man grinned.

"They all do," I told him.

"Heartbreaker," he said.

"It's why I live alone."

He had nothing to say to that.

6

The Cadillac Deville rolled slowly along the edge of the gutter. Inside, the three men, Caleb, Dale and Henry, scanned the street. There was a liquor store directly across from them, which was ironic, given what was going on inside the old Quaker Hall in front of them. A meeting, and not of the faithful.

Henry watched the addicts file in ready to stand up at the front of their junkie congregation and profess themselves sober for a day or a week or a month.

"What are we doing here?" Caleb asked, prodding at his teeth with a wooden pick that snapped as he rooted around. His incessant pick-pick-picking had his gums bleeding.

"What's the one thing we know about the delightful Raelynn?"

"That she's got a mighty fine ass on her, ripe like a peach," Dale offered from the driver's seat.

"What's the other thing we know about her?" Henry tried again.

"She's a junkie whore," Caleb said.

"And that, my friend, is why we're here. Where better to look for a junkie whore than in a crowd of junkies who're going to stand up there one after the other and tell their life stories?"

"Like taking candy from a stranger," Dale said.

"A baby," Caleb corrected him.

"Who you callin' a baby?"

And so it went.

"Park up, Dale. We'll make ourselves a new friend on the way out."

Dale did as he was told, putting the Caddy into park and killing the idling engine. He reached for the radio, but without the engine turning over there was no power. He looked across at Caleb, then back at Henry for permission to turn the engine over again.

"Knock yourself out," Henry told him, and a couple of seconds later they were suffering through Wang Chung's "Dance Hall Days." It was relentlessly happy, a stark juxtaposition to the world outside their window.

A hobo shuffled out of the liquor store with a bagged-up bottle that was at his lips before he'd made it to the corner. Wang Chung gave way to Strawberry Switchblade, who faded into Steven 'Tin Tin' Duffy telling them to kiss him with their mouths.

"Like you could kiss him with anything else, stupid song," Caleb said, staring out of the window.

There was nothing worse than waiting. He didn't do it well.

Henry was better at it. He'd learned patience inside. Good things were worth waiting for. Like the yearning that made the junkie's score all the sweeter.

Karel Fialka kept urging them to tell him what they saw and some sweet-voiced kid kept saying, 'The A-Team.' It was enough to have him clawing at the doors.

Mercifully they were spared too much more of the saccharine-sweet synth pop rubbish as the big old iron door of the Quaker Hall opened and the first of the recently confessed addicts filed out with their chips and twelve steps to follow.

Henry watched them go, like animals, two by two. He knew what he was looking for: one of them on their own, separated from the flock.

It didn't take long.

"Her," he said, tapping Dale on the bony shoulder.

The stick insect of a man moved the gear shift into drive and they rolled off the gutter, inching out to crawl along the curb beside the woman. She quickened her pace, just a little.

Caleb rolled down his window, and leaning out a little, smiled and called out, "Excuse me, miss?" Doing his best not to sound like the monster they all knew lived beneath his skin.

She turned, still walking, black curls falling across her face as she leaned ever so slightly to see if she recognized the man talking to her.

"We're looking for an old friend. She lives round here."

"Not sure I can help you," the woman said, not realizing that the worst thing she could possibly have done was talk.

Victims never understood that.

"We thought she might have been at the meeting," Caleb went on.

The woman stopped walking, and looked back at the Quaker Hall with its dark windows. It was amazing how quickly the place had emptied out. Or maybe it wasn't so amazing. How many people would willingly linger around a building full of addicts?

The woman shrugged. "What's her name?"

"Raelynn," Henry said from the backseat.

"Can't say I recognize it," the woman said. "Sorry."

"I've got a picture," Henry said, taking the creased photo from his back pocket and passing it forward to Caleb, who held it up, but didn't pass it out through the window. He wanted the woman to come closer to get a better look.

She did.

Everything happened so quickly after that.

Caleb's hand snaked out and grabbed a handful of her black curls, pulling her face down toward the window. She slapped at his wrist and pulled back but his grip was vicelike. No matter how fiercely she fought him, he wasn't letting go.

Henry got out of the car. He walked up behind her and punched her hard in the base of the spine. Her legs buckled, and as she tried to rear up and fight free of Caleb's grip, he yanked her forward again and her forehead cannoned off the top of the window frame. The impact staggered her. Henry's second punch dropped her.

He hooked his arms under hers and hauled her up, bundling her into the backseat of the stolen Caddy. She grabbed at the sides of the door, screaming loud enough to earn a savage elbow to the side of the face and another punch to the kidneys that beat the fight out of her.

It was all over in less than ten seconds. He glanced around. No one was looking their way.

He clambered into the backseat, the woman's head on his lap, and slammed the door.

"Drive," he told Dale.

They peeled away from the sidewalk in a shriek of burned rubber, the Beastie Boys telling everyone there'd be no sleep til Brooklyn.

7

T he headlights of Wayne's truck lit up the cabin. We'd concluded the more-beers-or-more-work argument. Wayne had prevailed.

Not that I'd argued hard. I knew what families were like—in theory—and was more than a little familiar with the panic that went along with a prodigal returning. The least I could do was hammer in a few more nails and heave a few more timbers if it made the difference between his grandkids having somewhere to rest their heads and not.

The long shadows made it more difficult to do any sort of precision work, but a lot of what we were doing was just grunt stuff. A few spikes driven to hold things in place, the nail gun doing the hard work.

"I promise we'll get beers when the last couple of timbers are laid," the old man said.

I smiled. He'd been saying that for the last two hours and, best I could tell, would probably be saying it in his sleep in two hours' time, like some sort of mantra. Truth be told, I was happy enough to go through till dawn. One thing I'd learned in special forces and intelligence work was that the best way to ingratiate yourself with the local community was to do the hard work, no questions asked, and be seen to be happy about doing it.

I grabbed another two by four and dropped it into place. It was like putting together a huge three-dimensional puzzle. Every timber had its place and every joist and crossbeam and brace slotted together just so. It wasn't exactly handcrafted pioneer stuff, even though we'd assembled a pretty impressive array of circular saws, jigsaws, sanders, planes, work benches and the like. Ideally, we'd have had another ten days to finish the frame, make it weather-proof and start on the inside. We'd be lucky if we had three.

Wayne had a hunting lamp shining up at me. Grinning down at him, I cut a pose, pretending to be a Wolfman howling at the moon. That earned a chuckle.

"You're a strange one," Wayne said, after a while.

"That I am, my friend," I agreed.

I could tell he wanted to talk. Again. And I knew the direction the conversation would go because his eyes kept drifting to the hole his foot had made.

"You're in pretty good shape for a geek," he said.

Not subtle. I laughed. I'd been interrogated by some of the nastiest bastards on the planet and could fend off a few questions about my past easily enough. "I used to work out a lot," I said.

"I can see," Wayne said. "Seriously, though, thanks, you know." Again with the meaningful look at the hole.

"No worries. You'd have done the same for me."

"No, I wouldn't," he said. "Not even close. I wouldn't have been able to get that beam into place on my own, never mind move fast enough or have the presence of mind to grab you before you fell."

"I got lucky," I said.

"Bullshit," he said. "That wasn't luck, son. That was instinct. That was the kind of thing they can't teach you. And if you're a desk jockey I'm banging Halle Berry."

"How is she?" I said.

"Surprisingly flexible." Wayne grinned, shaking his head. The old guy knew better than to press too hard.

Over his shoulder I saw the twin white globes of headlights turn down onto our long drive. The trees obscured the car itself for a good two hundred yards, but it wasn't as though the driver could sneak up on us in the dark with at least three thousand lumens burning bright from their full beams.

We had maybe sixty, ninety seconds before the car pulled up at the cabin.

My backpack was on the ground. My weapon of choice, a loaded SIG Sauer tucked inside.

It was no good to me up there. Without a word, I dropped into a tight crouch, swung down, landing lightly on my feet, and walked over to my pack to fish out the gun. The familiar feel of the heavy-gauge mill-finished metal in my hand never got old. Watching the headlights approach, I slipped the barrel into the back of my jeans.

Better safe than sorry.

8

They switched off the headlights and drove another six hundred yards in darkness, with only the moon to guide them. The suspension on the stolen Cadillac was ridiculously soft and on the pothole-pitted road it had them rolling around like they were at sea.

Dale switched off the tape deck. They drove on in silence, only the crunch of stones under the tires for company. No one said anything.

Henry stroked the dead woman's hair. As gestures went it was almost tender. She stared up blindly at the padded roof. She'd died badly. Dale had played rough. The radio had played that damned Madonna song right the way through it. Henry hoped never to hear it again.

She hadn't recognized Raelynn Cardiman's face, so letting Dale have his fun before they disposed of her body had been the least he could do. It was always better to feed Dale's proclivities in a controlled environment than ignore them and leave them to boil over when they least expected it. The guy was dangerous at the best of times, unpredictable and dangerous at the worst.

They reached the end of the dirt track and Caleb switched off the engine. He let the Caddy roll to a stop to avoid the flare of brake-lights. "This ought to do it," he said.

Henry nodded. He already had the door open and was clambering out. It was colder than a witch's tit out there. "Give me a hand," he said, reaching into the car to manhandle the body halfway into the road before Caleb clambered into the back to help push her all the way out. She fell onto the ground, legs wide open, skirt up around her waist.

"Grab the shovel out of the trunk," Henry told Dale, who didn't look any too happy at the idea of digging a grave, but they had an arrangement: if you killed it, you buried it. He popped the trunk and came back around the side of the car with a pick and a shovel. He tossed the pick to Caleb.

"Sooner we get this done, sooner we get back on the road," Henry said.

Caleb bent down for the pick. By the time he straightened up, Dale had already broken ground. He watched them work, silhouetted against the Hunter's Moon.

It was hard labor. It hadn't rained for a while, and beneath the layer of cracked top soil the dirt hid a wealth of sins. And rocks. But the dead woman wasn't going anywhere in a hurry and they had sins aplenty between them.

Caleb's pick struck stone over and over again, each blow ringing out loudly in the darkness. Beside him Dale dug, whistling a Gloria Estefan song while he worked.

Henry walked over to the trees and took a leak. The thick yellow stream pattered against the hard soil, running off the surface around his feet.

"Can't we just weigh her down with rocks and throw her in the lake?" Dale grunted, breathing heavily as he sank the shovel into another six inches of black soil.

"No," Henry said, putting an end to the argument before it began. "And we can't cut her up and leave her out here for the animals, either. Dig."

"And torching her's out of the question?"

"Unless you want to light up the sky from here all the way to kingdom come."

"Whatever you say, Henry. Whatever you say."

He went back to his whistling. Henry didn't recognize the tune this time.

Dale danced around the shovel like some sort of pole dancer.

Henry shook his head. "You're one strange little man, my friend."

"And don't you forget it." Dale started digging again.

9

The vehicle's headlights went out. A big burly guy clambered out of the sheriff's car. He had a buzz cut and a beer belly. I knew him. Everyone did. Jim Lowry represented the town's entire Sheriff's Department.

Wayne called, "Hey, Jim, what can we do for you?"

"Wayne." He raised his right hand in greeting as he slammed the car door. He scratched at the back of his buzz cut as he walked toward the old man. He had the look of a man who wanted to be anywhere but there, but whatever he had come to say, it was obvious it had nothing to do with me so I took the opportunity to drift back to my rucksack to make sure my SIG Sauer was tucked away before his attention turned to me.

Lowry was always going to say howdy, it's what old-timers like him in small towns like this did. They used to call it breeding. Lowry raised a hand again, his shadow stretched out all the way to the cabin wall. "Howdy, Mike," he called, like clockwork.

"Jim," I said, dusting my hands off, and walked over to them.

"Working late, boys?"

Wayne nodded.

"Mind if I ask why?"

"My little girl's coming home," Wayne told him.

Lowry didn't look surprised. Bad news had a way of traveling fast, even in small towns. Wayne had taken the call in Maeve's, and his last word before hanging up had been "When?" and his first three after hanging up had been "That was Rae." It didn't need rocket science to piece together that puzzle, and gossip was Maeve's stock-in-trade. If anyone could decipher half of a conversation in the name of tittle-tattle it was her.

"When?" the sheriff asked, mirroring Wayne's own question.

"Soon as," Wayne said. "She's on the road now."

Lowry nodded thoughtfully. "Then you boys better get a shift on. That shack's not gonna make itself watertight, is it?"

"You can always lend a hand, Sheriff," I said, earning a cockeyed grin from Lowry.

"My manual labor days are long behind me, son," he said, although he was only ten years my senior. Maybe less. It was part of the small-town-sheriff shtick. He played the part well. "Don't take this the wrong way, Wayne, I'm pleased for you, I really am. Family's everything. But I gotta ask, is she okay? You know, after last time ..."

"It's all good, Jim," Wayne assured him.

But Wayne couldn't be sure. I knew that. The sheriff knew that. It was one of those pillow promises made to lovers, filled with good intentions but with absolutely nothing to back it up.

"That's good to hear, Wayne. It really is. Rae's a real spitfire of a girl. It'll be good to have her smiling face back around town."

"I hear you." Wayne nodded.

Neither of them acknowledged the simple truth: no matter who you are, what your experience, what shit life has thrown at you, you can never go home. It just doesn't work. And if you're hopping a midnight bus, you're running from something, not to it.

"Besides," Lowry said, "we've already got our resident stranger in Mike here." He smiled at me, but it was plenty obvious he didn't trust me. He was right. I was a stranger in town, and for all any of them knew, I was running from something, so I could hardly blame him for being suspicious, even after a few weeks of my charm to wear him down.

"A stranger's just a friend you haven't met yet," I said, matching his grin with one of my own.

"Very Hallmark of you, Mike," the sheriff said. "Anyways, like I said, I'm really pleased for you, Wayne. A man needs his family around him. You know me, all I want is a quiet life."

"Don't we all?" I said.

"Amen to that." Wayne rounded off the agreement for everyone. "She won't be any trouble, Jim. You have my word."

More of those promises that couldn't be kept.

Wayne Cardiman was really good at making them, I realized.

One of them would end up breaking his heart.

That was always the way with rash promises and old hearts.

10

Raelynn tossed and turned all night, gripped by fever-sweats. Despite the cold room, the sheets clung to her skin. She'd cranked the air-conditioning up as far as it would go, and that wasn't enough. There was no blessing in oblivion.

Behind her eyes images flashed. In one fractured moment she was a fox being chased by hounds, in another a rabbit racing from a dog. On and on it went, in each version the predator capturing its prey in a savage circle of death.

"Mom." She felt a hand on her shoulder, shaking her awake. She grunted, pulling the sheet up over her.

"Mom," the voice came again. "We've got to go or we'll miss the bus. The alarm didn't go off." Words, just words. She didn't want to open her eyes. Not now. Not for ever.

"Just a minute," she mumbled. "Five. Just a few. I'm so tired."

"You've got to get up, Mom." Anna pulled back the blankets, leaving her all but bare to the morning in her bra and panties. She groaned again, but opened her eyes.

The ceiling fan turned lazily over her head, wobbling as it finished each new rotation. The screws must have worked themselves loose. One fine day the whole thing would come down and make a mess of the sleeper below.

The fake wood paneling was straight out of the 1970s. So was the orange carpet. It wasn't a room to wake up in with a hangover.

Anna was dressed. Chase was still in his PJs, playing with his action figure on the floor at the foot of the bed. He liked to escape to his own little world, one where he had a normal childhood. No doubt the orange pile was some sort of lava pit for the caped crusader to fly back and forth over. She had no idea what went on in her son's mind half of the time. He seemed to be capable of making an adventure out of anything. She envied him that. Sadly, the world would batter the innocence out of him soon enough.

She swung her legs out of the bed as Anna grabbed hold of her hands and helped her sit. The world swam around her, the grain of old panels taking on a psychedelic life of their own.

Her clothes were laid out over the back of the motel room's only chair. She shuffled through to the bathroom to splash water on her face. She couldn't look at herself in the mirror, not like this, not almost naked, because there was no way to hide the line of bruises around the crease in her left arm, which reminded her she wasn't anywhere near as clean as she needed to be, and that her last fix was too long ago now for her body to pretend it wasn't in withdrawal. The sweat still glistened on her skin. She was a mess.

She turned the shower on, only for Anna to shout through, "We don't have time, Mom. The bus pulls out in seven minutes!"

"Shit," Raelynn muttered to herself. She splashed some water under her pits and soaped up, let it sluice away, and then was done.

She didn't have a toothbrush. Or toothpaste. She'd buy a coffee when the bus pulled into a rest stop along the way. Someone had written a name in blue on the wall beside the mirror, with a heart and an arrow through it.

She dried quickly and dressed even quicker, but still had less than four minutes to get out of the room, across the street and into the bus station, and then she had to find the right bus.

And Chase was still in his PJs. Well, there was nothing she could do about that. She gathered up his clothes and stuffed them into a plastic bag, then scanned the room quickly to make sure she'd left nothing behind. The clock on the wall said three minutes and twenty seconds. She grabbed Chase by the wrist, and ran out of there, Anna two steps behind her.

Their room was on the second floor, which meant clattering down an iron fire escape and racing head down across the parking lot out front, playing Frogger across the four lanes of traffic and into the back of the bus station. There were six silver buses in the different bays, all identified at the back by numbers rather than destinations. Only one had people waiting to board. She ran toward it, making it with seconds to spare.

"One adult, two children, all the way," she said.

"Three tickets to Charleston," the driver said, parroting it back to her. "Four hundred and seventeen bucks," he said.

She fumbled in her pocket for change. She didn't have anywhere near enough. The room had left her short. She fumbled out what she had anyway, feeding it into the dish between them until there was no money left. She didn't even have enough for her own ticket. "I don't ..." She glanced around for a Good Samaritan. "I'm sorry. I'm short."

"How old is he?" The driver nodded at Chase.

"Seven," Anna said, from behind her.

"Try again," the driver said.

"He really is."

"No, he *isn't*," the driver said, leaning forward to tap the sign beside his change machine, which said that children under two rode for free.

"Two," Raelynn said.

"That's what I thought," the driver said. "And the girl?"

"Two," she said again.

"Looks like you've got just enough money then," the driver said, not printing out tickets for them. "If we fill up he'll have to sit on your lap."

"Thank you," she said.

"Don't thank me. They're two, right? Rules are rules." The driver nodded for them to go take their seats. Over the PA he said, "Settle in folks, we've got thirty-one hours between here and Charleston, plenty of time to get to know each other far too well for a Wednesday morning. So, kick back, relax and enjoy the sights, read a good book, stare at your iPhones. We'll be in Tampa before you know it."

The door's hydraulics hissed as it closed behind them.

11

L ike so many veterans of war, I no longer welcomed sleep. I didn't dream well. Not anymore.

My subconscious was like a best friend who had decided to screw you over one time too many, then left you holding a big old bag of shit and expected you to smile about it. This time it served me up a foreign field and, in the middle, a girl with an explosive suicide vest strapped to her chest. She was crying. Then she saw me, and her expression changed. Suddenly she had hope.

That was the worst part of the dream, the hope. Because I knew how dreams like this played out. They always ended the same way: the girl died and there was nothing I could do about it. The only mercy was that my dreaming mind didn't dwell on the horror, sparing me the details. I didn't feel the wet flesh hit my skin or the visceral heat of the detonation or the razor cuts of the shrapnel.

I woke suddenly, disoriented, part of my mind still in the field, but the primitive hindbrain had gone over into survival mode: there was someone else in the room.

There had been no obvious movement, no tell-tale sound to betray the intruder. They might have succeeded in sneaking up on a lesser man. My enhancements outstripped every imaginable evolutionary leap. My mind raced. The two-room shack I called home had one way in and one way out. I hadn't felt a drop in temperature when the door must have been opened. No kiss of the cold or faint brush of a breeze on my skin.

I'd taken to sleeping on the small couch in the room, which served as kitchen, dining and living space, rather than retreat to the bedroom. There was logic in the choice. It was all about making the best use of the residual heat in the potbellied stove. Even in the summer the bedroom couldn't shake off the damp and cold that clung to it. The smell was what got to me, though. It was just there. In everything. Permeating it all. The place was musty. Like a critter had crawled in there to die.

I'm a suspicious soul. It's part of my charm. It keeps me alive. I slept with the SIG Sauer tucked beneath the cushion, in easy reach, but I didn't want to risk any sudden movement in case the intruder was trigger-happy. Things would change once they realized I was awake, though, and making a move would be too late. It needed to be natural, the kind of tossing and turning a normal sleeper might make.

"Byron," a voice called, breaking the silence. It sounded so loud, like it was inside the plates of my skull and forcing its way out, not the other way around. I finished my roll, half on my stomach, half on my side, completely uncomfortable.

I was in another place, another time. I snatched at the gun, instinct taking over. Even in the gray early-morning light, I *knew* who it was. I didn't need to see her face. But her name wouldn't leave my too-dry lips.

She moved closer, stepping into the thin smear of light filtering through the grime-streaked window. Snow already fell out there, making the light struggle to find a way through the glass.

The girl reached out to me. I couldn't take my eyes away from the hollow, pleading look in her eyes.

The eyes. It was always the eyes.

"Please, help me," she begged.

I had heard her cries more times than I cared to remember, and experienced every shred of her agony so many more times than that. It should have been my pain not hers. A red bloom began to form on her stomach, a rose that grew too fast, blossoming impossibly bright.

I hated myself because even as I witnessed her death again I had a gun in my own hand, almost as though I'd pulled the trigger and caused those horrific injuries.

I tried to call her name, but it wouldn't come. It was as though she was drifting away from me, leaving me alone in the cabin with my shame and guilt.

I wanted to yell at her that it wouldn't work, that I was inured, immune, that they'd stolen everything human from me, but I didn't.

Something moved outside the window, or perhaps it was just a sudden flurry of snow caught up in the wind. It pushed at the glass. It was enough to steal my attention for a heartbeat—the only real measure of time worth a damn. When I looked back, the girl had gone.

I still had the SIG Sauer in my hand. The elements had been enough to keep me in the here and now, on the mountain, and help me maintain my grip on reality.

The stove was still warm, but no longer too hot to touch. The fire was more or less extinguished, but unlike the girl it wouldn't take much to resurrect it. There was kindling and a couple of logs stacked beside it, but not enough to keep the stove burning through another night.

Given the weather was about to turn, I needed to bring some more wood into the dry. The low lean-to I'd built onto the side of the shack was enough to keep the logs out of the worst of the rain, but snow and ice had a way of creeping into places rain feared to soak.

I was reluctant to put the gun down.

The cabin was a fair distance out of town. I was the stranger. I would be the stranger in town if I lived the next three or four years of my life on the mountain. That was just the way it was in places like this. I tucked the weapon into the back of my jeans before I slipped my coat on and stepped out into the night. The girl might have been some relic of my mind, but that didn't mean something out there hadn't woken me. Better to be prepared.

A gust of wind almost took the door out of my grip as I stepped into a world of white that took my breath away.

There was already a thick blanket of snow on the ground, easily four inches deep, and banked up much thicker where it had drifted against the walls of the shack. The wind kept the newly falling flakes in the air, bullying and swirling them as if it was playing some game with them.

I could make out fresh tracks running along the side of the cabin. They passed beneath the window. I crouched and reached out with one hand, tracing the outline of the hooves with a sense of relief. For now, at least, the only enemy was inside my mind.

"Deer," I said, not realizing that I had spoken aloud.

The tracks led a short distance further up the mountain before they disappeared into the tree line.

The thought of being close to Nature and her world of creatures, which posed no threat to my hidden existence, was comforting. The deer brought with it the kind of calm that people rarely did. That was partly why I had chosen this place to rebuild my life. It was healing.

Day by day, I'd felt more and more at peace: I was leaving my past life behind. I could rebuild myself, and the time to do it was one thing I had in abundance.

As long as I was left in peace.

That really shouldn't have been a lot to ask from the world.

The shelves weren't bare—there was enough fresh stuff to last for a couple of days if I was snowed in, maybe three at a push. The wood wouldn't last half that time. I was going to have to swing the axe before I thought about doing much else. There were canned and dried goods so I wouldn't starve, even if I was cut off from civilization. There was a stream of clear water running nearby that would be more than adequate for my needs, even if it froze. I had enough oil for the lamps to see me through the winter. Who needed electricity?

Twenty minutes later the stove was warming my quarters and I'd made a mug of coffee, which I took back outside.

The snow had stopped for the time being. The sky was gray and heavy, threatening more to come.

12

For Henry, life was good. They'd driven in silence for the last hour—the Caddy's cassette player had finally given up the ghost. The ancient deck had chewed up the magnetic strip. Better still, the radio hadn't managed to conjure more than a few crackles of white noise.

Still, Dale was intent on ruining the precious silence. He found a pen and tried to spool the tape back inside the plastic case, slowly turning the wheel to suck the magnetic strip back inside, but it looked like a relief map of the Rockies. There was no way it was going to play, even if he managed to get it back inside the deck. That didn't stop him trying. And it didn't stop Henry snatching it from him and tossing it out of the open window.

Caleb watched as it disappeared in the rearview mirror, the brown magnetic tape fluttering in the car's wake. A bird swooped down to examine the cassette but, realizing it wasn't some enormous worm, took to the wing again.

Dale shot Henry a look. When Henry stared back at him, his chin dropped to his chest, and he went into a sulk.

Five minutes later, they stopped. They were still twelve miles or so from their destination.

"What are we stopping for?" Dale whined. "Can't we just get this over with and go home? I miss home." He rocked in the plastic seat, the sweat pulling at his shirt.

"Because we need to blend in," Henry explained patiently. It was like talking to a child sometimes. "If we show up dressed like this we're going to stand out. People will remember us. And that, my friend, is exactly what we don't want. We need to go native."

"So, we've got to dress up like hicks?" said Dale.

"Can't be worse than what you're wearing," said Henry.

"What's wrong with it?" Dale took a moment to look down at his dark suit, the white shirt and the wingtip shoes. He liked it, Henry knew. It made him look smart. It made him look like a man who deserved respect, even if it did hang on his wiry frame like he'd left the coat hanger in it when he'd put it on.

"There's nothing wrong with it if you want to look like an undertaker," Henry said. "Which is fine as long as you stay in the car. But the minute you step outside someone is going to look at you, and remember the skinny dude who looked like Papa Death walking through town. We don't want people to pay us any attention, not now the world is full of cell phones and cameras that remember everything. You know what a bunch of suspicious bastards country folk are. They see something that don't belong, they remember it, they talk about it in the post office, then argue about it later in the bar. The fewer raised eyebrows, the better." It was hard to argue with that.

HALF AN HOUR later they were back inside the car wearing their new gear. It was cheap stuff. Work clothes. All three wore identical jeans and heavy-duty boots, but they'd managed to find three different shirts. Henry felt like a logger or a miner, someone who made a living with his hands. That was exactly what they wanted others to think. He ran a hand through his hair. Their suits were in the trunk, carefully folded in the brown-paper bags their new clothes had come in.

"We'll have to move them if we need to put another body in there. I don't want blood on my suit," Dale said.

"Let's see if we can get through the day without putting anyone in the trunk, shall we?" Henry asked.

"No promises," Dale said, grinning. "I mean, look at me." He raised his hands to make the Y of YMCA above his head.

Caleb laughed. Henry didn't. He hated Dale when he acted up.

There was no doubt their new clothes would stand out less than the Mormon missionary suits they'd worn in the city, because that's exactly what three men rocking into town dressed in black suits and white shirts would look like to the locals. So, sure, the three of them all wearing brand-new clothes would raise an eyebrow or two, but only if people really looked at them, and he wasn't about to encourage a bunch of strangers to do that. It wasn't his style.

Dale argued, but his whining was still an improvement on the music. Just.

13

By morning, the snowfall had melted, leaving behind a slick, icy sheen on the timber. I wasn't looking forward to working on the roof, so instead I concentrated on prep work, getting the timber in place to haul up there. It was backbreaking labor, and we were up against it, but Wayne wanted the place fit for habitation, and a month had become a week overnight, or at least the best part of one.

For his part, Wayne spent the morning grinning like the Cheshire Cat. I could understand his excitement, even if I didn't share it. His little girl was coming home.

It didn't matter how old Raelynn was, she'd always be his little girl. The same one whose hair he'd braided and whose knees he'd picked tiny stones out of. She'd always be the same one he'd taught to read with *The Cat in the Hat* and whose face he'd watched light up as she tore into the wrapping of the Christmas gifts he scrimped and saved all year to buy her. That was how it went with dads and their daughters, the sense that all we have is each other, no matter what.

Those thoughts took me back to Julia, the wife I'd left behind, along with all the other remnants of my old life. I'd had no choice, but that didn't make it sting any less. It was a wound that would never heal. Picking at it wouldn't help. I grabbed a fresh piece of timber, focusing on the feel of it in my hands, and pushed her from my mind.

I looked up at the cabin. With a little luck, we'd get the last of the joists in place before the day was out. That was my focus. And then there was the added work of patching the damage Wayne's near miss had caused, but that was two hours at worst. Anything beyond that was gravy.

"What do you reckon?" asked Wayne, following my gaze. "Think we can get her watertight in time?"

"I'm the wrong man to ask. It's not like I've ever built anything. I figure we're racing those clouds."

"And all the others," Wayne said. "Hey, would you be okay by yourself for the rest of the day? Only Raelynn called. I'll need to pick her up in a few hours."

"No problem. I'll be fine here."

If I wasn't being watched I'd be able to move faster, and get more done. A few hours to push myself would be good. Holding back was frustrating, but I couldn't risk powering through the work with him watching if I didn't want those difficult-to-answer questions, like "Who the devil are you?" Or, more accurately, what.

"You're sure you'll be okay by yourself?"

"I'll be fine. Don't worry. Go get your daughter," I reassured him.

"I've really missed her," Wayne said. "Still miss her mother too. Every day. They say it gets easier with time. It doesn't, it just gets different. I don't much like different."

"You don't talk about her," I said. "I've wondered, but it wasn't my place to ask."

"She was an addict, just like my little girl. We wonder what we give our kids, you know. Is she going to get her mother's eyes, her gramps's chin and cheekbones, her old man's hairline, or her mom's addictive personality? I always hoped she'd get her mother's smile and maybe her spirit, the stuff that made me fall in love with her, but blood is blood. It was in her personality. A flaw. She would have been okay if it wasn't for the quack treating her."

"How do you mean?"

"He got her hooked. She'd had a bad back. Compressed verte-brae. Her doc prescribed painkillers, but they only lasted a few weeks before they stopped helping, so he prescribed stronger and stronger meds. The stronger the pills, the more addictive they are. It's a vicious circle. She needed the pills for the pain, and when she was hooked those bastards in Congress told doctors they needed to cut back on the prescriptions they were handing out. Her supply was cut off, just like that, but the problem was she was hooked. And that meant looking for another way to feed the itch. Anything that would take the pain away."

I knew the story all too well. Who didn't? Opioid painkillers had been handed out like they were candy. Doctors got rich. Then the government ordered a crackdown. The pill supply dried up. But the demand they'd created was still there so people transferred to heroin.

"I'm sorry," I said again, for want of anything better.

14

Maeve wiped down the counter for what must have been the fiftieth time that day. She would do it a hundred more times before she closed.

The lunchtime rush had barely begun. Although "rush" was an optimistic choice of word. Even on a good day she'd see only a few dozen different faces roll through between twelve and two, with some ordering a bottomless coffee, nothing more. But that was fine. It was enough to keep her busy, people in seats and the community spirit of the place alive.

The diner was the heart of the town. It was a hub for gossip. All walks of life were there. That was one of the things she loved most about this time of year: instead of sitting on their stoops having an ice-cold brew, like they did in summer, the cold drove people through her door in search of warmth.

Even so, it was rare for a stranger to come into the diner. Rarer still if they were just passing through. No one just passed through Winter's Rage.

They came to visit family, or they came back here to retire. It wasn't on the way to anywhere. Maeve had a sixth sense for cars that did not belong. She didn't even have to look up—she knew every engine sound. When the battered old Cadillac pulled up curbside in front of the diner, she didn't recognize the engine or the misfiring muffler.

Now she did look up, and saw three men in the car. She didn't recognize any of them. Out-of-towners were always more of a pain than her regulars. They had their out-of-town ways. They wanted their coffee frothy or low-fat or non-dairy or decaf, anything to stop a simple coffee actually being coffee. There was an art to good coffee, and that demanded a thick black residue at the bottom of the mug, stubborn enough to stand a spoon up in.

She sighed, and plastered on her happy face to welcome the strangers.

Maeve was wise in the art of people-watching. It came with the job. She could spot a man who was comfortable in his clothes, whether they were a workman's wardrobe of jeans and a T-shirt, or a Bible-basher's smart suit and black tie. These men could not have been more obviously uncomfortable if they'd tried. Off the top of her head she could think of a dozen locals who'd struggle to hide their prejudices if they happened to see the newcomers, and a dozen more who'd like as not cause trouble. Luckily for them they'd rolled up outside the diner, not the bar.

The first man licked his palm and slicked back his hair before he barged through the door, opening it with more force than was necessary. It banged so hard against the hinges it bounced back against his hand. *Well, that's one way to make an entrance*, she thought.

The room fell silent, that kind of weird uncomfortable silence that comes with the weight of violence attached. All eyes turned in the direction of the newcomers.

The creases from the store were still in the shirts. They were all brand new. Three men wearing brand-new clothes. It was weird. Their boots squeaked on the linoleum as they walked in. She saw the store tag dangling from one of the belt loops. Over by the window she saw Larry Carter struggling to keep a smirk from his face.

"Village People auditions were last week, boys," he joked amicably enough. The old boy liked to get a rise out of the younger guys in town and, surrounded by his cronies at the window table, he felt safe.

"Told you," the stick-thin one of the trio said to the others. He made an M with his hands above his head, earning laughter from Larry's crew.

"Don't you mind Larry, boys, he's a harmless old coot," Maeve said, hurrying around to the customer side of the counter with three laminated menus in hand. "Table for three?" she asked, the smile back in place. A warm smile was the best way she knew to defuse a situation and, like it or not, this was in danger of turning into a situation. She could feel everyone looking anywhere but at the three newcomers.

She started to lead them to a quiet table in the corner, but realized they weren't following. She turned back to see the slick one sliding into a booth beside Larry.

"This'll do fine," he said. "Won't it, boys?"

His companions nodded.

"Just dandy," the skinny one said.

"Of course. Can I get you boys something to drink?"

"Coffees all round," the same man said.

"Three coffees coming up," she said.

But before she could turn for one of the pots on the counter, the man asked, "Maybe you can help us."

"I can try," she said.

"We're looking for an old friend. She lives around these parts, I think. Or did. We don't have an address for her. Might not even be this town. But we figured we'd swing by while we were in the neighborhood, pay our respects." It was an odd choice of words, but she didn't pick up on it.

"That's mighty neighborly of you, honey," she said, finding it harder to keep the smile in place. "What's her name?"

The man had both his hands on the table, palms flat to the laminate surface either side of the menu. He smiled up at her. It was one of the most chilling expressions she'd had the misfortune of seeing in all her years. "Rae. Raelynn."

She made a face, pretending to think about it. She wasn't about to tell these three where to find the girl, especially not as Raelynn had only told Wayne she was coming home the other day. Maeve was too old and too ugly to believe in coincidences when they came dressed in identical straight-out-of-the-wrapper new clothes. "Sorry, don't know her."

"Course you do, Maeve," Larry Carter said helpfully. He leaned back in his chair so he could get a better look at the trio. "Raelynn's Wayne's girl. He said she was coming home."

"And where might we find this Wayne?" Slick asked.

Maeve willed Larry to shut up. Her telepathy was on the fritz.

"Sure, you can't miss him, these days. He's walkin' around town with this huge shit-eatin' grin now his little girl's comin' home. He's got a place over in the shadow of the plant," he nodded toward the poorer side of town, "but spends most of his days out building that new cabin."

15

"When do you need to leave to get Raelynn and the kids?" I asked Wayne. The sooner he was gone, the sooner I could really get to work.

"An hour, maybe," he said. "Even if the roads are bad it's not exactly an epic quest. Hell, I'll be kicking my heels waiting for the bus to roll in, but I'd rather be early than late."

"I'm the same way," I said. If I needed to be somewhere at three I liked to turn up at two fifteen, better to scope a place out, get the lie of the land, establish a route out if things went south. That was something Uncle Sam drilled into you when he first put a gun in your hand. "What say we get as much done as we can before you need to leave?"

"Sounds like a plan."

For the next half-hour we worked *hard*.

It helped Wayne keep his mind off his watch at least, even if we didn't get that many timbers locked into place. I pushed him hard, so he needed to stop to catch his breath every few minutes. He was sweating profusely.

"You're a machine," he said, as we pushed the last of the roof trusses into place. He bent double, hands on knees, panting. It was the last of the two-man heavy lifting for the roof.

We stood side by side, admiring our handiwork. The place was starting to look like a house and less like the skeleton of a dead whale. Some of the internal structure was in place and the roof would be ready to take the shingles soon enough. The whole place could be watertight in a couple of days. Less if I was left to my own devices.

The only real issue was going to be the weather and the light. The lumber that had been cut to fit the part of the frame was fashioned like the trunks of the trees and, like the roof beams, would need two or more to fit them into place. I could have done it, but Wayne wasn't an idiot: my installing those alone would raise more suspicion than one man digging out a swimming-pool in a day with a spade.

The roof was a different matter. I was pretty sure I could convince him that I'd found it much easier than he'd figured, and made good time.

He'd already shown me how the pieces fitted together, and as long as we got the membrane and battens into place, I could press on when he left.

"No rest for the wicked," I said, grabbing hold of one end of the roll of membrane. "Let's get this up, then you can leave me to it."

He took in the woods around us and smiled. "Those kids will have a much better life growing up here than in the big city."

"Only if they've got a roof over their heads that doesn't show the stars."

"Funny boy."

"Just leave me with enough nails in the gun to get her done," I said, with a grin.

We had the membrane in place before Wayne left. I worked on securing it with the battens.

The wintry sun felt good against my skin.

I figured I wouldn't see him again that day—he'd have his hands full playing dad and grandad, unless he got it into his head to bring Raelynn and the kids to see their future home. That would very much depend what time her bus rolled in. He'd want to show the place off in its best light.

I waited until the grumble of his pick-up's engine had faded before getting back to work. I was determined to make sure there was a big grin on my friend's face when he next laid eyes on the cabin.

16

"They were a sour bunch, weren't they?" Caleb said, when they were back in the Caddy. "Still, that waitress was comfortable enough, had some dough on her bones."

"Built for comfort, not speed," Dale agreed.

Henry was still irritated because the woman had tried to seat them as far away from her regulars as she could, like they weren't good enough. Like they smelled or something. He cracked his knuckles, wrapping his hands around the wheel. He counted each ridge of his fingers, needing to focus on something, anything, other than the white-hot heat he felt building inside.

The plan had been simple: get close to some of the locals, listen, use them to find where Raelynn was hiding. Then find her and fuck her up. Simple. Clean. His kind of plan. It didn't have too many moving parts, not too many places for things to screw up. Life with Dale offered enough potential for screw-ups without adding any extra opportunities for things to go wrong. So, even if the smarmy old bastard at the window wanted to piss on their parade, it didn't matter. He'd spilled his guts, eager to please. In Henry's experience they always did that. They bent, they bowed. They tried desperately to keep the skin on their bones. Because they were weak. They were venal. They groveled and sniveled and licked his boots.

But he was smart. The last thing they needed was a scene. Not that he couldn't have handled one. A diner full of old folks was hardly a challenge. But making worm food out of them wasn't smart. It was the opposite. He needed to focus on the fact he'd seen a glimmer of recognition in the waitress's eye when he'd mentioned Raelynn's name, and she'd lied to him. Or tried to.

Henry didn't like people who lied to him.

It was a point of principle with him. There was a special place in Hell for liars. He might introduce her to it once he'd dealt with Raelynn.

He looked up from his knuckles, turning his gaze back toward the diner window. She had a decent little business going there. She was probably on her feet all day. He wondered how long she'd be able to keep it up if she was missing a couple of toes, or if her kneecaps were smashed to a pulp.

The old boy who had spilled the beans about Raelynn's old man had balls. Big fish in the small-town pond. He'd made his Village People joke and taken the smack-down, eager to please, but not exactly afraid. Maybe he'd seen action back in the day. Gone toe-to-toe with the yellow man. Maybe he'd even killed.

Henry liked to think you could tell, just looking at someone, if they'd taken a life. It was a bond. A brotherhood. It didn't matter if it was done in the heat of battle, in the throes of passion or out on the streets. It was all the same, wasn't it? Life, death, the whole sad parade.

Maybe he hadn't taken a life. Maybe he'd just dispensed a few beat-downs. It was enough to give the old fool a sense of bravado, at least enough to front it out, but not enough to stop him singing. All Henry had to do was sit back, sup his coffee and listen as the man rambled on and on, finally offering up directions to Wayne Cardiman's house.

Time to make the old man's acquaintance.

Henry ran the palm of his hand across his chin, scratching at the rash of stubble. Dale fidgeted uncomfortably in the passenger seat. He kept reaching instinctively for the tape deck, obviously tormented by the silence. Who wouldn't be, in his place, the amount of crap cycling around inside his head, the music his only way of drowning it out?

Henry looked at the house. There was a better than decent chance it was the right place, but that didn't mean the woman running the diner hadn't rung ahead to warn Cardiman he was about to receive visitors.

He assumed in a podunk town like Winter's Rage they'd have the whole stick-together thing down when it came to strangers, so the odds were good that they'd be greeted by the wrong end of a shotgun when they walked up the porch steps. Well, they could take counter-measures.

Henry reached into the glove box for the piece he'd stowed there when they'd gone into the store to buy their change of clothes. It wouldn't be too disappointing if he had to use it. After all, you bought a gun because you wanted to get some use out of it, otherwise why buy it in the first place? But bullets were always a last resort. There were plenty more entertaining ways of getting people to dance. And of silencing them.

He got out of the car, shielding his eyes to scope out the house.

First impression, it didn't look like there was anyone home. The place was a little way out of town, as the guy in the diner had said, on the plant side rather than among the nicer houses on the opposite side of Main. He didn't see a car out front, but there were tire tracks in the thin layer of snow that still clung to the ground. The guy in the diner had said Wayne had a place, not the Cardimans had a place, which Henry took to mean Wayne lived alone.

A thin wisp of smoke rose from the chimney, but there were no other signs of life. Likely Wayne had been home earlier, but the house was empty now.

Henry climbed the three wooden steps to the porch, then opened the screen door. Small towns were lax. They trusted the neighbors they grew up with, and plenty of times didn't bother locking their doors. After all, who'd rob from a friend? He tried the handle. It didn't give, but the whole thing was so flimsy all it took was a single sharp shove with his shoulder to pop the lock. The door swung open.

"What's the plan? We just gonna wait for him to come home?" Caleb said, planting himself on the couch. Dale took the matching chair opposite.

"What do you think?" Henry asked, starting to root around in the hidden places of the house. He pulled out the top drawer of a bureau first, spilling its contents to the floor. "First we're gonna make sure we're in the right place."

Henry reached down among the spread of paper on the floor, fanning it out to get a better look at the detritus of the old man's life and spotted the corner of a photograph. He plucked it out of the pile, getting all the confirmation he needed, seeing Raelynn's face smiling up at him. It was a less faded, less crumpled version of the same picture he carried folded up in his wallet.

"What you got there?" Dale asked, but before he could answer, the telephone on the top of the bureau rang. Then the machine clicked in. It was an old-fashioned tape recorder beside the phone, like something out of the late eighties, early nineties. The white plastic had faded to ivory in the sun.

"Hey, this is Wayne. I'm not here, or I don't recognize your caller ID and don't want to waste my life on robocalls or telesales. You can leave a message or not, it's all the same to me. I hardly ever check the machine."

There was a pause followed by a heavy inhalation, someone steeling themselves before speaking. "Hey, Wayne, it's Maeve. Pick up if you're there, I hate talking to machines. No? Okay, I figured you should know that there were three guys in here, asking questions about your Rae. They said they were old friends but there was something off about them that just didn't sit right. Anyway, Larry Carter's only gone and given them directions to your place. Might be nothing but, like I said, I figured you should know. You look after yourself, okay? Don't go getting into trouble." There was a pause filled with echoes and silence before the rattle of the receiver being replaced at her end.

"So much for blending in," Dale said.

"Can't be helped," Caleb said, from his seat. "People don't like strangers."

"And I don't like people," Dale said. "Does that make me stranger?" He smirked.

For a moment, Henry thought about taking the three strides to the couch and delivering Dale a slap hard enough to knock him into next week, but as difficult as it was, he resisted the impulse. There was nothing to be gained from that. Not yet. After they'd taken care of Raelynn, maybe. He was growing tired of Dale's shit.

17

Wayne was early. Even so, he wasn't alone.

The bus station was little more than hardstand with a single shelter on the far side for drop-offs, one on this side for pick-ups, and a ticket office that was pretty much a tar-paper shack with a single seat and a map of the state on the wall behind it. The office was unmanned. Nanci, who sold the tickets to people needing to escape the area, would be back in her seat in half an hour. She only worked four hours a day, timed around the comings and goings of the various buses that passed through the town.

A couple of people were waiting, their battered suitcases and backpacks leaning against the wall of Nanci's shack. There was a toilet block a little way behind them, where another couple of people were waiting. One puffed on an inhaler and pocketed it. There was hope in their stance, he figured, or anticipation, at least, so Wayne figured they were heading *to* something. Maybe, like his little girl, they were going home. Or maybe they were off to college or something equally life-changing.

He occupied himself with thoughts of nothing very much, mainly about how they could fix up the cabin to make it homey. All of those little touches his wife had been responsible for that had landed in his lap. He had even bought a couple of magazines for ideas, which was unlike him.

He saw Nanci walking across the hardstand to the ticket office. She spotted him and waved. She was a fine-looking woman. A fella could do a lot worse, he thought, then stopped thinking as he heard the low rumble of an engine in the distance that could only be an approaching bus.

It took a few seconds to swing into view around the side of the garage building, then rumble to a halt in front of the drop-off, the old engine giving an exhausted sigh as the doors eased open.

Wayne scanned the faces at the windows for his daughter. He couldn't see her. His heart sank. Then Anna stepped off the bus, and saw him. Her mother was next out, holding the boy's hand. Raelynn had changed since the last time he'd seen her. She looked gaunt. Haunted. Even from this distance he could see the dark shadows beneath her eyes. But that wasn't the most shocking aspect of seeing her for the first time in forever—she looked as if she hadn't eaten a proper meal in weeks. She was like a brittle-boned bird walking across the hardstand.

"Hey, Dad." She waved, the boy, Chase, clinging. Two steps ahead of her Anna looked so grown-up. Not a teenager, not a child, but caught somewhere awkwardly in between. She was the spitting image of Raelynn's mother, not that he'd tell her that. Those poor kids had been dragged from pillar to post for so long they probably didn't even know where they belonged.

Wayne wanted to rush across the hardstand and sweep them all up in his arms and hug them until they burst, but the sheer exhaustion on their faces kept him back. He nodded at the pick-up. "Your chariot awaits."

The driver hauled a shabby suitcase out from the hold and put it on the asphalt.

"That it?" Wayne asked.

"Traveling light," Raelynn said. "You know me, I'm not a material girl. That's the sum of our lives in a suitcase and a backpack. Not much to show for all my years on the planet."

"But you've got these two," Wayne said, smiling at the kids, "and they're worth all the fancy gadgets in the world. You guys hungry?" Anna nodded. Chase just stared at him. "We could pick up some fried chicken, if you fancy, or how about pizza? What do you think?"

"Chicken, please," Anna said, grinning. Chase nodded approvingly.

Wayne noticed for the first time that he was clutching a small plastic toy. "Well, then, chicken it is," he said. "But, first, I've got a surprise for you. You want to know what it is?" The kids nodded. "Well, I'm not telling. You'll just have to come here and find out."

Wayne lugged the suitcase to the rear of the pick-up and lifted it in, then opened the door on a selection of toys that would have rivaled the display at FAO Schwarz.

"I didn't know what to get," he said, with a rueful smile, "So the nice lady in the store helped me pick some stuff. Hope you like it."

The kids looked at their mom for the okay, then climbed into the back. They were good kids, wary of strangers, like they should be. Sure, it stung that they thought of him that way, but it was hardly their fault. It wasn't like he'd chosen not to be part of their lives, or them his.

The kids opened the bags, pulling out a set of Lego, a doll, a board game and a couple of coloring books and crayons. Their faces lit up as if in disbelief. "Can we keep them, Mommy?" the boy asked.

"Of course you can," Wayne said, but Chase still looked to his mother for confirmation.

"Sure, honey," Raelynn said, then reached out finally to give her father a hug. "You really didn't need to do that."

"Oh, I did. These kids are owed a lifetime of birthday and Christmas presents as far as I'm concerned. And I intend to spoil them rotten."

"I'm sorry, Dad. Things have been ... tricky."

He resisted the temptation to say: *So tricky that you couldn't call?* But instead said, "You're here now."

"I am."

He looked into her eyes and saw a shadow of the same hollow, haunted look he'd seen far too many times in her mother's. "One thing, and I won't ask again, I promise. You're clean now, right?" He asked the question in a quieter, softer voice that barely registered above her whisper, like he wasn't sure he actually wanted her to hear it. He didn't know how much the kids knew or understood, but it wasn't his place to enlighten them.

She glanced through the window to see the kids engrossed in the gifts before she nodded. "I'm clean," she said.

He'd longed to hear those words. Problem was, he wasn't convinced.

There was something in her voice that reminded him of all the times she'd tried to pull the wool over his eyes as a kid. He might have imagined it, of course. Hearing things to worry about when there weren't any. Because, really, how much could he remember from back then? Raelynn trying to cover for breaking a window or crashing his truck? It was only natural she'd be on edge. This was a big thing, coming home. He had to trust her. And if she wasn't clean, surely that meant she'd come home to *get* clean, which was almost as good. He resolved there and then to do everything he could to help her, no questions asked. He wouldn't repeat the mistakes he had made with her mother.

"Are you in some kind of trouble?"

"Just man trouble," she said, with a smile, and in that moment Raelynn Cardiman looked like any other single mom, a little frazzled, a little disappointed with how life had turned out, but mostly just content to be herself and not sweat the small stuff. It was a good look on her. "I need to be somewhere he's not going to find me, at least for a while. Give us a chance to make a fresh start. And what better place to do that than here?"

"I don't want any trouble following you, Rae."

"Don't worry, Dad. I've left all that behind me. I promise."

"You don't know how good it is to hear that, kiddo." He hugged her again, impulsively, then smiled sheepishly. "Sorry, I don't have any of those fancy kid's seats."

"They're too old for them, anyway," she told him, and he smiled again.

"See? What do I know?"

She gave him a peck on the cheek, then slid in beside the children, picking up Chase and settling him on her lap.

Wayne walked around to the driver's side and climbed in behind the wheel. "Buckle up. Next stop, fried chicken. Then when our bellies are full it'll be time for the real surprise."

18

Within an hour of Wayne leaving, I'd finished securing the remaining battens and started fixing the shingles in place. His brief tutorial had been enough for me to make progress at my more unnatural rate, and without having to worry about being seen I was able to get on with stuff.

When the nail gun finally clicked emptily I knew I'd done a full day's work based on the old man's calculations. I clambered up to perch on the roof and took a moment to enjoy the view. I was jealous of the simplicity of life it offered, like Thoreau going out into the woods to live deliberately. This was a good place to live deliberately. Even from this vantage point I couldn't see another house for miles, though I could just make out a thin wisp of smoke that curled up from behind a distant stand of trees not so far away from the towering behemoth of the plant.

It took me a moment to realize that the smoke could quite easily be coming from Wayne's house. That was typical of him. He'd be thinking about making sure the old place was warm for when he brought his family home, not about the safety issue of letting an open fire burn when no one was home to tend it.

To get to the house from the cabin you needed to drive a couple of miles down the winding track to the main road, head back toward town, then turn off the main road again to circle round the outside of town, as though you were going to the plant, then follow a well-worn track to his door. It was maybe seven or eight minutes by car, but a fair old trek on foot.

From this angle, though, it looked as though it should be fairly easy to cut through the woodland and follow an as-the-crow-flies short-cut to reach the house in half the time. I figured it was less than a mile cross-country. I wasn't sure if the intervening land was private, or public forest, but either way I didn't think anyone would be particularly put out if I decided to save a bit of time.

Two miles or so altogether, over rough terrain, I could probably be there and back in less than half an hour, get enough nails to go on with the job, and be back before I was missed. And it'd offer a different kind of exercise. All the lifting and carrying in the world couldn't replace the freedom and liberty that came with a good run, pushing yourself hard, driving yourself on as the muscles burned and knotted and your lungs ignited. I couldn't remember the last time I'd run properly.

I'd already made up my mind before I started toward the ladder leaning against the far end of the roof. I stopped. There was no one around to see me, and the ground below was clear, save for the thin dusting of snow. The drop was less than eight feet.

I jumped, landing easily, knees bent, boots hitting the ground hard, and rising in an instant, upright without so much as the slightest jarring ache from the impact. I felt adrenalin surge, as if the activity had triggered some buried muscle memory. I embraced it. It was who I was. I started to run.

The landscape was caught between seasons. There was snow on the treetops, but no trace of it on the ground beneath them. I wove a path through the shadows of the forest. The light was thin, casting coins across the dirt as if some leprechaun's pot of gold had been overturned. I hurdled an outcropping of roots, then ran lightly through sucking peat-bog, almost slipping before the ground firmed up again. It felt good, weaving in and out of the trees, arms and legs pumping furiously, driving myself on. I hit a large uprooted trunk that was riddled with decay, planted my hands on the bark and bounced over it, coming down on the other side, barely breaking my stride.

High in the canopy above, a bird took flight, startled at my approach. Somewhere deeper in the woodland I heard the sudden flurry of movement as something larger bolted. I caught the briefest of glimpses, a ghost between the thick boles of the distant trees, and figured it had to be a deer. Perhaps it was the same one that had visited my sleeping place.

I loved the paradox of the forest: despite the oppressive sense of the trees closing in on all sides, there was something incredibly wild —free—about racing through this unchanging woodland. It was as though I was moving through a world that hadn't changed for hundreds of years. It was primal. Primeval. It was easy to understand why other ages of man had considered such places mystical, worshipping woodland sprites and forest gods.

I pushed myself on and on, the landscape locked in my mind. I didn't doubt for a second that I was heading in the right direction, although it would not have been difficult to get lost with the smoke to guide me. I could picture the lie of the land pretty much perfectly, and knew I had no more than a few hundred yards before I hit the town road where it crossed the track leading to Wayne's house. It was easier to find a road than a house: more points of possible intersection for my path and its meandering. A house was different. You might overshoot, race straight past even when you were less than a hundred yards away, tricked by the geography, missing the place altogether.

I covered the ground much faster than I'd anticipated. My boots barely touched the mud. A mile was nothing, even weaving in and out of trees and negotiating obstacles. My breathing was good. My pulse was good. I was good. Better than good. I zigzagged to avoid another fallen tree.

I heard another flurry of movement in the undergrowth as I raced through it, wildlife running for cover, desperate not to be seen because that was how they survived. And for a moment there was just me and Nature, an empty world.

Then I heard a car's engine.

19

The sky grew darker in the distance, but the sun was still high in the sky. There was a kiss of snow in the air, but no more than that, the odd flake swirling to land on his upturned face as he closed the car door. Wayne sent a silent prayer out into the universe, hoping the weather would hold a while longer.

He really wanted to take them up to the cabin later to show them how serious he was about them being home now, but really all that mattered was that they were there. Safe.

Raelynn and the kids had fallen asleep.

He was tempted to keep driving for a while, let the rhythm of the road rock them and soothe them. Raelynn had always loved to sleep in the car growing up. When she was teething, it was the only way they could get her off. He smiled at the memory. He'd thought about taking them to Maeve's place, but he'd promised fried chicken and he was nothing if not a man of his word. But now, looking at them in the rearview mirror, he thought they'd be straight to bed as soon as they walked through the door, the promise of chicken or no.

He phoned in an order for a bucket of chicken with all the fixings, and fries, lots of fries, as he drove, then picked it up from what passed for the drive-thru window at the Chicken Shack up by the cloverleaf where the local road hit the freeway. It'd stay warm forever: they nuked it with so much radiation that it had a half-life of six months.

The weather was closing in. The wipers flicked away a smattering of flakes from the windshield. Give it twenty minutes and it would be full of snow.

Showing them the cabin would have to wait until morning. He'd been a little optimistic in thinking they'd be able to fit everything in on the first day they got here. The only important thing was food. They didn't stir when he wound the window down, oblivious to the sudden flurry of cold air that found its way inside. He was handed his bucket along with a large bottle of Coke, which he placed on the floor in the passenger foot well.

While the pick-up was stationary, Wayne took the opportunity to check his cell phone. He wasn't expecting a call, and coverage was spotty at best this far out of town, with the one cell tower some distance away, but he'd felt it vibrate in his trouser pocket while he'd been driving. Missed call, the screen said, from Maeve.

Occasionally he had parcels dropped at the diner: it was easier than trying to give directions out to the cabin when he wasn't home to take them. He figured that was why she was calling, even though he wasn't expecting anything.

She had left a message.

He listened to Maeve's voice telling him about the strangers asking for Raelynn, and explaining that Larry had told them where he lived. She tried to reassure him it was nothing, saying the same thing or variations on it, three times in the short message, but the more she tried to convince him otherwise the more certain he became that there was something to worry about. Especially when she explained that she'd left a message on the house phone too. You didn't do that if you weren't worried. And he trusted Maeve's instincts. She was good at reading people. It went with the territory.

He blew out a slow sigh. Raelynn had more reasons than she was letting on for the sudden urge to return home. That was a conversation he really wasn't relishing. The last thing he wanted to do was scare her off again, but what kind of father would he be if he didn't worry about his little girl?

He looked at her now. She'd taken off the flimsy jacket she'd been wearing and used it as a blanket to cover the three of them. One of her arms was exposed, bare where the baggy jumper had ridden up enough for him to see the inside of her elbow and the telltale bruising of fresh track marks in her skin.

He wanted to weep.

There was every chance she was still using, he'd always known that, but he'd been clinging to the hope that he might be wrong. She'd looked him in the eye and promised him she was clean. He'd wanted desperately to believe her. Those bruises meant she'd lied to his face. That hurt. But addicts were liars. They couldn't help themselves. It was what their addiction did to them. And that transformation was a bigger betrayal than all of the rest of them combined.

Raelynn stirred. She reached out protectively to pull her cubs closer. Her sleeve slid down, covering what he'd seen. He wanted to be wrong. He would have given anything to be wrong. Just this once. She opened her eyes and smiled at him, and in that moment he felt a swell of protective love. She needed him. He wouldn't let her down. Whatever it took, he'd be there for her.

Raelynn snuggled her head into the seat and closed her eyes again. His questions could wait until tomorrow. Today was all about coming home. He wasn't about to let anything spoil that.

Wayne turned his attention back to the road. Everything would be all right. It had to be. He deserved that. Just this once. He deserved a happy ending. So did those kids back there.

20

I slowed my pace. The trees ahead were thinning.

The light improved, promising a clearing. I figured it had to be the edge of Wayne's property, or at least the track leading to it. The plant couldn't be too far away.

The engine noise had ended a couple of minutes ago. Something didn't feel right.

My first thought was that it was Wayne coming home, but the math didn't add up. There was no way he could have made it to the bus station and back again in such a short time, not given how early he'd set off to be sure he wasn't late. So unless he'd turned back because he'd forgotten something, it wasn't him. And if it wasn't him, it was someone else.

Friend or foe? That was my first paranoid thought. That kind of thinking had been drilled into me by Graves and his sort, in all of the labs and all of the test zones and all of the parade grounds and combat zones and green zones, demilitarized zones and every other kind of zone.

I stopped long enough to catch the final sounds of the engine dwindling to nothing. It wasn't new but it was big and powerful. A gas guzzler. Something big and American. A Pontiac maybe, or a Caddy.

I stuck close to the tree line and crouched low to get a better view, but before I could really get a sighting I heard the familiar *thunk* of car doors slamming. Instinctively, I ducked back into cover rather than risk being seen even though the odds of that happening were between slim and non-existent. I was less than fifty yards from Wayne's house, much closer than I'd anticipated. That wasn't necessarily a good thing.

Parked outside Wayne's house was a battered Cadillac. I hadn't seen it before. It was like a boat on wheels, or one of those amphibious landing craft the navy used. It was held together by rust, but once upon a time it must have been someone's idea of a status symbol.

Two people got out. One was thin, uncomfortable in his own skin. He twitched like a tweaker. The other was a brute of a man who towered over the stick insect. They left one person sitting in the backseat of the car. That increased my concern. Something really wasn't right. One guy might have been a salesman, two, holy rollers on the look-out for souls to save, but three was a crowd. The guy in the back got out. He slammed the door.

Wayne was expecting only one visitor today, and he was picking her up at the bus station. So if not Wayne, who? Me? That was the only reasonable explanation: some government agency sniffing around, a three-man team sent to track me down and try to bring me in. Emphasis on the word *try*. Well, if that was the case, they were in for a world of hurt, because I wasn't going anywhere. Not now. Not because someone wanted to bring me in. Not because they needed something from me or were frightened of me. I was done. Out. Through.

But ignorance wasn't bliss. I needed to know. If I didn't, the doubt would just gnaw away at me, and I'd start thinking dark thoughts, bringing my own ghosts back to hunt me. I wasn't stupid: I knew plenty of the damage in my brain was down to meddling, but that didn't mean I'd just ignore it and think happy thoughts. I crept closer to the house, keeping low, conscious not to draw the eye with any jerky movements. Part of me wished I'd brought the SIG with me.

In any case, sometimes evasion was the smart move. Do a bit of recon, move out, regroup, circle back.

I watched the three of them. They weren't salesmen or missionaries. They weren't Wayne's friends either—it was painfully obvious they'd never been to the house before by the way they scoped it out. They didn't seem particularly edgy, though, which I liked to think they would have been if they were there to bring me in. That either made them elite, or idiots. I hadn't made up my mind yet.

One option, the sensible one, was to get the hell out of there, and keep moving. There wasn't anything I couldn't leave behind. That was my new life. I didn't own much, and needed even less. I wasn't quite the rootless wanderer with only a toothbrush and the clothes on my back, but it was close. And had been closer before I'd turned up in Winter's Rage.

I'd let myself plant a few roots there. Nothing major, but enough that disappearing would leave a few hints to go into my psych file. And when it came to psych warfare, the guys who'd come looking for me were right up there with the meanest bastards on the planet. So, I could split, lay down false tracks, use what I knew to make it difficult to find me, but what about Wayne? Would they leave him be?

I didn't want my friend caught up in the middle of things. He didn't deserve that. All he'd done was reach out a friendly hand. It wasn't his fault I'd allowed myself to take it. That was all on me. And it made me remember the home truth I'd been running from forever: I couldn't have anyone in my life because, when it came right down to it, they were just weapons that could be used against me. Why give the enemy ammo? It was a simple enough mantra to live by.

I looked back up the hill toward the cabin, not that I could see it through the undergrowth. I *could* run. I could stay hidden in these forests for months, foraging off the land to survive. All I needed was food, and I could make do, eating what I killed. I was getting ahead of myself. The soldier's brain kicking in, thinking ten steps ahead of where I was, but working off a false premise: I had no idea if these three people were government, or if they'd come looking for me. They could have been anyone.

They didn't knock. The first opened the screen door and tried the handle, like he had every right to walk on in. There was a slight hesitation, a change in his stance, and the door opened inwards. I heard the tear of wood and knew he'd forced the lock. That convinced me. I wasn't going anywhere. The break-in focused my mind. I knew what I had to do.

I kept to the trees, moving a little closer to the house until I was at the edge of the clearing and had only one choice: go forward or back. I couldn't stay where I was. I broke cover, moving fast, head down, keeping low, rushing across the killing ground until I hit the Caddy.

I took the fact that all three had gone inside as a good sign. They hadn't left anyone to keep look-out. One less problem for me to take care of.

The door was still open. I could see where the latch had been forced, splintering the surround. Neither army nor FBI would have forced their way in. They had to deal with pesky things like the law when they acted—even hunting a man like me their hands were tied in certain ways. And that was only right. You didn't want law enforcement with carte blanche to do whatever it wanted regardless of the legalities. To be fair, there was no way the Feds would have rocked up in a battered old Caddy either: they'd have come into town in the obligatory black Crown Vic with radio antennae broadcasting their credentials.

I let my fingers linger on the ground, my touch enough to melt the thin layer of snow. I could make out three separate sets of tracks leading from the vehicle, all merging as they reached the porch steps. These were men who knew they weren't going to meet any resistance inside, or didn't care if they did.

I looked up at the windows, trying to get a view of them. The angles were all wrong. My brain was still chasing connections. It kept coming back to the same thought: men with this kind of arrogance were dangerous, not least because they had a habit of pulling triggers without any real thought of the consequences.

That was enough to convince me they weren't there for me.

But why come for Wayne?

Raelynn was the only answer that made any sort of sense.

I broke cover, moving from the side of the Caddy to the wall, determined to get a better look at what I was dealing with. Keeping low, I risked a quick glance through the glass.

Two men sitting, one on the sofa, one in Wayne's tired old armchair. The third stood at the bureau, rifling through the drawers. He didn't care if Wayne knew they'd been there. He turned out the drawers, scattering papers across the floor.

What was he looking for?

The fact they hadn't moved through the house first, securing it, suggested a lack of organized thought and training. I discounted law enforcement once and for all. Up close, it was obvious they'd dressed to try to blend in, but they were so obviously uncomfortable in the cheap shirts and too-blue jeans. Some people just didn't do casual well. These three were strange bedfellows. They weren't easy in each other's company, obviously deferring to the guy rooting through the contents of Wayne's life.

He held up something, I couldn't see what, and seemed happy with his find.

I left the window, working my way around to the open door as quietly as I could. I placed the weight on every step evenly, careful not to make any of the old boards creak. The trees were thirty yards away. I could cover the distance before the three intruders made it out of Wayne's living room and down the steps, but I didn't want to engage. Not yet. This was recon. Threat assessment.

And if—only if—I judged them dangerous, I'd think about how best to neutralize the threat they posed.

Right now, I was thinking about how best to use local knowledge to my advantage.

The idea of playing Ten Little Indians with them crossed my mind. It wouldn't be particularly challenging to lure them into the woods and pick them off one at a time. But where was the fun in that?

I tried to hear what they were saying, but even with the open door it was a muffled conversation. The only thing I could be sure of was that they weren't in agreement. Their voices were sharp, tones clipped, occasionally rising. I used their arguing as cover to climb the porch stairs. A lot of it was still probability and numbers. Sure the guy had found something, but was it the one thing they'd come looking for? It wasn't like the old man hid his secrets, but this had been in the first drawer they'd turned out. It was a calculated risk, but I was banking on them not walking out while I was hunkered down on the porch.

That gamble crapped out in less than fifteen seconds as I heard them moving. Sticking around wasn't worth the risk. I left. Two quick steps across the decking, planting one hand on the wooden rail and vaulting to the ground, scrambling around the side of the house and out of sight before they reached the door. There was always the risk they'd see my tracks leading from the trees to the car to the house, but there was nothing I could do about that.

They came out onto the stoop, arguing hard. I couldn't see who was saying what, but they weren't happy. I moved around so I could watch them, unseen. They walked with the swagger of men used to meaner streets than these, and looked ridiculous in their borrowed clothes.

I caught the briefest glimpse of the driver's face as he turned to open the car door, but I wouldn't forget it in a hurry.

Nor would I forget the Glock jammed into the waistband of his jeans.

The other two climbed into the Caddy on the passenger side, giving me less of an opportunity to get a decent look at them. It didn't matter. One was enough.

21

The brief layover at the drive-in window, combined with the tantalizing aroma of fried chicken in the cab, was just enough to lure the kids back from sleep.

"Mm, that smells *good*," Anna said, stretching as she eased herself from beneath the comfort of her mom's coat.

"And it tastes even better," Wayne promised. "We'll be home soon enough."

"Mom, Mom, look," she said, suddenly even more excited. Wayne couldn't see what had got her so wound up. Her peered out through the windshield, scanning the road. The sky had grown darker with every mile, but there was nothing remarkable out there. A fresh flurry of snow had started a mile back. Now it came thickly enough for Wayne to need his headlights on and have his wipers sluicing the windshield clean every second or so. The beams turned the snow into dancing winter sprites twirling and swirling ahead of them.

"It's snowing!" she said. "Real snow!"

And he realized she was seeing his world with the eyes of a child who had likely never seen snow apart from on a screen. "That's right, honey," he said. "And looking at those clouds, I reckon it's safe to say there's a lot more of it to come."

"Enough to make a snowman?"

That made him smile. "Enough to make an army of snowmen," he said. "But not tonight. We can get up early and make one before breakfast, if you like?"

"You hear that, Chase? We're going to build a snowman." She nudged her younger brother, who didn't seem quite as enthusiastic as she did at the prospect of waking up early. He stared out through the side window, though, watching the snow with all the rapt wonder of his sister, which was good enough for Wayne.

"Remember when you were young, Rae?" he said, looking back at her. "You used to love making angels in the snow."

She nodded. "On the bank alongside the road?" Her smile was genuine. A fond memory. "I'd forgotten about that."

"Your mom used to make a great long row of snow angels, all lined up on the side of the road to the house, just so they could look for me coming home from work."

"We can do that too," Anna said, loving the idea of doing something her mom and grandma had done together, like it was some ritual being handed down from generation to generation. "That will be fun, won't it?" It was almost as though the girl was asking permission to enjoy herself. He wondered, not for the first time, what those kids had gone through in their young lives. Whatever it was, it was as if they'd woken up completely different children. The doubt and suspicion had morphed into tentative excitement and wonder in their new environment.

As he watched them in the mirror, it was pretty obvious that Anna was used to looking out for her brother. He got the impression they were the only friends they had, which was sad. Things were going to change, he promised silently. This was going to be a new beginning for all of them. They deserved that much out of life.

By the time they passed the population sign at the town limits of Winter's Rage the snow was falling heavily. Large flakes filled the air, making it harder to see the road ahead.

The snow was settling on the ground at either side of the road. That didn't bode well for the cabin. The road itself was clear, not that it would stay that way. It wasn't exactly the most trafficked highway, but big Jim Burges would have the plow out later to make sure it was clear after nightfall, or it would be impassable by morning.

That was life on the mountain. It could change on the whim of the wind, a change of direction, the north wind blowing, and a warm front rolling in or out could make all the difference.

He turned onto Main. The road was deserted. The cars parked up alongside the curb were dusted with a not-so-fine coating of snow. The streetlamps puddled yellow in patches, with large dark spaces in between. Most of the store fronts were dark. It was funny driving past them now. A hundred memories were attached to each one, things he'd done with Raelynn, with his wife, with both of them. It didn't matter if they were the most normal things in the world, like the three of them walking hand in hand, a very young Raelynn swinging between them every third or fourth step, her feet kicking up into the air as she giggled, or the most unnatural things in the world, like stumbling along the street consumed by grief, knowing he had to go home and tell his little girl her mom was dead. All of his life was there, reflected in those dark windows.

The lights were on in the diner, one bright spot in an avenue of darkness. Wayne had an urge to stop and check in with Maeve about the strangers who'd come looking for Raelynn, but with the snow thickening, and the fact he hadn't put the chains on the tires yet, he didn't want to risk getting stranded halfway home and them having to hike through the wind and the snow.

This time of year the town really earned its name. It didn't take a lot for a sudden snowfall to isolate it, and once it was cut off that was invariably that for the season, not just a day or two. The banks could get to waist deep in a matter of hours during the worst nights of the year. He remembered all too well the winter of '84 when the walk from the main drag out to the house—less than six hundred yards—had taken him the best part of two hours battling against the elements. It wasn't something he wanted to go through twice. Not if he could help it.

As he crawled past he saw Maeve through the window, her face obscured by the curving letters on the glass. She was alone. It looked like she was cashing out. Made sense. It wasn't like there'd be a rush of diners in this weather. Better she get home rather than sit around in the empty diner and end up stuck there for the night. Though he knew from experience she had a cot in the back where she could sleep if things got too hairy outside. He'd sobered up on it once or twice after Raelynn had run away.

He drove on, taking the turns that led down to the power plant, and the woodland beyond where he made his home.

Wayne took his foot off the gas as he approached the turning to his house, giving the car plenty of time to slow long before he needed to turn. It would have been easy to go off the road: it was a tricky little hairpin bend. Ice on the surface turned it deadly. He needed more fingers and toes than he'd got to count the amount of times he'd seen the tow truck pull someone from the ditch down the years. Wayne wasn't about to let that happen to him. He'd never live it down.

He took the turn.

"Home sweet home," he said, long before the house came into view.

He started up the track, the world around them turning white. Out of the shelter of the town the snow was doing a good job of turning everything into a winter wonderland. The pick-up's old heater had the windows steaming. The kids were fogging the glass with heavy breaths and wiping it clear. Another hour and they might not have been able to make it up this far.

He took the last turn, the house coming into view, and followed the drive down to the loop of road out front. It was only when he drew closer that he saw the mesh of tire tracks in the snow. He'd almost missed them because the blizzard had already begun to fill them in, but they weren't as deeply covered as the ground on either side.

So Maeve's strangers had come a-calling. Judging by the tracks they'd been and gone. But that didn't mean that they wouldn't be back.

He pulled up outside the house. "Do me a favor, wait here a

second." Clambering out of the car, he realized that the screen door was open, and the front door ajar. He closed the car door behind him quickly, but softly, not that it mattered. If they were still here, they'd heard the car approach, crunching through the virgin snow. Three meant it was more than possible they'd left one behind to wait for him. That almost felt like a best-case scenario. They could just as easily have moved the car around the back, hoping to take him by surprise on his return.

He crossed himself, a habit he'd dropped since he'd become a widower, before all the gods in the sky had given up believing in him, and took the half-dozen strides to the porch steps he'd taken so many times before. His heart pounded in chest. He almost managed to convince himself he could hear it, or at least the thunder of blood in his ears, so still was the world around him, so frightened was he to his core.

Up the steps, one at a time, wincing as they creaked and groaned beneath his weight.

He saw the damage to the frame where the lock had torn free of the hasp.

Wayne placed a hand on the door and heard the unmistakable sound of someone moving about inside.

Shaking, adrenalin surging through his system, he pushed the door all the way open, having forgotten just how loudly it creaked on its old hinges. Any hope of surprise was ruined.

As the door swung inwards he saw a shape standing in the room.

22

"Mike," Wayne said, when he realized who was on the other side of the door. "What are you doing here?"

His smile was warm enough, he liked the guy, but there was something weird about him just letting himself in. It wasn't like it was the first time he'd been in the place, and Wayne had gone out of his way to tell him to treat it like his own because he trusted him completely.

NOW HIS FIRST thought was of hope, because the last thing he wanted to think was that he'd misjudged the man he considered a friend. It was a fleeting thought, banished before it could take hold. Of course Mike was a friend. He might not be a burned-out Silicon Valley vet, but he was a friend.

"You had some visitors."

Wayne nodded. "I heard. Maeve rang on the cell. You see them?"

"Yeah, not the kind of guys you want paying you a social call. The three Caddy drivers of the apocalypse," he said, with a wry smile.

Wayne got it. "They were in the diner earlier, asking a lot of questions about Rae. Larry told them where to find me."

"You got any idea who they were?"

Wayne shook his head. "Not a clue, but I'll be brutally honest, you deserve that much. This wouldn't be the first time trouble has followed my daughter home."

"Roger that," Mike said, clearly joining the dots.

"Not that you're unwelcome, but how come you're here and not out there killing yourself on the cabin?"

"Ran out of nails so I came over to pick some up, and saw your visitors."

"Please tell me you didn't do anything stupid, Mike."

"Scout's honor."

"Good man. Last thing I want is you to get caught up in whatever mess Rae's brought with her."

"It's all good, Wayne. All good."

"So, the wrong kind of people, yeah?"

"That just about covers it. But they didn't see me."

"Any damage?"

Mike pointed at the door. "They popped the lock, but I think I've made it at least as secure as it was before. Not that that was particularly secure. I think you might want to invest in something a little more substantial."

"Can't say I ever felt I needed to before. Hell, there's nothing in here worth stealing."

"Right, but looking out there, I'd figure there's two little things worth keeping safe."

Wayne nodded. "Can't argue with that. So, what about inside? They mess it up?"

Mike shook his head. "Nothing to get worked up over. They'd pulled out a drawer, upturned it and spread the papers out over the floor. That was the sum of it. I just gathered it all back up, put it away. I couldn't tell you if they took anything. They were only in here a couple of minutes. I figure they found what they were looking for and split."

"Makes sense. Thanks for cleaning up."

"I didn't want you guys coming home to a broken door and crap all over the floor."

"Appreciated . . . Tossing out one drawer doesn't sound like burglars to me," Wayne reasoned. He placed a hand on Mike's arm in gratitude. It was one of those silent communications that passed between men and spoke volumes, more than any of the words they exchanged.

Mike didn't answer him immediately: he seemed distracted, his attention caught on something over Wayne's shoulder. He was smiling. Wayne relaxed as he heard Raelynn call, "You going to leave us out here all day? The chicken'll go cold."

Wayne turned to see the two kids climbing up the porch steps, eager to get inside. Anna clutched the bucket of fried chicken and fries to her chest. Beside her Chase struggled with the large bottle of Coke. He clung to it like it was the most precious thing in the world and he'd never let it go.

"And who might this be?" Raelynn asked, and pushed her bangs out of her eyes. She let a smile form on her lips. It was the first time Wayne had seen that sparkle in her eyes since she'd climbed down off the bus with the kids in tow. It was great—so utterly normal. A glimpse of the kid she'd been all those years ago. Back when things had been simpler. Innocent.

He smiled and stepped aside so the kids could run in. "This is Mike. He's been helping me out with your surprise."

He gave Mike a look, pretty sure he'd read between the lines and not spill the beans. It was one thing to say she'd always have a home with him, but something else entirely to say, "Surprise!" and pull your hands away from her eyes so she could see the best present ever.

He'd owned the plot of land for more years than he could remember. It had always been his plan to build her a place of her own. He loved the idea of her just being up the hill from him. His wife would have loved it, too. But, like the old song went, you couldn't always get what you wanted. Thing was, right until a couple of days ago, he hadn't believed you ever got lucky enough to get what you needed, either. And it had been that way ever since she'd run away. Raelynn calling to say she wanted to come home, that changed everything.

"Why don't you stay and have something to eat with us, Mike? I'm sure Dad bought more than enough to feed the five thousand." The smile grew wider.

"It's okay, thanks. I'm going to head back before the weather gets much worse."

"This is Winter's Rage," she told him. "It's already worse. Tell him, Dad."

"For once I agree with my daughter," Wayne told him. "You can't have had a decent meal all day, not that this is decent. I'll put some coffee on, then run you back to your place when we've finished. How's that sound?"

"If you're sure?"

"Of course I'm sure."

"That snow's looking pretty nasty. I can walk."

Wayne laughed. "Dear God, just take the lift, my friend. That old pick-up of mine has driven through more snow than Santa's sled. Trust me, it'll be fine. It's going to be a fair old while before the road's impassable, especially if Jim's out later with the snowplouw. So, stay, eat some chicken, warm yourself up by the fire, listen to us tell stories about the good old days when Rae was knee high to a grasshopper, and I'll find some embarrassing photos. We'll worry about getting you home later."

So that was what they did. They went through to the living room. The kids sat cross-legged on the floor in front of the open fire as they tucked into the chicken. Wayne wouldn't have been surprised if it was the first meal they'd eaten all week. Mike took a proffered drumstick but seemed more interested in cradling his hot mug of coffee than eating. He sipped it while it was still steaming.

It didn't take long for the fresh logs to have the place verging on uncomfortably warm, but the kids didn't seem to care. They licked their fingers and smacked their lips and grinned around the secret blend of herbs and spices.

While the kids were busy tucking in, Wayne gave Mike a nod and drew him back into the hallway. He eased the door closed, to give them a little privacy. Even so, he kept his voice low. "Okay, man to man, I'm asking you, do you think they'll be back?" He wondered if it was obvious how rattled he was.

"Honestly? Depends if they got what they were looking for. If that was whatever they stole, then, no, they won't be back. But if they're looking for someone, not something, then maybe. Probably."

"Shit." He knew Mike was right. "There's nothing in there of any value. Some old bills, bank statements, finance agreement on the truck, that kind of thing. A few old photos. Nothing you'd break into a man's home for."

"Meaning they'll be back."

He hadn't noticed the door open. Raelynn looked at him, one hand on the frame. "These things aren't exactly soundproofed, you know. So, is one of you going to tell me what's going on?"

23

"Well, thanks for the chicken. I think I'll get out of here now, before the snow gets too bad."

Mike grabbed his coat from the rack just inside the door and shrugged into it. Wayne opened the door. He thought it was like one of those movies where they blurred the stars to make it look like they were going so fast light couldn't keep up, only here the stars were snow, though the adage about no one being able to hear you scream was a good fit for the mountain, too.

Mike buttoned the coat, not that it was going to make much difference out there, Wayne thought. At a certain point cold stopped being anything other than cold. There were no varying degrees to it. "Look, you sure you don't want a ride? It's no trouble. Seriously. I don't like the idea of you out there in this." He glanced outside.

"I'll be fine."

"Are you sure?"

"You worry too much, old man."

Wayne grinned.

Outside, the last traces of the strangers' car had completely disappeared and the windshield of the pick-up was hidden beneath an inch and a half of white.

"I've lived through worse than this. What you need to do is get back in there and enjoy the grandkids. You only get one first night with them. Don't waste it worrying about me. You got enough wood for the night, or do you need me to bring some round before I go?"

"We're good, but you could give me a hand with Rae's bags before you head off?"

"Sure."

It was an excuse to move away from the house and talk to Mike without Raelynn and the kids being able to overhear. As they crossed the snow, Wayne asked, "Did you manage to get much done?"

"The roof's finished, more or less."

"I'm guessing less, surely." He shook his head. "How the hell did you manage that?" It strained credulity that the man had managed to get even half of the roof finished in the time Wayne had been gone, never mind running down to the house to look for supplies, fix the door and everything else.

Mike just grinned. "I found a short-cut," he explained, pointing up through the woods.

'I can't remember the last time I went that way. There's no paths, not even worn trails to follow.' He shook his head, feeling like one of those nodding dogs on the back shelf of a car. "I'm trying to wrap my head around this, pal, but I can't. You're telling me you came here, saw those three goons, went back to work on the roof, finished it, then came *back* again to fix the door? Did you stumble into a time-warp or something? I mean, it's not that I'm not grateful, hell, you know I am, but who are you, really? Because I'm not even sure Usain Bolt could move that fast."

"You know who I am," Mike told him.

"I really don't," Wayne said.

"I'm Batman," he said, in a gravelly voice, doing a terrible Christian Bale impression.

Wayne couldn't help himself. He laughed. "Of course you are. Anyway, given this," he pointed up at the sky, "I can't see us getting much done over the next few days, so thank you. For all of it. But mostly for just being here." He offered his hand.

"Have faith." Mike shook it, then trudged down the track toward the road. Wayne called a farewell and Mike raised a hand in acknowledgment, but didn't turn.

24

Wayne wanting to keep that little home invasion from his daughter didn't sit well with me. For one thing, I was fairly certain she'd have some idea who the three men were, and right now, my top priority was still intel gathering.

They needed to talk to each other. Clear the air. And there was a lot of it to clear, as far as I could tell, going back years to Raelynn's dead mom, the women's shared addictions, Raelynn's disappearance and all the days in between. There were two kids and however many tragedies to account for. I just figured it'd be easier if I wasn't there.

I could still see the footprints the kids had made in the snow as they went to the door with the bucket of chicken and the bottle of Coke. Their little feet scuffed the snow aside, making exaggeratedly long prints in the snow, some deep enough to look like dark scars on the track as they went down to the asphalt. Everything else was pristine white. I turned my face up to the sky. At the rate the snow was coming down, I figured it'd take maybe half an hour to wipe out any sign of the kids' footprints, a little longer to obscure the pick-up's tracks on the driveway. It was hard to credit how utterly the Caddy's presence had been eradicated. But that was Nature in the microcosm. I walked on, thinking bleakly that we were all like those tire tracks. It just took longer for the world to forget us, but eventually it'd be like we'd never been there at all. And after a couple of generations no one would be left who even remembered our names, never mind our faces.

Sometimes my mind went to dark places. There wasn't a lot I could do about it. It wasn't PTSD. I'm not even sure it was down to whatever messing they'd done to the chemistry of my brain in the lab. It was just me.

I ran through the little I knew. Raelynn had come to town. She hadn't been expected. It had been a prodigal-daughter moment. The same day three misfits had turned up asking about her, then broken into Wayne's place, stolen something and gone. I had an idea what they'd taken, but nothing to back up the supposition. Wayne had mentioned photographs.

My gut told me they'd found one of Raelynn and decided they were in the right place—or the wrong place—and hadn't waited around for her to appear. Which meant they'd be back. I didn't see another way this worked. It was way too much of a coincidence, otherwise. Strangers, questions, a random break-in? Nah, didn't work. In all the time I'd been in Winter's Rage barely a handful of people had passed through who didn't belong. The rest were relatives or old friends, and they didn't count. They weren't strangers.

These guys were strangers, no matter that they'd known Raelynn's name. It didn't take a lot to find out someone's name if you set your mind to it.

The thing with the clothes bugged me. Why change? Why deliberately try to blend in, unless you thought it might mean you'd be forgotten? And why worry about being forgotten unless you intended to do something memorable? I didn't like the way my thoughts were going, especially given the Glock stuffed down the back of that guy's jeans. Sure, there were plenty of folks who carried. This was the heartland, but open-carry like that was still weird.

You didn't see guys with AK47s strapped to their backs walking into Walmart, or guys with Walther PPKs putting them on the bar counter as they asked for a beer. Sticking it down the waistband of the jeans felt off. It felt like something that a man who spent most of his days obsessing over Tarantino movies might do, same as holding the gun sideways. It didn't make sense. It wasn't functional. And, in my experience, good guys liked things functional. Bad guys, less so. Sometimes with them it was just about image and wanting to look the part.

I kept my SIG Sauer tucked away in my kitbag. The last thing I wanted to do was draw attention to myself. And guns on strangers did that. A local carrying a handgun is perfectly normal: you don't get immediately suspicious of them like you would with a stranger. So, I kept it hidden because I needed to fit in. It was the invisible option. Those men didn't fit in, but they'd still taken the time to change their clothes. It was the contradiction I didn't like. I like things to make sense. I like to be able to look at a situation and reasonably extrapolate how it's going to play out. And this scenario made me uncomfortable as much for what I didn't know as what I did.

I thought about Raelynn.

Wayne's daughter was a troubled soul. That much was obvious—and not just because she'd come running home with starving kids. She had a pretty smile that went all the way to her eyes, but there was some hard living back there, too. I knew all too well what that kind of smile meant. I had no intention of doing anything about it. There were a million good reasons not to. It wasn't even about feelings, or being a good guy. It wasn't as if I hadn't slept with women I barely knew. It was just that I had a good thing here and I didn't want to fuck it up. This woman was burdened with a whole battered suitcase full of complications.

Wayne hadn't said much about her, beyond some of the old troubles with drugs the last time she'd been home, and how she'd run. He didn't talk much about his family. He gave no indication of even knowing who the father of his grandchildren was. I figured he didn't know, or didn't like what he did know. I wasn't a shrink. I couldn't easily guess why she'd kept the kids out of his life, if she was punishing him for something, maybe failing her or her mother, or shame. Sometimes the hardest thing in the world was to walk down familiar streets, knock on a familiar door and say, "I'm sorry, I was wrong." And instead of getting better, wounds turned septic.

I walked on, reaching the road, but before I could make the turn for my place, I heard Wayne's shout. I mistook it for the wind at first, but it took on the shape of my name, so I turned.

He stood in the middle of the road, yelling and waving frantically. My heart sank. I started to jog back toward him.

25

"Everything okay?" I asked, as soon as I was close enough that I didn't have to raise my voice. My first thought, I hate to admit, was that something had happened when we were outside, that the Stooges had snuck in around the back, or left a darker message, like a rat nailed to the bedroom wall or something I'd missed. I kicked myself. I should have checked the whole place was clean, not just focused on the room I knew they'd been in.

Raelynn stood in the doorway, her face a match for her old man's. Confession is good for the soul, right? Maybe not, judging by the pain behind the woman's eyes. Wayne had told her what had happened. I'd been gone less than two minutes. There was no way it could have been anything else. Raelynn confirmed it, walking barefoot down the wooden steps ignoring the snow, to stand beside her father.

"Dad said you saw them?" She didn't seem surprised that there had been someone to see.

I nodded.

"You think they'll be back?"

I shrugged. I did now. For sure. The look on her face was all I needed to convince me of that. She knew who they were, and she knew where they were looking for her. I'd have put good money on her knowing why as well. I said, "Maybe. Maybe not. I don't know who they are. I don't know what they were looking for. That's not a lot to go on."

"Did they have guns?" she asked. Not the first question I'd have expected.

"One, for sure," I said. "All of them, probably."

It was enough to bring fear to her eyes.

"Maybe they've got what they came here for and that's the end of it," Wayne said hopefully. I could tell that what he was really worrying about was spooking Raelynn and her taking off again. He wanted to pretend that everything was fine and dandy. "No real harm done. The door's fixed. It's warm inside. Why don't we just forget it ever happened?"

I knew he was wrong, willfully so, he knew he was wrong, and Raelynn knew he was wrong, but none of us said anything.

"What do you think, Mike?" Raelynn asked.

I couldn't tell if she wanted me to show her father up, contradicting his naivety, or if she really was hoping I'd say something other than the obvious. I had no intention of lying, but looking at her, then at my friend, I knew that it wouldn't be much of a challenge to spook her. And spooked, she ran—or carried on running. I didn't reply.

"Why don't you give us a minute, Rae," Wayne said, going inside. I followed him up the porch steps. Raelynn's feet were bright pink with the cold, and left wet prints on the floor. She gave me a look I didn't like: rabbit in the headlights. Her brain was racing. Weighing it up, the oncoming headlights and the speeding wheels, the impact they promised. She wanted to run. That much was obvious. But she couldn't look away.

Even so, she went back through to the living room to sit with the kids.

Wayne closed the door behind her.

"I'm not an idiot, Mike," Wayne said. "This is about her. But I don't know what to do. We can't just stay here. There are two little kids in there. If it was just me and Rae maybe it'd be different, but it's not. So, what do I do? Where do I run? How do I fight? How do I protect my family?"

It was a good question, better than any his daughter had asked.

"You need to get her away from here," I said. It was the most obvious thing to do. "Get in the pick-up and drive out of town. Go take a vacation."

He shook his head. "I'm an old man. I can't protect her. And I don't have the stamina to run, not for long. Not for long enough."

"What are you thinking?" I asked.

He wiped at the side of his nose, a self-conscious gesture if ever there was one. "I wouldn't normally ask . . ."

"Go on."

"You go. Take Raelynn and the kids home with you, please. Those guys don't know about you, so she'll be safe with you. I'll stay here. I'll take my chances if they come back. It'll be enough to know they're safe."

"I'm not loving that plan," I told him. I didn't need to spell out why. He knew that by moving Rae and the kids out of immediate danger he was putting himself in the line of fire, but that's what fathers did, I guess. At least, fathers like Wayne Cardiman, looking for a second chance.

"I can take care of myself," he said. "If they come back, they'll find themselves looking at the business end of my shotgun. And before you argue, I won't give them time to draw their own."

We understood each other.

"I'd be happier if you went with them to my place and I stayed here to wait for whoever they are. No offense, but I'm younger, stronger, and more likely to put the shits into them."

"Sure you are," he agreed. "But there's an ace up my sleeve," he reassured me. I waited for him to explain his thinking. "A man has the right to defend his home in this great land of ours."

Bless him, he was actually smiling when he said it, like he figured three on one were decent odds for an old man and his shotgun. In my hands they were. In his, I wasn't so sure.

"Please, do this for me, just for a couple of days. Keep them safe.

I've never asked anything of you. I've never even pushed to hear your real story, Mike. I've opened my home to you. Help me protect my family."

And, despite every instinct telling me to say no, telling me if I walked away from there tonight I'd never see my friend again, I made that dumb promise. I owed him too much not to. "You got it," I said. "I'll need the keys to the pick-up."

"They're in the ignition," he said. "I'm trusting you with the most precious things in my life."

"You can trust me," I promised.

"I know."

26

"You really didn't have to do this," Raelynn said.

"I didn't have a choice," I said, not meanly. I was being honest. "I owe your dad. A lot. He called in a favor. I'm not the kind of guy who says no when someone asks for help. I'm a bleeding heart."

She looked at me in a way I really wasn't comfortable with. "Somehow I doubt that," she said. "The bleeding heart, that is, not the whole stand-up-guy thing."

My lean-to wasn't exactly the luxury home they'd just left, and there wouldn't be enough room for the four of us, but all things considered, the kids would have their toys, Rae my cot and I'd take a chair. There were worse family homes all over the state.

We'd make do.

The kids hadn't been eager to leave the relative warmth and comfort of their grandpa's place, and it wasn't like I had a bucket of fried chicken to tempt them with. But when Raelynn said they were going, like kids used to being dragged from pillar to post, they grabbed their few things and were ready to move in a couple of minutes.

They occupied themselves while I did my best to concentrate on the road ahead. Heightened reflexes, increased perception, none of it mattered if I plowed into a tree because I'd taken my eye off the road.

"So, what's your story?" she asked. "I mean, how did you end up with Dad?"

"Not much to say, really."

"I'm sure there is."

I shook my head. "Really, there isn't. I was passing through, he offered me some work and a place to rest my head for a while. I needed the work."

"So, you're just another drifter? Like a Lone Ranger kind of guy?"

"Something like that. Though not as glamorous. I don't ride into town to fix people's problems."

"And yet here you are, trying to fix mine." She laughed, but she was half serious in her assessment. She was quick. She'd pegged my weakness.

"Guess so," I said, changing gears.

The headlights cut through the snow, but even so I couldn't see more than thirty feet ahead, and the road was single-track in some places, twisting and turning like a slalom slope—or, at least, that was how it felt. It demanded all of my concentration. I really didn't want to be splitting it between making up lies and trying to stay on the road, so I stuck to the same old story, Mike, Silicon Valley escapee, burn-out, running away from it all.

"We're not so different then," she said. "Both running from something."

"I guess not." I reached the turn where the road divided, though you would never have known it from the whiteout up ahead. I slowed to a crawl and, without hitting the blinkers, rolled slowly on, tires crunching snow under them.

The flakes were coming thick and fast. The wipers worked at full speed. Even so they barely kept the windshield clear for a couple of seconds before the glass started to fill up. I negotiated the camber in the road, which, in normal circumstances, would have scraped the sump without braking, but the tailgate of the pick-up still slid beneath me as I straightened up. I fought the wheel, keeping up the revs as I tried to control it. The kids gave out a whooping yell as we slid, enjoying it far too much.

Raelynn didn't seem quite so comfortable. She had her hands braced on the dash and stared straight ahead. "I don't want to ask where you learned to drive," she said.

"I learned playing video games," I joked.

"I can quite believe that," she said, when I had the vehicle back under control. In that whole maneuver my heart rate barely increased by a single beat per minute. I was dead calm. Absolutely relaxed. It took a lot more to rattle me these days. Nothing got under my skin. I didn't have the luxury of the endorphin rush or any of that. And I still hadn't gotten used to it.

"They call it defensive driving," I said.

"Doesn't feel like there's a lot that's particularly defensive about it," she said.

"You'd be surprised."

"You done a lot of this kind of thing?"

"What? Driving? Some."

"Rescuing damsels in distress."

"Are you trying to tell me that's what you are? A damsel?" This time I couldn't stop the smile reaching my lips though I had the feeling it was more like a smirk.

"Are you saying I'm not?"

"I'm not saying anything. I'm just driving."

"You should do that more often, you know, smile."

I let my expression fall blank. "It's not a good idea," I said.

She knew what I meant. But she chose to be deliberately obtuse and, looking at the side of my face, said, "Oh, I don't know, it won't break any mirrors or anything."

"You're a lousy flirt," I said.

"No, I'm not," she said. "I'm really rather good at it."

I felt a hand on my thigh, but didn't take my eye off the road. "Besides, there's not a lot to smile about at the moment."

"There's always something to smile about, even if it's just the fact that the Cubs finally won the World Series."

"I didn't take you for a sports fan."

"I'm full of surprises," she promised, and I didn't doubt it for a second. Not all surprises were good.

The headlights picked out the dark shape of my shed through the whiteness of the snow.

"Here we go, home sweet home."

27

"A veritable palace, as you can see," I said, as I hauled the luggage back out from underneath the tarp. "Your quarters are in the West Wing."

"The Presidential Suite?" Raelynn offered, with a grin, and I nodded along with the joke. She was quick. That was a good quality in anyone, but it was a great quality in a woman. I admit I'm a bit of a misanthrope, but if I have to be in the company of others I'd always choose intelligent, funny, quick-witted women. They see the world through different eyes, and I like to learn.

There was not so much as a wisp of smoke rising from the metal chimney. The fire in the potbellied stove would have died eight or nine hours ago and there was no hope of residual heat still being trapped inside those four walls, but mercifully it heated up pretty quickly. I couldn't remember how much dry wood was inside, enough for the night at least, though. I'd meant to bring in more that morning but had got distracted. "So, according to your dad, the snow has a habit hanging around."

"You could say that," Rae said. "Give it a couple of weeks and you'll have forgotten what it feels like to be warm." She smiled that damned smile again. "I've got a theory about it. Wanna hear it?" I nodded. "It's evolution, see. Places like Winter's Rage have good-looking women and shit-for-brains guys, so that new blood is attracted to the area to breed. You get a better-looking lay than you'd get in LA or Florida, say, where everyone is beautiful and you're just one of the regular Joes, because even a good-looking guy isn't good-looking enough in that kind of place. But come to a place like Winter's Rage and you're an Adonis. The evolutionary combo has to be hot chicks and dumb-as-hell dudes, or it doesn't work. But done right, it lures in better-than-average drifters who might get lucky and improve the gene pool."

"I'm not entirely sure that's how evolution works," I said.

"Then you explain to me how someone ends up staying in a place like this."

I ushered all three of them inside and quickly closed the door behind us, not that there was any heat to keep in.

The kids didn't seem to care that everything was crammed into such a tiny space. With the curiosity only kids could show they were already into every nook and cranny before we were halfway into the room.

On my hands and knees, I raked out the ashes then set about lighting the stove, filling the top with kindling and yesterday's news, then dropping in a Firestarter. I watched it burn for a moment, making sure the vents were set for decent airflow. It took a couple of minutes to get going properly, and after one, I dropped in another short piece of kindling to get the heat up, then a couple of logs. The stove crackled and cackled, the fire rising quickly. It didn't take long for the heat to start filling the shack.

Done, I dusted my hands off and stood up again. I didn't own much, but it was more than I'd owned in a while. Still, my lack of stuff made me feel inadequate. I saw the place through the kids' eyes. I didn't like what I saw.

"Where are we all going to sleep?" Anna asked, as she put the bag of toys on the floor. Chase seemed less concerned about that than he was about tearing through the shrink wrap on the game Wayne had bought him.

"There's a bedroom through there, but it gets cold so I sleep out here. We can put blankets down and make up beds for you by the fire, or you can crash with your mom in the bed. I'll take the chair."

"Sounds like a plan, doesn't it, kids?" Raelynn said. "We can bunk-up together in there. We'll keep the door open, and if it gets too cold we can snuggle up. It should only be for a couple of nights. We'll make do."

"I'll get some clean sheets for you," I said, then headed toward the bedroom.

"How about you just tell me where they are? I'm not completely helpless."

"There's a blanket box by the bed."

I put a hand on the stove. It was warming nicely. I watched the embers do their fire dance through the hatch, then pushed the iron poker into the ashes of the kindling, stirring it up, and felt the warmth in the air increase.

It took maybe ten minutes before the small room was properly warm, and most of that was down to the kids running about rather than the stove.

"Where's the bathroom?" Anna asked.

"Ah," I said, and couldn't help but grin. I thought I'd have a little fun. "You have to go outside, honey."

The look of shock on her face was priceless. "You mean in the *woods*?" She sounded mortified.

"Like bears?" Chase laughed.

"Don't be mean," Raelynn said, from the bedroom doorway. "There's an outhouse."

"You take all the fun out of life," I told her.

"Not all of it," she promised, and I kicked myself, but it was the first time I'd heard either of the kids laugh. Sure, they'd been delighted when they tucked into the food and excited to play with their new toys, but there hadn't been actual laughter, no squeals of joy. It was an infectious sound.

"You got me." I chuckled. "There's a shed around the side of the house. It's a chemical toilet, so it doesn't flush, but it works just fine as long as you're careful not to get splinters in your behind." I winked at Anna.

"I'll go with you," Raelynn said. She'd already spread the clean sheets across the back of the sofa to let the warming air get to them. She held out a hand for her daughter to take, and in that moment I was struck by the physical similarity of the two. It was like a little window into the past, offering a glimpse of the girl Raelynn had once been before life had beaten the innocence out of her.

28

The brothers had driven more than twenty miles before they found a place they liked the look of. A sign had lured them off the highway, like a naked siren on the rocky outcrop above a sea of snow. The flashing neon sign promised "Girls, Girls, Girls." The reality was a rundown bar where strippers went to die.

On the opposite side of the run-off was an equally seedy motel that advertised an hourly rate. It would do just fine. All they needed was a place to lay their heads for the night. If they laid anything else, well, that was just gravy.

"You think I'm setting foot in there dressed like this? You touched in the head, H?" Dale grumbled. "We don't need a disguise and, more importantly, we don't need to look like Hicksville idiots."

"You look like an idiot no matter what you're wearing," Henry snapped. "You've got a choice. You can either come in dressed as you are, sink a beer and see some titties, or you can go back to the motel room and jerk off. But you're not going anywhere in your suit, understand?"

"No need to be a dick about it."

"Then do me a favor and shut the fuck up for a minute. I just want to have a beer and enjoy the view. I don't want to have to worry about you fucking things up. Again. So, how about you use your head? We're half an hour away, we're in the only titty bar as far as the eyes can see, ain't nothing to say someone from Winter's Rage isn't propping up the bar drooling at some double Ds. Gotta think smart, Dale. So just do what I tell you."

Dale grunted but didn't argue.

Sometimes Henry needed to lay down the law. Dale had attention deficit disorder so he kept forgetting shit. He was like a magpie attracted to shiny objects.

"So, how long are we going to hang around here?"

"Long enough," Henry said. "We ain't going anywhere before morning. The snow up in the mountains is going to be a lot worse than down here. Wouldn't surprise me if that town gets cut off before too long."

Dale still didn't seem satisfied, but at least he shut up long enough that Henry didn't need to give him a slap.

Henry fished out his cell phone to check if he had a signal. The coverage had been non-existent in parts of Winter's Rage. It was like stepping back in time. He needed to check in with their employer. He was very specific about wanting regular updates. He got itchy if he didn't feel in control, and the last thing Henry wanted was the boss getting the idea they couldn't do the job. That way lay a whole heap of shit he didn't want to swim in.

He punched in the key combo that called through to the boss. It had been years since he'd had to learn any numbers by heart.

"It's Henry," he said, before the man at the other end had the chance to say hello. "We've found her father's place. He wasn't home, neither was she. But we know she's on her way."

"And you're telling me this because?"

Henry listened to the silence, his mouth dry and his throat tight. The boss didn't like wasted words. He wasn't a fan of excuses either, and most certainly didn't deal well with disappointment. And that was what he was phoning to deliver. "Just letting you know what's what. We're closing in. Won't be long now. But the weather is pretty shit out here."

"I really couldn't care. You've got a job to do, get it done. And be smart about it."

"She'll be there tomorrow. It's a small town. Nowhere to hide."

"You're not there to play hide and seek, Henry. You're there to kill her. And do those kids while you're about it. No one messes with me and walks away. They suffer. And you, Henry, are my tool. You make them suffer."

"The kids? Seriously? I don't like that. We don't do kids."

"You need me to send a man to do the job, Henry? You wouldn't want that. I want the entire bloodline wiped from the face of the planet. The old man, too. Get it done, get it done fast, and get out of there. I don't accept failure, Henry. Not now. Not ever. You know what happens to people who fail me? They wind up with a bullet in the back of the head."

Henry said nothing. He didn't have the luxury of protesting: the line was dead. And he was left in no doubt the same fate awaited him if he screwed this up.

Caleb and Dale stared at him expectantly.

What was he supposed to say? They'd heard him say they didn't do kids. They knew what the boss would say to that. You didn't say no to him. Ever.

"Nothing's changed," he said. "We need to find her and take her out."

"Which is a job for tomorrow," Dale said. "Tonight we see titties."

"I'm right there with you, brother," Henry said. "Anything to make what we have to do tomorrow more palatable."

"What do you mean, H?"

"You know what I mean, Dale."

Dale twitched, scratching at the scuff of stubble growing out of his sallow cheeks. He knew. "We getting a bonus for the extra blood?"

"We don't do kids," Caleb said.

"We do if we know what's good for us," Henry said.

Silence settled between them. It was anything but comfortable. Dale looked at Henry. Henry looked at Caleb. Caleb looked from Dale to Henry and back again. Henry had seen that look before. It was the moment when someone realized they were being asked to cross the line. Everyone had their own version of the line. For some it was as simple as taking an extra drink before getting behind the wheel of their car, for others it was walking out of a restaurant without paying. For him it was killing kids. Pretty much anything else was doable, but kids ... There was a special place in Hell for men who did shit like that.

"You're joking, right?"

"No way. Not happening," Caleb said. Henry was with him on that. "We don't kill kids, that's not what we do."

"Here's the choice we've got, Caleb," Henry said. "We either do what we're told or we paint a big red target on our backs. The boss has promised to send someone to clean up our mess if we don't do as we're told. So, I don't know about you two, but given a choice like that I need a drink, because there's no way I can even think about killing some kid sober."

They went inside the strip joint. There was an old woman on the pole in skimpy black lace bra and panties. He could see her Caesarean scar as the hard skin glistened in the spotlight. He held up three fingers, meaning three beers. The barman balanced off a thick foam and put the icy glasses on the counter one at a time. The amber liquid looked and tasted like piss. The music ground on, the woman on the pole moving disinterestedly.

Dale watched her do her thing.

Behind her, on the edge of the curtain, Henry saw the next act getting ready. She had snow-tips frosted into her hair and more folds in her belly than he had in the notes in his wallet. She sucked at a cigarette, blowing smoke.

They took a booth at the back.

Up on the stage the woman fumbled with her bra strap and huge pendulous breasts spilled out of the lace cups as she lowered into a squat.

Henry put his drink on the table. The music was supposed to be seductive. It sounded like cats being strangled. The whole place did nothing to improve their moods.

"So, no one's saying it, so I will. How much extra are we getting paid for doing the kids?" Dale said, when they were approaching the end of their first drink.

"Extra? You can't seriously think there's a price that makes this okay, man?" said Caleb. "They're kids."

"How much?" Dale asked again.

Henry looked at him. Dale scratched at his nose and sniffed. There was a wildness in his eyes the dark bar couldn't completely hide. "Nothing. Not a single cent. The price is the price. Same as it always was."

Dale took a slug of his beer, finishing it, and waved to the bar, signaling for three more. "What we do is an art," Dale said, leaning forward. "It's a gift. That's why they pay us, coz we're good at what we do. And we can do this. But it's gonna cost."

"Is it?" Caleb asked.

"We do this thing for the money, don't we?" Dale said. Henry knew he'd already rationalized it in his head. "We don't pick and choose the jobs we take, we just pocket the money if the green's right. And it's always right, coz if we don't do it someone else will, and that someone will be the one the client turns to next time. And if we're gonna pretend some kind of morality, well, screw that. You kill someone you kill them. Don't matter none if they're nine or ninety. They're dead. The money spends just as good. Done and done and on to the next one. It's who we are. It's what we do."

"Maybe it's who you are," Caleb said.

But Dale was right. It was who they were. There was no point pretending at morality or ethics. They weren't good people. They'd given up the right to any sort of moral quandaries a long time ago.

Henry turned to Caleb. "He's right. But if you want out, now's the time to say. I won't stop you walking, brother. I'll miss you, but I'll understand."

"But you don't get your cut," Dale said, still thinking about the money. "Your call. It's a take-it-or-leave-it situation. And as far as I'm concerned, we took the money, so we're obligated to do the job right."

"And if we do it wrong," Henry said, "we better be ready to run for the rest of our fucking lives, because the boss ain't exactly the forgiving kind."

29

Morning came, crisp and bright and bitterly cold.

There was no sign of the snow melting, but after the initial flurry, things had settled down, so we weren't snowed in, which was a major plus. Part of me had half expected to open the door to a huge drift that I'd need to dig us out of before breakfast.

I was up before the others stirred. I'd woken up twice in the night to put extra wood in the stove. The chair wasn't the most comfortable piece of furniture in the world, so my neck and lower back felt as though they'd been pummeled by an army of Buzz Lightyears—or whatever Chase's action figure was called.

The room was still reasonably warm. There were a dozen split logs beside the stove, drying out in the heat. More than enough to keep it going for the day. I'd bring some more in from the store to keep us warm tomorrow and the day after. I figured that ought to do it. Any longer and we were moving into dangerous territory. I wanted them gone, not least because their still being here meant the three Stooges were still out there, and that wasn't a thought I wanted to entertain any longer than I had to.

Right now my biggest concern was making sure we hadn't had

any visitors during the night. I stepped outside and closed the door behind me as quietly as I could. I didn't want to wake Raelynn and the kids. They'd been absolutely wiped when they'd finally hit the sack. I could only imagine how wrung out they really were with all of that running, especially Raelynn if she'd known she was being hunted. That kind of pressure, the constant need to look back over your shoulder, wore you out pretty fast. Still, they were here now, and there was no rush for them to go anywhere.

I'd promised Wayne I'd swing by for him in the pick-up as long as I could get it down to the road. He wanted to see the cabin. I wanted him to see it. And I wanted to see his face when he did. It was starting to look like a proper home.

The only fresh tracks in the snow had been made by a deer. No doubt it was the same visitor who'd called by before. We were becoming old friends, him and me. Apart from that and the slight impressions made by a few birds that barely broke the crust of the surface and could only be seen close up, the whiteness was flawless and endless.

I hadn't expected the Stooges to find this place, not yet. It'd take a while for them to join the dots and trace Wayne to the cabin, to me, to here, even if someone with loose lips had decided to spill their guts. The weather just made that even more unlikely. For now. But now wasn't forever, so I was going to need to take measures to secure the place soon enough.

"You want coffee?" Raelynn called from the doorway.

I hadn't heard her come out. I was getting sloppy. It had been too long since someone had hunted me, I guess. I'd started taking things for granted. It was a good lesson to relearn. Even so, she was lucky the SIG Sauer was in the pack, or she'd have seen the beady black eye of the barrel instead of my smile of thanks as I spun around. That wouldn't have made the situation any more uncomfortable, though.

She wasn't exactly dressed for the elements, and I could see every curve through the sheer fabric of her nightgown. It reminded me of a line I'd read somewhere. She had a body like a country road, loads of curves where I wanted to stop off and take a picnic. Raelynn

Cardiman was bad for the soul. "Sure," I said. "But you could have stayed in bed a little longer, you know."

"You're joking, right? Once the kids are awake, there's no stopping them."

She rubbed her arms against the cold. It was a reflex. Brisk. But I suspected there was more to it than that. I'd seen my share of addicts overdue a fix. It wasn't my place to parent her, and I wasn't her sponsor, so what she did with her own body was her business. Who was I to judge? But I wouldn't keep her secret if I thought she was getting stoned and putting the kids at risk. There were limits. I figured Wayne knew what he was getting himself into in bringing his junkie daughter home. But then again, maybe he didn't. They did say love was blind.

I took a quick walk around the shack before I went back inside. I wanted to make sure I hadn't missed anything. I saw where the deer had headed off into the woods, but nothing else, which was just fine by me. I walked back around to the front, kicked the snow off my boots and went inside, just as the kids burst out, laughing and screaming, intent on making those snow angels they'd been promised. I stepped aside to let them pass, not that I'd have been able to stop them if I'd wanted to. They wriggled and squirmed and ran, then threw themselves to the ground laughing even more as they swept their arms and legs out.

There was a mug of piping hot black coffee waiting for me when I closed the door on their noise.

"They've been desperate to get out there from the moment they opened their eyes," Raelynn said.

"That's kids for you. Give it an hour and we'll have a snowman the size of King Kong looking down on us."

"I don't doubt it," she said. "Hope you've got a carrot in here somewhere. Every good snowman needs a nose."

I smiled, and looked out of the window at the kids. I could see the sheer joy in their auras, halos burning bright. It made a change from the fear and anger I was used to seeing on people. I could have watched them for a long time. Even so, it was disconcerting to have such a sharp and unexpected reminder of the implant and how different it made me from the rest of the world. Not for me a normal life playing father to giggling kids. Not for me a life without the threat of violence lurking in someone's shadow, the blazing hot red of rage, the insidious, almost gangrenous green of jealousy, and somewhere in between the color lurking around Raelynn's body that marked the stirrings of lust.

It wasn't clear cut a lot of the time. Sometimes it was a stirring, a kind of blur around someone's head, with no obvious color, if it wasn't driven by the extremes of emotion, but other times I was in no doubt what someone was feeling. Like Raelynn. Every time she looked me up and down.

I consciously willed myself to ignore it. It wasn't like she knew she was giving off her heat in waves. But maybe she wouldn't have cared if she had known. Hard to say about some people. What I did know was that kids deserved a life where they could enjoy themselves without the adults having to fret over them every minute of the day, imagining the worst. This place was much better for them than the city could ever have been.

I saw Chase scoop up a handful of snow and run at his sister. She responded in kind, cackling, as she buried her hands deep in the snow and threw up a thick plume of white for him to run straight into. They were having fun.

"Don't suppose you could drive me into town this morning? I was hoping to meet up with an old friend," Raelynn said, watching me watching them. "I wouldn't ask normally, but what with the weather and everything . . . It's a long walk."

There was something about the way she asked that seemed a little peculiar. I didn't want to read too much into it, but this was her first morning back and she was itching to meet up with a friend she couldn't have seen for years, rather than spend the time with her kids while they were having fun. I might have understood it if she had asked me to take her up to see Wayne, but she hadn't even mentioned him. In her place this morning I would have asked right away if he'd been in touch. We'd left him alone in a house that had been burgled a few hours earlier by people almost certainly looking for her. That she didn't ask was telling.

"Sorry," I said, but I wasn't. "I promised your father I'd pick him up first thing. I'm already running late. You can always walk."

"It's miles."

"Good exercise," I said.

"You're a very strange man," she said.

"I am," I agreed. "Stranger than you could ever imagine."

"I've got a good imagination," she said. Again with the flirting.

"Not good enough," I promised her.

She let it drop.

Over the next few minutes she tried to convince me to change my mind, but gave up pretty quickly after the third time I said no. I finished my coffee without taking my coat off and headed for the door. "There's bread and eggs and a few cans in the cupboard, nothing fancy, but you're welcome to help yourself. I'll try and check in with you in a few hours. If I can manage it I'll swing by and drop you and the kids at your dad's later."

"Thanks," she said, through a smile that was painfully forced. "Have fun."

I closed the door behind me, made a fuss of the kids, then climbed into the pick-up and turned it around. I headed for the road.

30

—————

Wayne stared at the cabin, trying to process what he was seeing. He shook his head, started to ask how, then just shook his head again. "I was only gone an afternoon, Mike. How on earth did you get even half of this done?"

He was up the ladder examining my handiwork. The rungs beneath his feet were still coated with a thin crust of ice, but I had my eye on him. He was testing a couple of the batons to check they were secure.

"It's just discipline," I said, like that could make sense of it for him. "Once I got into a rhythm it was just a case of keeping going. I didn't think about it. It's pretty straightforward."

He was smiling now. "You're a natural, son. Once word gets around what you're capable of I'm pretty sure half the town will have work for you."

"But not till we finish up here," I said.

"Of course." Wayne laughed. "Hell, I'll even give you references. I'm sure we can find enough work to keep you busy for a while. It'd be nice to keep you around, let you put some roots down."

It was a seductive idea. It's a natural state for most people, that feeling of needing to belong. It was an important part of what guys like me got out of the armed forces, the whole brothers-in-arms ideal. That was the last time I'd ever felt like I belonged anywhere. And it was a long time ago now. I had to admit that I was enjoying working with my hands, too. "Careful, I might just take you up on that."

He clambered down. He did a circuit of the cabin, admiring my work from the ground. "We just need to tidy up the edges and that roof will be done," he said, patting me on the shoulder. "Not long until it'll be ready for Rae and the kids to move in."

"You planning on bringing them out to see it today?"

"Not yet. In an ideal world I'd love to be able to surprise them with it finished, but there's no way we'll get it done. She'll just bombard us with questions about where we're sneaking off to, and drive us nuts long before we're done. Besides, I'm no good at keeping secrets."

"Soon, then," I said. "Before she wheedles the surprise out of you."

"Soon," he agreed.

We started to move planks into position. The last thing I'd done yesterday evening was pile them up beneath the shelter of the roof and cover them with a tarp. Wayne either didn't notice or didn't want to know how I'd managed to do even more than he already thought was impossible.

WE WORKED for a couple of hours, fixing them in place, not talking much. We'd made good progress, and with a bit of luck we'd have the whole back wall in place before the day was out.

Wayne started to flag.

"Why don't we take a break?" I suggested. "You brought the coffee?"

"Sure have," he said, and went to retrieve his bag from the truck.

I was trying to make up my mind whether I should meddle or not. I asked myself what I'd want in his place: my friend to keep secrets from me or for him to tell me an ugly truth I didn't want to hear. I decided just this once maybe ignorance could be bliss. He deserved a few days at least to enjoy having his little girl home, no matter how screwed up she was. I'd find out who she was so eager to meet in town, and then I'd reassess my decision.

"We may as well have it in here," he called, from the cab of the pick-up, and beckoned me through the open driver's window. As I walked across the snow-covered ground to the vehicle, he fired up the engine and wound the window up to get some warmth back into his old bones. Sometimes it was easy to forget he was seventy-something.

"So, how was last night?" I asked.

"Quiet. Yours?"

"Noisy," I said, with a grin. He laughed and I joined in. "No return visit then?"

"Nah." He sipped at the still too-hot coffee. "Whoever they were, they're long gone. Maybe we're just jumping at shadows thinking they're something to do with Rae. Nothing to say they're not just addicts from further down the mountain looking for something they could cash in to feed their habit. People like that get desperate." It was wishful thinking, I knew, and I'm pretty sure he did too, but it was a bubble I didn't want to pop just yet. That whole shooting-the-messenger thing had become a saying for a reason.

Still, the three men I'd seen hadn't looked either desperate or addicted. And if they wanted cash they wouldn't have walked out leaving stuff they could have pawned to feed their habit, even if they'd found a wad of notes bundled up in the drawer. They'd have kept looking until they were sure they'd cleaned him out, including jewelry, portable electronics, anything easy to offload.

"Rae and the kids no trouble?"

"Good as gold," I said. "They bunked up together in the bedroom. I slept in the chair. Didn't hear a peep out of them once they settled down." I told him how the kids had been full of it this morning, making snow angels, building a snowman and having a snowball fight when I left. Picturing it was enough to bring a smile to his face.

"Sounds like they're having fun."

"They're good kids," I said.

Wayne took another sip of coffee and stared out of the windshield at the cabin. "You know what I'm going to ask," he said.

I nodded.

"But you're going to make me ask, aren't you?"

I nodded again.

He sighed.

"Okay, you mind if they stay with you for another couple of days? Just until things blow over."

"For as long as they need to. You don't have to ask," I said.

"Then why make me?"

"Because I'm an ornery bastard," I said, and grinned.

"That you are," he agreed.

"I'm going to need to go into town to pick up some groceries. It's like Old Mother Hubbard rented out my place. Those cupboards are bare."

"Don't worry about it. I've got you covered. We'll swing by my place on the way to yours. I bought enough to feed the five thousand. No idea what those kids eat or don't eat, so I bought everything. You may as well make use of it."

"Thanks."

There was the faintest trace of yellow around him, like he was just slightly blurred and hard to look at. He was frightened. Not sudden fear. Not the kind of panic that came with the fall from the roof. This was just there, an undercurrent, but strong enough for me to see it.

31

There was no sign of the kids outside when I got back to the shack, but they'd left plenty of evidence to prove they'd been there. Both sides of the winding track were crammed with snow angels. Their attempt at a snowman stood sentry outside the door. He didn't have a carrot for a nose, but he did have two big black stones for eyes. It wasn't exactly Christmas-card perfect, but it was the closest I'd been to any sort of domestic bliss in a very long time.

I grabbed the bags of victuals Wayne had insisted I take, including a six-pack of Pabst that went above and beyond what I needed to feed his family, unless he knew something about the kids that I didn't. Like maybe they drove you to drink.

I'd tried to get him to come back and eat with us, but he insisted he had a couple of things he needed to take care of. Again, as with Raelynn, I was surprised he didn't want to spend every second he could with his daughter and grandchildren, but in his case it maybe wasn't as surprising as it might have been. It was easy to forget how something as relatively commonplace in the city could be so utterly invasive and alien out here. He'd been putting on a brave face about the whole thing. I'm sure his errands were related to the break-in, so I didn't push it.

"Here's Johnny," I called, as I pushed the door open. I kicked the snow from my boots and trudged inside. There'd been no fresh snow so far today, but the kids had managed to scatter what there was just about everywhere. Including inside.

I felt the blast of heat from the stove.

"Hey, Mike," Chase said, without looking up from what he was doing. He had that new game of his spread out across the floor, taking up most of the free space, while Anna sat with her legs tucked under her, coloring intently between the lines on a geisha-like maiden with flowers in her hair. The book was perched on the arm of the sofa. She glanced up and smiled.

Again that unwanted feeling: the notion that I could get used to this.

That way lay madness for a man like me.

The door into the bedroom was wide open, but there was no sign of Raelynn. I figured she was in the outhouse, but asked anyway. "Where's your mom?"

"She'll be back soon," Chase said, this time glancing up from his game long enough to see concern flit across my face. "Want to play with me while we wait for her?"

"Not right now, son," I said, mind racing to all the worst conclusions.

"You just don't wanna lose like Anna. She always loses," the boy said. His sister smiled indulgently at him. It wasn't hard to figure out that she let him win. She was a good kid, older and wiser than her years.

"Where has she gone?" I asked Anna.

She looked at me and, without blinking, told me, "She's gone to buy her stuff. She won't be long. She never is."

"Stuff?"

"You know, pills, painkillers, whatever she can get.'

"You sure, kiddo?"

"I know that look she gets. It's always the same. She'll go out and get what she needs, then pick up some Red Vines and Twizzlers for us. She always says she's going to get some candy. Sometimes she forgets. But most of the time she comes back with something." The kid was so matter-of-fact about it, like it was an everyday occurrence and there was nothing out of the ordinary about a mom going into town to score and bring back some treats for the kids. It was the kind of thing that broke your heart to hear. You didn't want to imagine the complete loss of innocence that was needed for something like that to be normal.

How could someone be so desperate for a handful of pills they didn't stop to think about the kids and the crap they were putting them through? I didn't need to ask that one out loud: I knew just how easy it was.

I retrieved the cheap pay-as-you-go cellphone I'd picked up in a Walmart along the freeway before I'd settled in Winter's Rage. I'd bought it on impulse, not because I was planning on needing to make any calls, but more because, the way the world was changing, I knew it was going to become more and more difficult to buy a burner as the authorities tried to track anything and everything in the name of Homeland Insecurity.

My first thought when I'd charged it up was that I would make one call, just to let someone know I was okay, but that was a bad idea. I stripped it, keeping the Sim card and battery separate, not giving anyone a chance to track it. And every now and then I'd charge it at the diner. I hadn't made a single call on the burner in the months that I'd owned it. Wayne had given me his number. It wasn't in the phone. I'd committed it to memory even though I'd never called him.

I quickly reassembled the phone, slipping the Sim into place beneath the battery and sliding the back on until it clicked in place. I thumbed down the power button and waited for the boot sequence to pick up the signal from the nearest cell tower.

Nothing. The one time I actually needed to use the damned thing and there was no signal.

I went outside, holding the burner up like I was dowsing, in the hope that it would improve things. *Nada.* Damn.

Why couldn't the woman have done as she'd been told? She knew there were people out there looking for her, and that they'd be drawn to the same kind of dirtbags who traded in pills and weed and anything else, because they knew about her habit, yet she'd still gone looking for her fix in a town with a population of a few thousand. It wasn't like a dealer could hide in Winter's Rage, though at a guess I'd peg the self-destructive drug of choice in town to be meth. Nothing designer, just good old-fashioned homebrew shit.

I couldn't pretend to understand how the cravings of withdrawal could mess with someone's mind, causing them to do stupid things. Neither was I stupid enough to blindly ignore the cycle of misery that went with addiction. But those kids knew what she was doing. She didn't even attempt to hide it from them. That was unforgivable.

I had no way of knowing how long it would be before she came back or, more tellingly, what kind of state she'd be in.

I walked to the end of the track, holding the burner phone up as I turned in a full circle, looking for the little bars of a signal to appear. Nothing. I looked up and down the road. There was no sign of her.

There was no sign of anyone.

I headed back inside.

"You kids hungry?" I asked, starting to shelve the various groceries on the counter. I didn't have a fridge or freezer, but given the subzero temperatures, anything that needed to be kept cold would just have to go outside. The beers, I figured, would be just fine out there, unless my curious deer had a taste for the amber liquid.

"You bet," they echoed in unison.

"You eaten anything since breakfast?"

A look of uncertainty passed between them, like they weren't sure which answer would get their mother into less trouble. "How about sandwiches? Nothing fancy. I've got ham, and I've got cheese. Or you can have both together, if you want." I winked conspiratorially, like I was offering them the greatest delicacy in the world. "Better still, I've got OJ."

In a matter of minutes we were tucking into our late lunch, chewing and talking around mouthfuls of food. I kept one eye out through the window, hoping that Raelynn would be back at any minute, and dreading that she wouldn't.

32

Caleb and Dale were bitching like little girls. Henry was tired of listening to them. Every couple of minutes he squeezed his hand so tight his dirty fingernails left deep impressions in his palm. He could happily have wrung the life out of one of those stress balls. No amount of alcohol had improved his mood, or things between them, and even a go-round with the C-section woman, up against the wall in the bathroom, hadn't mended his mood.

He'd crashed hard last night. They'd have had a better chance of raising the dead than getting him out of his pit. It wasn't just a few drinks. It was the weight of the argument. Knowing what he was about to become, and that he really didn't have a choice in it.

Caleb and Dale were *still* going at it when he opened his eyes. They didn't stop through breakfast, and he doubted very much they'd stop until a trigger was pulled.

It was endless round-and-around with the pair of them, money versus morality, mortality versus sentimentality, sentimentality versus reputation versus professionalism in a pointless dance that always came back to the same two things: money or peace of mind. Both of them tried their damnedest to convince him they were right. Henry was past caring. He just wanted them to shut the hell up and leave him alone.

"Look, it's not about what actually happens, is it? It's about what we tell the boss. If we just do the job we were hired to do, kill her and leave the kids alone, no one's going to know any different."

"Apart from the TV, the internet, the news reports, and the fact that there's no outpouring of grief in a small community for a couple of kids. Yeah, you're right, no one will know. Moron."

"Shut the hell up, Dale. How many times do I have to tell you this *isn't* the job? We've got a contract. It's very specific. Kill Raelynn Cardiman. When we've done that, we're done. End of. All obligations are fulfilled. We bank the dough and walk away."

"He ain't gonna pay up if we don't off the kids."

"Then he doesn't pay up, and we go pay him a visit. Turn the tables."

"Don't even go there," Dale said, twitching in his seat. "Are you out of your mind?"

"Why? We're sharks, bro. We're not the little fishes that swim around waiting to be eaten. So what? You worried it's the last job we're going to do if we piss off the boss? So be it. I won't lose any sleep over it. Bastard tried to change the rules halfway into the game. That ain't on. We're men of honor, Dale. You get that, right? Without honor we've got nothing."

"We've got cold hard cash," the other man objected.

"Man, that's all it is with you, isn't it? Money, money, money. I want to be able to sleep at night. I don't want to wake up at two in the morning coz I'm seeing their faces in my dreams."

"A killer with a conscience! You're such a cliché, Caleb."

"Will you pair just shut up!" Henry demanded. He braked hard and pulled the car over to the side of the road. The snow still obscured the edge of the asphalt. He could easily have run off into the ditch but didn't care. He was out of patience. "Listen to me and listen good, boys. Because my word is God, understand?" He didn't wait for them to answer. "We are doing this. And then that's it. The band's breaking up. You can move to Timbuktu for all I care, but we're done."

"And you aren't even gonna push for compensation? Man, that's shit. You want us to take three times the risk for the same money?"

"How many times do I have to tell you? It's not three times the risk. It's the same job. We find Mom and kids playing happy families, three bullets, no witnesses. Done. If the old man's there, then four. And that's an end of it. And you know why? Because I say so." Dale started to speak but Henry cut him short. "This isn't open for discussion. This is my job. We play it the way I want to play it. You get your cut. You do not give me grief."

"Hang on a minute ..."

"No, you hang on. If you don't like it you know what you have to do." He held out his hand for the cash Dale had already spent. "Yeah, I didn't think so. Now let that be an end to it. This is my gig. We're doing it my way."

Henry still hadn't let go of the steering wheel, his grip so tight that his knuckles were white. There was a rage building inside him he struggled to control. He counted out the lines along his knuckles, trying to regulate his breathing. If he let go of the wheel he was going to slap one or both of them, maybe worse if they didn't just shut up. It was getting harder and harder to think clearly. To see the end game. No matter what he said, things had changed. Now it was all about getting this done quickly and cleanly and getting as far from Winter's Rage as the roads would take them.

"We do this," he said slowly, barely keeping his anger in check, "and then we go our separate ways. This little arrangement isn't working for me anymore. Dale, you're a damn liability. Caleb, man, I just don't *like* you. So, let's go out in style, or go out dead, one or the other."

"I ain't gonna die," Dale said. "I'm going to live forever."

"Sure you are," Caleb said.

Before either of them could say anything else, Henry hit the wheel once. Hard. The horn blared then choked off.

Dale laughed.

He fucking *laughed*.

33

Leaving Anna and Chase was the last thing I wanted to do. But when Raelynn still hadn't returned after more than an hour, and there was no sign of her on the road, I didn't have a choice. There were too many variables at play. Too many things I couldn't control.

I *could* have taken them with me, or at a push dropped them over at Wayne's, but without explaining why I was anxious, and therefore bringing up the whole drug thing. He had enough to worry about without this. The problem with taking the kids along was that I didn't know what I was walking into. Chances were good I'd find her in the bar, but I could just as easily find her in a back alley, out of her mind, or worse. And I wanted to spare the kids that. And even after a few months I was still a stranger there. Wayne knew the town, and the people. He'd know where to start looking, and probably where to end looking, too. I thought about the sheriff, but that wasn't a call I wanted to make without a very good reason. And we weren't at that stage yet.

So, really, I wasn't sure what I could do apart from drive around town, street by street, and hope I got lucky. Maybe I'd meet Raelynn on the road, making her way back up. The question was, how was my luck?

"Okay, kiddo, I'm leaving you in charge," I told Anna. "That means she's the boss," I told Chase. "What she says goes."

He made a face at that. His sister just grinned. "Same as always," she said.

They settled down on the couch, squirming in like sardines, sharing the blanket I'd used the night before. I put another log on the stove, to be sure it stayed warm while I was gone. They had full bellies. In an ideal world I'd have put the TV on and left them to their own devices with a flatscreen babysitter. They looked ready to drift off to sleep, which was no bad thing.

I felt a pang of guilt, knowing I was doing to them exactly what their mother had done, but it wasn't my place to beat myself up over the quality of their lives.

"You going to be okay?" I asked, as I shrugged back into my coat.

"Course we will," Anna said matter-of-factly. "We can look after ourselves just fine."

And I didn't doubt that for a second. This was a kid who'd been playing the adult in her world for a long time now. "I promise I won't be long."

"You going to look for Mom?"

"Yep. Figure I'll meet her on the road. It's a long way from town. Give her a ride so she gets out of the cold and then you guys can show her the snowman you made. Sound good?"

Anna shrugged. "She'll be fine," she said, her eyelids starting to droop. "She always is."

"Okay, well, you guys have a nap. You won't have long enough to miss me."

Anna was already asleep before I reached the door. With a little luck I'd be back before they woke up again.

I stopped at the door, hand on the frame.

Something didn't feel right. I looked back at the kids, trying to think what I'd forgotten. I saw my bag on the floor: never a good idea to leave a couple of kids alone with a loaded gun. I grabbed the pack and slung it over my shoulder.

I closed the door quietly behind me, and went out into the cold. The air was bracing. I felt it deep in my lungs. Clean. There was no other word for it. It would be a long time before I got used to what fresh air tasted like after years of city smog, exhaust fumes and desert sands.

I threw my pack in through the open door, then clambered in.

Before I turned the ignition over, I took the SIG Sauer out of the bag and tucked it into the back of my jeans. I loosened my shirt, untucking it so the tail fell over the gun, hiding it.

I put the key in the ignition. As I turned it over, the wipers kicked in, the blades squealing across the dry glass. I killed them. I was banking on her coming home. I really didn't want to have to walk into whatever passed for a drug den in Winter's Rage and drag her out by the hair. But I'd do it if I had to. For Wayne. He didn't deserve to be fucked around. And once I'd got her, she and me, we were going to have some serious words about what kind of trouble she'd brought to town with her.

I turned the pick-up around.

I wanted to be angry at her, but a growing sense of unease was setting in. The longer she was missing, the longer I didn't know who those three Stooges actually were, or where they were, the more convinced I was that they'd got her. I could think of a hundred things she could have got herself involved in and a hundred more she might have run from, none of them good. A single mom who left the kids home alone to go out and score wasn't exactly role-model material. So, assuming her past was catching up with her, the question was just one of collateral damage and how much of it there would be before those chickens came home to roost.

So much for a quiet life, I thought, as I pulled away.

34

I drove slowly, alert, looking, I realized, more often than not in the ditches along the side of the road for a splash of color that said someone was face down in one.

Habit had me using the blinkers as I reached the turn, even though there was no one on the road. I pulled out onto the wider road, but didn't accelerate. Jim Burges's snowplow had broken the back of the last fall, but with the quickly dropping temperature and the melt still glistening on the road, black ice was a real possibility.

Hit that, and I could easily end up in the ditch myself.

A crow flew across my field of vision, banking in the blue sky with its wide wings unfurled, feathers a blur as the wings started beating again. I followed the direction of its flight across the road. A color that shouldn't have been anywhere in the landscape caught my eye. It was almost a hundred yards away. I immediately sensed what it was.

Raelynn.

"Shit, shit, shit," I hissed, pulling over to the side of the road.

I left the engine running and the door open as I ran across the road to kneel beside her. My first thought was hit-and-run, that she'd been flung to the side of the road like a ragdoll, broken, and the driver had powered off, damned if he was going to wait to see if she was all right.

But close up I couldn't see any sign of injuries. For one sickening second I couldn't see the rise and fall of her chest, but I leaned in close enough to feel her breath on my skin. I checked her pulse. It was weak but steady.

A picture began to form in my mind. She'd taken something back in town and hadn't been able to make it to my place. She was cold. I figured she'd been lying there for a long time. She wasn't even dressed for the damned cold. She was in the same clothes she'd come to town in.

She needed help. Without knowing what she'd taken, I wasn't sure what I was supposed to do. Or where I was supposed to take her. The nearest hospital was two towns over. There was a small Doc-in-a-Box in Winter's Rage, or the surgery, but the doctor was older than God, a doddery old soak who should have retired and handed the practice to someone younger a long time ago. We couldn't go home. There was no way I was letting the kids see her like this.

Which left Wayne.

I lifted her up and slung her over my shoulder, surprised at how light she was. It wasn't the first time I had carried someone like that. It was standard battlefield procedure. No one left behind. When you needed to get someone out of danger, and fast, it was more effective than trying to carry them in your arms, no matter the indignity of it. Winter's Rage might not be a war zone, but the ethos stood.

With one hand wrapped around her legs, I opened the passenger side door and lowered her in as gently as I could, without banging her head on the doorframe. Raelynn fell lengthways across the bench seat, her arm sliding down into the foot well. I had to push her all the way in and fold her legs up, wedging her against the door so that I could get it closed.

I jumped in behind the wheel. I looked over at her. "Don't you dare die on me, Raelynn. If you're in there, you listen to me. I'm serious. You've got two kids back there who I am not going to play Dad to, and a father who'll die if you don't wake up." The implant in my brain deadened me to so much, taking away the adrenalin surge of panic and all of the natural amplifiers that helped the human body cope with duress. It was meant to help me, make me more ruthlessly efficient in the field, but sometimes it felt detrimental, like now, where the pulse-pounding adrenal high might just be the difference between life and death for my passenger.

I couldn't let myself think like that. My focus had to be her. Everything from here had to be about minimizing the trauma of the drug on her system, on reviving her, leveling her out. And, first, waking her up. I remembered a conversation when I was much younger, at a party down in Chelsea where the girl I'd been chasing—it wasn't so much a date as a pity party for one— had ended up half conscious after someone had slipped her a roofie. I'd walked her round in circles, trying to keep her awake because the medic at the other end of the 911 call had said it was imperative I didn't let her fall asleep. And there was Raelynn, out cold. Pretty much the opposite of everything that medic had said was life and death. I slapped her, not hard, just a sting on the cheek, trying to wake her.

A second and third slap as I drove toward Wayne's, saying over and over, "Don't you dare, girl. Don't you dare. Those kids need you." I had no idea if it would make a blind bit of difference, but I had to figure she could hear me, even if she couldn't respond, and I wanted to give her something to cling to wherever she was, so I kept on talking to her. I said the kids names over and over again, telling her she had to come back. Open her eyes.

I accelerated, still not driving fast, but on the edge of the limit, and beyond what was safe, given the conditions. I wanted to call ahead to Wayne, but I still didn't have a signal. So, I had no choice but to accelerate, pushing the pick-up harder than it had been driven in years. It jounced and juddered down the track as I took the turn to his place.

Wayne was sitting on his porch with a shotgun across his lap. He didn't move even as he saw me approaching. He stayed in his seat right until I slewed the pick-up to a stop at the foot of the porch steps. Then he rose to his feet, holding the gun in both hands.

I jumped out, yelling at him to put the gun down and come and help me.

"What the hell's lit the fire under your ass, Mike?"

"It's Raelynn," I said, running around the side of the cab to get at the passenger door. "I found her at the side of the road. She's in a bad way." It was enough to set him in motion. He leaned the shotgun against his wooden rocking chair and came stumping down the few wooden steps to join me at the passenger side of the pick-up. I already had the door open and was holding Raelynn's inert body in my arms as she spilled out of the cab. He helped me steady her. I carried her up the steps and into the house. I didn't bother kicking the snow off my boots so I left wet prints as I took her inside.

"The living room," he said. "There's a fire burning. I'll get blankets."

Wayne snatched up his shotgun again, coming into the house behind me. He slammed the door harder than he intended. There was something in his voice, an edge to it, which led me to think this wasn't the first time something very much like this had happened to him. There was no surprise. No panic. I recognized what it was when he asked, "What happened?" Resignation. Like this was always going to happen.

I told him. "She wasn't there when I got back. She'd told the kids she was going into town to buy them some candy. Anna told me that's what she says when she goes to buy drugs."

He just nodded. No surprise again.

"When she didn't come back I went looking for her. I found her about a mile from the shack, in the ditch."

"She left the kids on their own?"

"And not for the first time. Those kids are old beyond their years, Wayne. I get the feeling Anna's the adult in that little family." He didn't argue with my observation.

"I can't believe she walked out on them," he said, looking at her like he didn't recognize her—and maybe he didn't. The junkie wasn't the little girl he'd raised, surely.

I went through to the living room. It was hot in there, almost oppressively so with the fire roaring in the grate. He went ahead of me, moving a pile of newspapers from the couch so I could lay her down. He made a pillow out of a couple of cushions for her head. I stepped aside so he could fuss over her. I watched him do the same checks I had done: airways, pulse, though he lifted her eyelids, too.

"You want me to take her to the hospital?"

He shook his head. "No point. It's miles away. The weather could turn at any minute."

"Okay. Want me to drive into town to fetch the doc?"

He shook his head again. "She's out of it, but she's fine, or as fine as she can be with that shit swimming through her veins. Trust me, I've seen this before, too often. The only thing that's going to help her is time." I looked at him, waiting for more in the way of explanation. All he said was "I should have seen this coming."

"Why? Because she's come back home?"

"She said she was clean, but I saw the marks on her arm. I *knew* she was lying to me. I knew what those bruises meant. I knew she was using again, or still using, but I didn't say anything. I let you take her and I didn't warn you. I should have told you."

"Yes, you should. But it's done now. We can't change it. So, we take turns and watch her. We wait and we hope she's fine."

Wayne nodded but he did not take his eyes from his daughter.

It was my turn to broach a difficult subject. "You know what I'm going to ask now," I said.

He nodded.

"Those men. They came looking for Raelynn."

He nodded again. No doubt in his mind either.

"They took a photograph of her," he said, which confirmed my suspicion.

"They were confirming her ID," I said. I knew plenty of different people who might look for visual confirmation that they'd found the right person, everyone from bail bondsmen, bounty hunters, skip tracers and private eyes to paid goons, hitmen and everything in between. I didn't say anything.

Wayne raised his head. He looked defeated.

"They aren't burglars," I said. "They asked around town about Raelynn. Remember that. They went into the diner, sat down in the middle of the busiest place, ordered coffees and chatted up Larry Carter. That's not someone who's looking at breaking into your place without you knowing. They're banking on word getting back to Raelynn that they're here. They want her to panic. To react."

"You may be right," Wayne said, then rubbed the back of his hand across his eyes.

"I'm always right," I said. "Even when I don't want to be."

"What do they want with her?"

"Good question. It's normally money," I said. "Nine times out of ten it's money. Did she say why it was so important she came home now?"

"Not a word. I guessed that she was in some kind of trouble. Why else would she be back here?"

"To be with you?"

"I doubt it. Raelynn's always done what's best for Raelynn. She doesn't think about me, her kids. That's how she got herself into this mess in the first place."

"We're going to have to have an honest chat with her when she comes around." I almost said "if." "She knows who those guys are. She knows what they want. And, to be brutally honest, she knows just how serious they're going to be about getting it."

In the moment of silence that deepened between us I heard a sound that seemed so absolutely familiar yet so utterly out of place. An engine. I glanced through the window and saw a beat-up Cadillac heading toward the house. "We've got company," I said. "We need to get out of here."

Wayne followed my gaze.

"I ain't leaving," he said, picking up his shotgun, ready to defend his property. He reminded me of no one more than a larger-than-life Elmer Fudd.

But he wasn't planning on shooting rabbits or ducks.

"I'm serious, we need to get out of here!" I snapped. "Use your head. There's three of them. They've got guns. They are going to come in hot. No questions. No stand-off on the porch. We're not driving them off. Not if they're looking for money," I said. "And she's the key. So, we've got to get her out of here, too."

"If we walk out now, they're just going to trash the place."

"Let them. Better that than leave you dead in front of the fire." I gathered Raelynn up into my arms. She stirred a little but didn't open her eyes. I started for the back door. "Don't be a fool," I said, without turning. "She's going to need you alive and so are those kids. Look at the state of her. You're all they've got. Don't make it so the next time they see youse in a box going into the ground."

"You don't argue fair," Wayne said.

"If it keeps you alive I don't give a shit," I said.

It was enough. It got him out of there.

35

Henry felt the hood of the pick-up parked at an angle outside. It was still warm. Snow filled the flatbed, turning the tarp into a replica of the mountain. It hadn't been abandoned for long, meaning someone was home. He walked up the wooden steps to the porch. The first thing he noticed was that the lock had been fixed. There was a strong metal plate where the wood had splintered the last time he had forced his way inside. It made no difference whatsoever because the door was unlocked. "Now ain't that just a puzzlement," Henry said. "Our boy's gone to all the trouble of fixing the lock, but hasn't used it. These country folk are something. They make my brain hurt. It's like they just don't get there are wolves out there."

"Or maybe they figure the best way to stay safe is just to let the wolves into the henhouse and hope they pick a different hen to chow down on." Dale laughed, a hysterical edge to the sound.

Caleb gazed down at the tracks in the snow. They told a story all of their own. He looked up at his skinny runt of a companion. "If they really wanted to help they'd leave a nice little note about how they couldn't face the world and put a bullet in their temples."

"No one's that helpful," Dale said. He pushed the door open, and leaned inside. "Come out, come out, wherever you are," he called.

No reply.

The house *felt* empty.

Henry drew his Desert Eagle as he crossed the threshold. It was a beast of a gun. It could quite easily put down an elephant. It was more than adequate for dealing with an old man and a junkie whore.

There was a misconception about guns, about how they were all about stopping power, but stopping power itself was pretty much irrelevant when it came to killing someone. You want to stop someone you might as well to hit them with a brick to the side of the head, or a bat. You could seriously mess someone up with a Louisville Slugger. A bullet, once it was inside you, was going to do the same shit to your vital organs and blood system whether it came at you from a Magnum or a Browning or a Glock. It was a matter of physics and biology.

"Caleb, circle round the back," Henry ordered. "Make sure no one gets any bright ideas about trying to sneak off before the party gets started."

Caleb didn't need to be told twice.

"We'll save you a live one," Dale mocked. "Wouldn't want you missing out on anything."

Whatever else he thought about Dale, he knew he could rely on his trigger-happy partner to have his back. He wouldn't think twice about putting a couple of slugs into a target if the situation called for it. No hesitation. No half-second delay as he wrestled with his conscience or struggled to differentiate between friend and foe.

Henry paused to listen to the silence. He heard the snap and crackle of damp logs burning in the fire, the sap sounding like the staccato rattle of gunfire.

He felt the heat coming off the fire. It was like a furnace.

He held the Desert Eagle in front of him, pushing the door all the way open with his free hand. He stepped into the room, hoping to see a touching family scene, Raelynn crouched protectively over her kids, arms around their shoulders, trying to hide in the corner, like he wouldn't be able to see them there.

The room was empty.

"Upstairs," he told Dale.

The other man padded up the risers, a grin of anticipation plastered over his cadaverous features. His elongated shadow made him look like a poor man's Max Schreck.

Henry moved through to the small kitchen diner at the back of the house. Like the living room, it was empty. Plenty of signs of recent habitation, including a pot on the stove where someone had boiled water for coffee. The jar of granules was open on the counter top and the water was still plenty warm.

The back door opened.

He turned fast, raising his gun instinctively, only to see himself facing down the wrong end of Caleb's Glock.

Henry saw footprints leading away from the house. They disappeared into the coverage of trees beyond.

"No sign," Caleb said.

Henry looked at the tracks properly. Two sets, both adult, both male, given the size of the impression. No kids. No Raelynn.

He went back into the living room, trying to think like them. Two people had been in that room until just a few minutes ago. He looked at the window. So, they'd heard or seen them coming and made a break for it, slipping out the back.

They couldn't be far.

And one of them was an old man.

He knew he should get out there and run the bastard down, because this was losing what little entertainment value it had—but the old man wasn't the target, the daughter was, and she wasn't with them.

Dale came down the stairs. "All clear up here, H," he said.

"This is such a fucking mess," Caleb said. "It was supposed to be an easy gig, Henry. Whack the girl, move on. This is turning into a freaking circus."

"Christ, all you do is whine, whine, whine, like a little bitch. If I hear one more fucking word out of you I'm going to drill a hole right here." He prodded Caleb in the chest, not hard but the jab caught him off guard and the big man dropped onto the couch.

He tried to get back to his feet, but Henry leaned over him, placing a firm hand on his chest and pinning him in place. For a moment he saw proper fear in the other man's eyes. And with good reason. Henry was the best of them. Or the worst. It was all a matter of perspective.

He saw something then that had him laughing. He reached over Caleb, and plucked a cheap earring from the sofa cushion. He held it up to the light like it was the finest treasure to be admired. He was laughing because he knew it as Raelynn's from the photo he'd found yesterday. He could smell her in the room, he realized. Her fragrance. He should have recognized it earlier but he'd been too focused on the fact there had been only two sets of prints in the snow.

"She's been here all right," he said, vindicated. "And she'll be back sooner or later."

"The kids ain't here, though," Dale said. Which was right. It was a fair observation, and might actually be important. If the kids were staying somewhere else that meant Raelynn was, too. So, what other places might she stay in town?

Or they were carrying the kids. That was possible, wasn't it?

There were people who could tell from the size of a print whether it was a man or a woman, how heavy they were, how fast they were going, and all sorts of other shit like what they'd eaten for breakfast. He wasn't one of them. All he had seen were two sets of prints that merged into each other as if their paths crossed, or maybe one was pulling the other along, like a soldier dragging a wounded man. Big prints, which was why he'd guessed male. But that was it.

"Shouldn't we go after them?" Caleb asked, back on his feet at last.

"They'll be back," Henry said, sure that they would. "This place is miles from town and they're going to need that pick-up out front to get there. They'll be back."

"So, we just wait?"

"We could do that, sure. It's nice and warm in here. We could just brew a coffee and wait for them. But we could also make sure there's no room for fuck-ups. Like taking the starter motor out of that pick-up, cutting the fuel line, disabling the brakes, whatever will crush their spirits if they actually make it that far."

"I've got it," Caleb said. He produced a knife and flicked it open.

"Your kind of job," Dale said. "Cutting something that don't fight back."

"Shut up, Dale, unless you want me to give you something to really smile about," the other man said, with a flick of the wrist making it obvious just how wide a smile could become with the help of one good cut.

36

I watched from the trees as the three men emerged from Wayne's house. I studied them as they walked, judging them. You can tell a lot about a man from the way he carries himself. It's not just about arrogance or confidence either. You can tell if someone's got a natural propensity to go left or right, for one, depending on their dominant hand and foot, which is worth knowing if you're anticipating a fight. It's about weight distribution.

You can also tell if a man's antsy or calm, even over distance. And only one of these men was calm. The other two were tense. They'd worked themselves up before they stormed the house, and now they were coming down.

I didn't move. We had a problem, in terms of being isolated in the woods with no easy way to cover distance, but in their place I wouldn't have come out to hunt us, either. We needed wheels; they had wheels. We could hardly cover the miles of forest in the snow carrying Raelynn between us.

One of them had taken the back door, but we'd been clear and in the cover of the trees maybe thirty seconds before he appeared. Close, but he'd never know how close. A second had emerged from inside. I'd seen him note our tracks. Both had their weapons drawn.

The guns were all Wayne needed to grasp the severity of the shit his daughter had brought to his door.

The second man seemed to stare straight at me without actually seeing me.

I didn't move.

For the longest time I didn't even breathe. I just stared right back at him. I still had Raelynn in my arms. Wayne stood at my shoulder, struggling to catch his breath.

In the darkness of the trees we were invisible.

"If we can get to the pick-up we can get out of here," Wayne muttered, but it was wishful thinking at its finest.

Even if we made it all the way to the vehicle unseen, we'd be sitting ducks trying to get away, and after their little display I didn't see these three as hostage takers. They wanted Raelynn. She was our insurance as long as they needed her to talk, and our death sentence from the moment words ceased to matter.

Wayne had his shotgun and I had my SIG, but with Raelynn's dead weight to worry about it wasn't as if we could rush them.

Plus, anywhere we went Nature was going to leave handy arrows for them to follow.

There was no getting away from the footprints in the snow unless we could learn to fly, or swing through the trees.

The problem was, we weren't getting out of there without the pick-up. They knew that. We knew that. It wasn't exactly a Mexican standoff, but it sure as hell made things more complicated than I would have liked.

By myself I could have taken to the trees and they'd never have found me. I knew how to get back to my shack avoiding the main roads, or up to the cabin where we'd be afforded at least a semblance of shelter, but with a whacked-out Raelynn, already verging on hypothermic, the last thing I wanted to do was stay out in the cold.

We needed to be around people.

No one pulls a trigger with dozens of witnesses. The safest place in the world for us right now was Winter's Rage, right in the heart of Main Street.

The two men disappeared back inside.

We took our chance, moving as quickly as we dared around the tree line, working ourselves into a position where we could make a run for the pick-up if, and only if, the opportunity arose.

It's the hope that kills you.

Always the hope.

The three of them emerged together, the bigger man moving ahead as they walked down the steps from Wayne's porch. He had something in his hand that glinted silver in the sunlight: a knife. He walked around the side of the pick-up. A moment later the screech of metal on metal filled the silence as he dragged his blade along the side of Wayne's vehicle, gouging deep beneath the paintwork.

Wayne jerked forward, shotgun raised and ready to put a few holes in the man for the sheer temerity of his wanton vandalism. I put my hand on the barrel of the gun and lowered it. "You wouldn't stand a chance from this range," I said. "A few scratches aren't the end of the world."

The knife man went down on one knee beside the wheel. It wasn't hard to put two and two together and get a flat. But before he could ram the blade home, the main man put a hand on his shoulder and stopped him. I was confused. Why? It was the smart play to disable the truck. Then I heard the not-so-distant sound of another vehicle approaching along the track.

37

The siren cycled through two calls, the sheriff alerting them to his presence. The lights on the top of the patrol car flashed on even after he climbed out of the car and walked toward them. Like a caricature of a donut-eating law-enforcement officer, the man carried a spare tire around his gut. He was an imposing figure, gone to seed.

"This is all we need." Henry sighed, and straightened up, ready to greet the man with a fake smile. "Jumped-up little shit stain in a uniform sticking his nose in."

"You think the old man called in the cavalry?" Caleb asked.

"Maybe." He checked his own cellphone for reception, saw the single bar disappear and shrugged. "Maybe not. Not from inside. Didn't have time."

"So the sheriff's making a house call, dropping by to share a cold one with his buddy."

Henry nodded. "We'll see."

The sheriff adjusted his belt as he walked toward them, making it obvious he was wearing a sidearm. The move only served to make it all the more obvious how out of shape he was: the belt barely moved beneath the roll of fat. Maybe his word was law in this place. It was a sleepy little hole, after all. Jaywalking probably ranked among the worst crimes he faced in a day. He had a swagger that meant, Henry figured, "Hey, shit-for-brains, look at me, I'm the king of rock and roll," but told Henry he waddled because he had bad eating habits.

Fifteen strides, more or less. That was all the distance he had to cover.

Henry didn't need this, and he certainly didn't need Dale running his mouth off and making things ten times worse when the lawman started talking.

The damage to the pick-up was obvious.

The house door was wide open.

There was no sign of Raelynn's old man or anyone else for that matter. Just them.

Ten strides.

His mind raced, searching for an easy explanation, something believable as to what they were doing outside Cardiman's place. Something that'd have the old boy tug the forelock and wish them a mighty fine day as he left them to it.

Six steps.

His mind drew a blank.

Five steps.

The point of no return.

"Howdy," the sheriff called, raising a hand in greeting.

"Fuck this," Henry said to no one, drew and fired in a single fluid motion.

It was a center-of-gravity shot, aiming at the biggest mass, taking the man high up in the chest. There was a moment of shock as realization took control of the sheriff's face, as his hand reached for his own weapon but wouldn't obey his brain, and that split second of sheer terror as his world came crashing down. Anything he tried to do was already too late. And then he staggered backwards, as though his body had finally caught up with his brain, understanding that it had been shot, and he sprawled on the ground.

Henry stood over him.

There was no cry of pain, no scream of fear, no whimpering or pleading, just a grunt as the air was hammered out of his lungs.

Henry let his gun fall to his side.

He looked down at the sheriff. His hand didn't move for his gun. Blood seeped beneath him into the snow, turning it crimson. There was a lot of it. There always was. It never ceased to surprise him how much a dying man could bleed.

The sheriff tried to turn, fingers of one hand clawing at the bloody snow as he struggled to haul himself back in the direction of his car. It was pitiful. Pathetic. He managed maybe six inches. It probably felt like six hundred yards to him.

Henry didn't move. He wasn't going anywhere.

The sheriff stubbornly clawed at the ground, trying desperately to drag himself another precious inch away from his killer.

Henry put his boot on one of the man's hands, crushing his fingers into the hard dirt, before he bent to relieve him of his weapon.

"Where would they go?" he asked, reasonably enough, like he was catching up with an old friend.

The sheriff barely managed a grunt as his face twisted. He tried to raise his head to look up at Henry. He wasn't going anywhere. Henry pressed down with all of his weight on the man's hand, hearing the unmistakable sound of bones breaking, then dropped to his haunches, close to the dying man's face.

He could smell his fear. It reeked of piss. But he stubbornly refused to answer Henry's question.

"Want me to loosen his lips?" Caleb asked, waving his knife close to the sheriff's face.

"Why not?" Henry said. "A little gentle persuasion."

Caleb bent down beside him. He had no qualms about killing a cop of any stripe. They were fair game. The moment they strapped that badge and gun belt on they made themselves a target.

Henry stood up to give him room to work.

"Little pig, little pig," Caleb said, resting the blade against the dying man's cheek. "I know it hurts. It hurts like a bitch. But the pain will go away. I promise you. The only question is, do you want it to go away quickly, or do you want it to get much, much worse before it does? Because, see, I'm a priest in the Church of Pain. A devotee of the knife. I can make you suffer in ways you can't even begin to imagine."

"Not least by talking the man to death," Dale said, behind him.

"I am going to open you up and remove one organ at a time, like in the most delicate surgery, and I won't let you die until I want you to die. Or you can tell my friend what he wants to know and I'll show you mercy. It's up to you, little pig." Caleb moved the knife slowly from the man's cheek down along the line of his fluttering pulmonary artery to where his uniform opened in a V at his neck. He cut the top button away.

Caleb moved the tip of the knife to the sheriff's cheekbone again, applying pressure this time. A bead of blood started to form against its edge.

"Just cut him and be done with it," Dale suggested.

"No," Caleb said, a slow smile spreading across his face. "There's an art to this work. It's delicate, like peeling the petals away from a flower to get at the bud of pollen inside."

Caleb drew a line down the side of the man's face until it almost met his mouth then did the same on the other side with perfect precision, opening it into a face-wide grin that bared the meat and bones of his teeth and jaw.

The sheriff gave a wet squeal, blood gurgling in the back of his throat.

Henry wondered idly if this torture was something Caleb had picked up in the joint. It was ugly enough, and permanent. That was the kind of thing cons did to mark their territory.

"I'm asking you again, where might we find Raelynn Cardiman?"

The man couldn't form any actual words, but blood gargled in his throat as he choked on it trying to speak. He shook his head, just a little, enough to say no. Either he didn't know or he wasn't saying. Given the state of his face and the gaping hole in his chest, the odds were he didn't know and didn't believe there was a miracle on offer even if he did.

"Finish him," Henry said, turning his back on the grim scene.

"You sure? I can do more."

"I'm sure you can, but he doesn't know anything. Just put him out of his misery, then drag him out back and dump his body in the trees."

38

The gunshot echoed across the mountains, taking Henry by surprise. Stranger still, he couldn't see a gun in Caleb's hand.

He had expected the ruthless efficiency of Caleb's blade, not the more brutal bullet. Caleb liked to savor the kill. Henry turned, fully intending to chastise his partner, as half of Caleb's face exploded in a brutal and ugly exit wound that took his features away.

There was a moment, the echoing silence of the report running across the mountains from peak to white peak all the way to the Blue Ridge, and in it Henry realized what had happened.

Caleb sagged forwards, onto his knees, already dead. His hand still held his knife, as though his nerves were intent on finishing the job on the sheriff that he had started. As his hand twitched uncontrollably he fell on top of the sheriff's corpse. More blood joined the slush.

"Move," Henry barked, but Dale was already moving.

He'd been spurred into action even before Caleb's corpse had hit the ground, running at the trees rather than away from them. He fired a shot blindly in the direction of where he thought the lethal bullet had originated, for no other reason than to suppress a second easy shot coming their way.

His spindly stick-insect legs ate up the ground.

A second shot rang out.

Dale threw himself to the ground, using the Caddy for cover.

A bullet opened a hole in the fender six inches from his head, which had Dale scrambling about on the deck.

Henry mastered his breathing. Panic was a killer. He pressed himself flat against the ground, scanning the tree line for a glimmer of light, reflection or movement. Something that would give the shooter away, without making himself an easy target.

He counted to eleven, one more than ten, out of superstition. Others counted to ten and got their heads blown off by patient snipers. That extra beat could make all the difference.

There was no sign of movement in the trees.

He waited.

No more shots came.

"Draw their fire," Henry said.

Dale looked at him like he was insane, then grinned, like *he* was insane, and nodded. He was sitting on the ground with his back against the Cadillac, his gun in his hand, cradled and ready to return fire. He eased his way along the side until he was close enough to reach up for the silver door handle.

He pulled on it.

As the door swung open another shot shattered the glass.

Had he been trying to crawl into the car it would have put a hole through the top of his head and drilled a path out through his backside. It had served its purpose: Henry had got a glimpse of where the shot had come from.

He returned fire, squeezing off a rapid volley of shots, into the general vicinity of the shooter. Maybe he'd get lucky. Maybe not. Didn't really matter. Returning fire changed the game. Whoever it was out there, he'd moved, at least once, changing the line of fire. In his place Henry would have moved up and down the cover of the tree line making it just about impossible to guess where the next shot would come from.

Unless both of them are armed, Henry thought, adjusting his thought pattern. Two shooters were trickier. It changed the combination of angles and cover, meaning he and Dale were almost always going to be exposed to one or the other.

But they had a box of tricks in the back that would even things out.

Dale knew what was expected of him. He crawled into the backseat, and where the padded central armrest was meant to come down and offer comfort, this time it opened a hole all the way into the truck where three assault rifles, among other things, were stashed. He fed the first out through the hole and handed it to Henry, then got a second for himself. These things were as close to weapons of mass destruction as one man could hold in his own hands.

They'd cut through a forest like a scythe, laying down enough fire to cut clean through the middle of anyone hiding behind the trees.

All he needed was a sighting.

"Work your way around the house," he said. "I'll lay down covering fire. We're going to get these assholes. I don't give a shit if Raelynn is with them or not."

"For Caleb," Dale said, and Henry couldn't tell if the other man was taking the piss or genuinely intend to honor their fallen comrade, such was his way with words.

No questions asked, though. Henry liked that. Dale was a good soldier. He didn't think for himself too much. As long as the money was right he'd do what it took to get the job done. Where Caleb's forte was the blade, Dale was a shooter. If anyone took a pot shot at him he'd make sure they never took a shot at anyone else. It was a matter of honor. Same went for witnesses. Dale was a stone-cold killer.

On the count of three, Henry rose and released a spray of bullets into the trees.

On four, Dale started to run. Head down, arms and legs pumping furiously, his gangly legs covered the killing ground faster than Henry could have.

Henry laid down a second burst of fire.

As the cartridge spat out its last round, Dale reached the house, hit the wall hard and spun, around the side of the building and out of sight of the shooter. He crouched and checked his weapon, satisfying himself it was good, before circling around and heading into the trees.

Henry needed another cartridge if he wanted to lay down more suppressing fire, which meant scrambling into the car to retrieve it from the trunk.

He managed it without getting his head blown off. He sat with his back against the wing, breathing hard, thinking harder.

Henry needed to keep the shooter's attention on him. If they were looking his way, they weren't looking for Dale. It was as simple as that.

He fired off another short volley, half a dozen shells whistling through the air to hit home in the trees. He didn't care who claimed the kill. He wasn't vain like that. Dead was dead, whether he delivered the killing blow or Dale did.

He fired again, but this was the fourth time he'd shot without any return. There could have been any number of reasons for that. Maybe they were low on ammo. Maybe he'd got lucky with one of his bullets and Dale would find a dead man waiting for him in the woods.

Or maybe they'd made a run for it.

39

"We need to move," I told Wayne. "Now. Fast."

I kept my voice low, I didn't need to shout to convey the absolute urgency of our situation. There were two dead bodies less than two hundred yards from where we were hiding.

Wayne surprised me. He hadn't been fazed by the shot, or by the addition of a second corpse to the funeral pyre. Far from it. He'd hissed out a gratified "Yes!" at the sight of the big man going down on his knees and the spray of blood that reached his eyes fractionally before he even heard my shot.

There had been a moment when I might have been able to take a second shot, but the awkward, gangly shooter made a break for cover as soon as his partner laid waste to a good chunk of woodland with his fifty to sixty rounds per minute as he emptied his clip. And with him, the moment had gone.

I'd had no real choice but to put Raelynn down when I wanted to shoot—I'd propped her up against the trunk of a tree, like she was sitting. The first shot, the one that killed Jim Lowry and put an end to the entire Winter's Rage Sheriff's Department, had laid down the rules of engagement. The immediate area between us had become a kill zone. There was no way forward that didn't involve at least one more death.

I wasn't averse to killing another of them, or even all three. I've got no moral objection to ending someone's life when they're trying to end mine. At that point all bets are off. And that first shot of mine had more than evened up the odds. However good they were, I was better. I'd always been better, even pre-enhancement, but post-enhancement there wasn't an enemy combatant that had a prayer. Not when I was fully engaged.

I was ice cold. Inside and out.

My brain raced through the permutations out there. The likelihood of us being flanked by the skinny dude, where he'd most likely come from, how long it would take him to move with any kind of stealth through the undergrowth, how many rounds his partner had fired, the probability of him following the skinny dude into the trees, and just how far we'd get with me carrying Raelynn and our asses out of there.

This wasn't our Alamo moment. Not with Raelynn out of it, and Wayne clutching a shotgun, which at this distance was pretty much as effective as a paper condom.

I gathered Raelynn into my arms. We weren't getting to the truck, not without perforations, which meant Plan B. I hadn't worked out exactly what that was, yet, but it began with hauling ass through the trees, as far and as fast as we could manage.

I started to run.

She had made a few encouraging sounds that I really hoped meant she was beginning to come round. But I wasn't a doc. It could have meant she was blissed out, or just as easily checking out. The ground was uneven. Icy. I couldn't think about it. I had to trust my instincts and not consider the possibility that any tree root rising up out of the hard-packed earth might trip me, turning an ankle or worse.

It was all about buying fast time.

She'd have her chance to recover, but not here.

"Pick it up," I urged Wayne, trying to hurry him along. He moved carefully. Not slowly, but nowhere near quickly enough. But then he was seventy not seventeen.

Raelynn gave a groan of complaint as I hoisted her over my shoulder into a better position to carry her, but she didn't fight me.

"There's no way a few weeks working on that cabin got you in this shape," Wayne grunted, losing his footing as he stumbled through the trees. He was leaving a trail behind him that any fool would be able to follow, but there was nothing we could do about it.

My gamble, and it was looking a bigger gamble by the second, was that the two men wouldn't follow us once they lost us in the trees.

Right then, it was in our interest that they were professionals, which I assumed they were. Professionals wouldn't run headlong into a blind. Not when they had wheels, weapons and options that we didn't. I couldn't run forever—they had to know that. I had an old man and a junkie with me. They had to know that, too.

"You'd be surprised," I said, but no more than that. I needed to keep my breath for getting us out of there.

Local geography came together in my head. We were moving up the mountain, keeping a steady pace even if it wasn't a punishing one. My feet sludged through the mud as I drove myself on. If my bearings were right we'd bypass the cabin, arcing around the wider base of the mountainside to come out closer to mine. It wasn't an as-the-crow-flies run, but we'd be moving without roads across some pretty rough terrain. It'd take time, but that was better than risking our necks out in the open or trying to double back for the pick-up.

Wayne grasped where we were heading without having to be told. He wasn't happy about it. "We go this way, we lead them straight to the kids," he said, looking at me like I was mad.

I couldn't blame him. It was a risk, and the reality was I was putting them in more danger but, selfishly, I figured they had a better shot if I were there to protect them than if they were alone. They'd coped with plenty on their own, no doubt about that, but they were a pressure point for Raelynn. These guys were as serious as a cardiac infarction. They weren't messing about. They wanted Raelynn. Those kids were a way to get at her and make her compliant. So, I was getting back to the shack come hell or high water. And if need be I'd make that my Alamo. I had a plan. It wasn't great, but it gave me something to work toward. And that was all I ever needed. Better, always, to act than react in a combat situation, and until now, everything had been about reacting to a situation we didn't understand.

"What's happening?" Raelynn said suddenly, wriggling against my shoulder as she tried to free herself. I held on tight and kept moving. The words came in slurs. Her attempts to free herself were feeble.

"I've got you," I said, maybe not as reassuring a notion as it might have been to someone being dragged through undergrowth, but I doubted she was sober enough to work out the meaning behind anything.

Beside me, Wayne was breathing hard.

For the first time in as long as I'd known him, he looked every one of his seventy years. "I need a minute," he said, and I could see he hated himself for it. He was struggling. Each breath came short and sharp. He had a hand on his chest, and for one long-sliding second I thought he was going to clutch at it and fall, he was so pale. He didn't. I slowed up, giving him half a minute. We couldn't afford more.

The trees were sparser on this stretch of the mountain, offering less cover, but in turn offering more in terms of a view. I looked back down the mountain, dreading the sight of pursuit.

Wayne was on his knees, hands planted in the snow, breathing so hard I thought he was going to burst.

I lowered Raelynn to the ground. She was at least able to sit upright now. A glance back down the slope confirmed my second-worst fear: our tracks were like a black scar on the mountainside. A blind man could have followed them. And the more snow there was, the more obvious our passage became. We couldn't keep going this way, not without changing the way we were moving.

I scanned the hills for an alternative.

The trees started to grow a little denser again closer to my shack but by then our destination was obvious. We might as well have sent them GPS coordinates.

I was thinking on the fly. "You two think you can find your way to the shack?"

"What do you think, given I've lived here all my life?"

I nodded. "Good. You think you can get Raelynn there?"

She still wasn't with it. She looked at me, eyes struggling to focus on my face and asked, "What's going on?" She had no idea where she was.

I tried to ground her as quickly as I could. I didn't bother trying to spare her or pretty it up. "I found you in a ditch at the side of the road. I have no idea how long you'd been there. But for my impatience with your shit you'd still be there, face down in the snow, freezing to death." I left it at that. I could have said so much more, about abandoning her kids, about lying to us, all of it. I didn't. It wouldn't have helped.

Wayne put his arm around her and helped her to her feet.

She looked about, still trying to understand what she was doing in the middle of the forest. "But why are we *here*?" she pressed. "Why was Mike carrying me? And ... was that gunfire?"

"I was carrying you because the three men you brought here want you dead," I said. "They've killed Jim Lowry, so there's no law in Winter's Rage right now. And we're here in the woods because we're trying to get back to your kids before those men do. Because those two kids are your weakness and if they get their hands on them there's nothing I can do to save you."

40

I sent them ahead of me. I had my SIG Sauer, even if I was short of a few rounds. It was important Wayne had something to defend himself, and in the confines of the shack the shotgun was a much more formidable weapon than it had been out in the open. Not that I intended to put him in a position where he had to use it.

I lurked within a thicker stand of trees, watching the mountain. Alone, I had options I hadn't had before.

The first was heading back the way I'd come, looping around to cut the two men off and give them something more to worry about than chasing us. The risk there was that I'd get snared in my own cleverness if I misjudged it and emerged in the wrong place. It was a rock-and-a-hard-place quandary. The second option was waiting them out. If they didn't appear in fifteen minutes I'd have to assume they'd given up the chase or gotten lost. Neither alternative meant the problem had gone away, just that dealing with it had been deferred.

There was no escaping the fact I'd killed one of them. They wouldn't let that go. In their place, I wouldn't.

I dropped down, making myself as small a target as possible, checking there wasn't an angle where I was betrayed by the light, and settled in to wait them out.

Less than ten minutes later I was rewarded by my first sight of our pursuers.

They were following our tracks, but not rushing. It made sense to conserve their energy for the inevitable confrontation. I watched as they stopped, scanning the near-distance, eyes shielded from the winter sun, talked, gesticulated, and finally broke cover of the trees.

They separated, moving in opposite directions across the tree line, creating two separate targets, just as they had done at Wayne's place. It was the smart move.

I watched patiently. Patience is the best weapon in the world.

Let them move closer. Wait until they are exposed. Vulnerable.

Think like them. What was going through their heads?

They'd see the same two sets of tracks moving on. That was the key. Those prints, from a distance, wouldn't look any different. No obvious change from two big men moving through the landscape to a slight woman and an old man continuing that path. There was no obvious place for an enemy to peel off from the main party, and because I wasn't shooting at them, no reason to suspect anyone would. Even so, they were cautious, moving with their assault rifles in hand, combing through the undergrowth, looking everywhere, listening, reading the land.

Which was the perfect time to take the first shot.

I didn't take it.

I waited.

The snow began to fall.

It came softly at first. A single flake landed on my hand, a presage of more to come.

Within a matter of a minute they were coming heavily enough to carry a muffled sound of their own. Dug in, I might become invisible beneath a blanket of white, but so would they. When I broke cover to move, however, the whiteness would highlight my presence and exaggerate the effect of my movement, drawing the eye. Which meant it was now or never.

I'd kept my eye on one of the men. My enhancements meant I could comfortably track him, in no small part because of the shadowy shape of his heat signature and the angry halo of red that clung to him.

The snow was an added variable. It was never easy to factor in Nature: it was as unpredictable as it came, and over a distance started to exert influence on a shot, even with a decent sighting. Wind speed, angle of shot from high to low ground, gravity, natural slowing of velocity, all of it came into play over extremes of range. The P320 was a solid weapon. Striker-fired semiautomatic; 9mm threaded 5-inch bull barrel; polymer frame, nitron slide finish, but the important stuff was all stainless steel. Six point five pounds in the hand; forty thousand pounds per square inch of pressure behind the shot; 124-grain NATO spec ammo. It was capable of doing some serious damage, even at a hundred plus yards. They were maybe three hundred yards away, down the slope. It was a long shot. Even guns like the SIG Sauer are most effective up close. It's what they're designed for. They're defensive combat weapons. Three out of every four shots in life-or-death moments miss the mark, even in skilled hands. There's so much going on. Three hundred yards was a huge shot, even on a range. But my heart rate was steady, my breathing good, my grip rock-solid. I counted the shot down, watching the red halo creep relentlessly forward, factoring in every possible variable I could.

At less than two hundred yards, I squeezed the trigger.

The shot echoed in the near silence, the sound folding back on itself as the sound wave hit the next mountainside and rippled back toward me.

Answering gunfire rattled blindly in my general direction, coming from both sources, neither of them effective. They'd wasted a decent amount of ammo spraying high and wide.

I took my time and fired again.

The shot drove the man back. I saw his halo retreat, looking for cover. It didn't drop him, but I hadn't expected it to. I just didn't want them thinking they were getting everything their own way. It was about turning the hunter into the hunted, at least in their own heads.

I couldn't see the other shooter, and not just because the snow was thickening. He wasn't giving off the same burning-hot heat signature. There was no blazing yellow of fear. Nothing. He was utterly calm. Or dead. And, sadly, I knew that wasn't the case. Interesting. What sort of man got into a firefight and didn't exhibit any sort of powerful emotion?

Me.

That was the answer.

And if not me, then what else?

A stone-cold psychopath?

In the time it had taken us to trade bullets, the snowfall had thickened to the extent that it had all but obliterated Wayne and Raelynn's tracks.

If they were going to keep coming the weather was going to have a major say in how this played out.

It was on the verge of being a full blizzard.

I could hear my own breathing, and nothing else beyond that.

I couldn't see anything beyond maybe thirty feet away with any clarity, and visibility was getting worse by the second.

It was the kind of weather that had frozen Neanderthal hunters in ice floes to be discovered millennia later by snot-nosed kids and thawed out in true horror-movie fashion.

The one good thing? A couple of city boys were going to struggle to follow me in this.

41

"Down!" Henry yelled, as a bullet whistled past him. It was close. So close he'd felt the displaced air. That bastard, whoever he was, was either a decent shot or a lucky son of a bitch. Both options were troublesome. You didn't want to hunt someone who was lucky. Luck wasn't something you could factor into a kill. And a good shot just increased the likelihood of the prey doing some damage before you took it down.

It was a lose-lose situation as far as he was concerned.

And, judging by the mess the son of a bitch had made of Caleb's face, his money was on a proper shooter. Ex-military, maybe. Nothing they'd known had hinted at that sort of background for anyone in or around Raelynn Cardiman. That made him the unknown, and in any equation the unknown was the core of the problem. Twice now this guy had managed to pin them down. Henry wasn't about to give him a third opportunity to get lucky.

The snow fell faster. It thickened, swirling all around them. It was a suffocating blanket smothering the mountain and everything around it. And cold. Dear God it was unholy. Why would anyone in their right mind choose to live in this hellhole? He was shivering and wishing he'd brought a coat.

The snow was soaking into his new shirt. It clung wet and heavy to his skin, making it uncomfortable. He'd freeze to death out here if he didn't get warm sooner rather than later. He shook his head. Freaks, the lot of them. He couldn't see more than a couple of feet ahead of him clearly. Dale was a ghost. Lost in the white. He couldn't even hear him out there.

Henry wasn't an idiot. He knew when it was time to cut and run. Regroup, confront the bastard on their terms, not his. He didn't want to be going up against some dueling banjo player when he couldn't even see where the bastard was hiding.

A dark shape moved closer to him.

He had his gun trained on it, finger on the trigger, realizing almost too late that it was Dale, not the other guy.

"This is nuts," Dale grunted.

He didn't argue. "There's got to be a better way of doing it than this."

"We need to get the hell out of here," Dale said bluntly. He scratched at his arm like a junkie. Fingers digging in hard. He was already plastered with snow, white wetness clinging to every inch of his clothing. He didn't bother trying to brush it away. It was a waste of time with more settling on him all the time.

"We ain't gonna find him in this, unless it's the same way Caleb found him, bullet first. We've got more chance of shooting each other," Henry said. This was a waste of time and energy. "Let's head back. Get the Caddy, drive into town. Get ourselves a room. It's time we took control of the situation."

Dale nodded. "Sounds good to me, amigo."

More than once, they almost lost their way: the light was fading fast, casting lying shadows that changed the mountain and its damned forest into something out of Shakespeare's twisted imagination. Henry hated the country. Give him the canyons of the city any day of the week. Streets went to the same destination no matter the weather—they didn't twist you around and leave you disoriented, stumbling back the way you'd just come, or have you following your own trail because you couldn't see a foot before your face.

But there were only so many places they could get lost, even in the snow, and finally, stumbling, freezing, soaking, on the point of exhaustion, they were back with the two corpses and three cars outside Wayne Cardiman's place.

"What d'you wanna do about those?" Dale asked, pointing to Caleb and the dead sheriff.

Henry was about to say leave them—he was so wet and miserable he just wanted to go inside, get dry and get warm—but he thought better of it. "Let's get them out of sight, at least. We don't want the UPS guy stumbling over them." It was purely practical. He couldn't give a shit if the coyotes stripped Caleb's bones. Thinking about it, he wasn't even sure if they had coyotes in West Virginia.

Dale grabbed Caleb's body by the ankles and dragged him unceremoniously off the track, leaving a trail of blood. The snow would fill in the drag marks soon enough, given the mounting intensity of the snowstorm. It was a whiteout. His sorry ass was back at the Caddy a few minutes later. He looked down at the bulk of the dead sheriff. "Man, he was one fat bastard. Gonna need some help shifting this lardass."

He was a two-man job, no argument.

Henry took the arms, Dale the legs. The guy had shat himself in death. He absolutely stank. Henry hated that. It was the one thing about killing someone that really got under his skin, the way the sphincter loosened and whatever shit was in there just leaked out. There was no dignity in it. He couldn't understand why they wanted to make sure a guy on Death Row had a hearty breakfast. It only meant there was more shit to stink the place up when they juiced him.

"Get in the Caddy," Henry said, looking at the other vehicle blocking their way back to the road.

"What you gonna do?"

He smiled.

"I am the law," he said.

"What?"

"Always wanted to drive a cop car. Get the Caddy warmed up and

I'll be with you in a sec." Henry crunched across the track to the sheriff's car and climbed inside. He had to ease the seat forward, because he wasn't a match for the big man's bulk. The leather on the seats was worn as smooth as the Caddy's. The key was still in the ignition. He turned the engine over. As it roared into life he got the distinct impression it had a lot more muscle under the hood.

He flexed his fingers on the steering wheel, and for a minute he might have been sitting behind the wheel of a Lamborghini or a Ferrari, test-driving the car of his dreams, not ditching a cop car. He smirked. This, he decided, was better.

With a crackle, the radio came to life. The sudden burst of static caught Henry by surprise, but after that first heart-attack sound, he took the handset from the hook, and decided to play along.

"Sheriff Lowry? Are you there?" The dispatcher's voice had a faraway hard-to-hear quality, as though the weather distorted the connection.

He could work with that. He thumbed down the button, and said, "Lowry here," trying to his best not to laugh.

"Boss? That you?"

"Sure is."

"You sound different," she said.

I'm sure I do, Henry thought, *given I'm coming to you from beyond the grave*. "Weather. Making it a bitch to hear what you're saying." Henry clamped a hand over his mouth to hold back a bark of a laugh. "What do you need?"

"Just checking in. Hadn't heard back from you. Figured I'd make sure everything was good, what with the storm coming in."

"Yeah, all's good up here," he said, then glanced at the two bodies slowly being covered by snow. "Quiet as the grave. Guess I'll just wait out the worst of the storm before I head back down to town."

"Good luck with that. Weather report reckons it's in for the rest of the day, and only going to get worse. Want me to put out an advisory on the roads? They're gonna start getting blocked pretty soon."

"Why don't you do that?" he said, and signed off.

42

They were drenched in snow by the time they reached Byron's shack. Wayne had tried to give Raelynn his coat, but she had refused it. Instead, she'd just pulled her flimsy jacket tighter around her and staggered on, every third or fourth step a slight stumble, a slip or a lurch as the ground threatened to undermine her. Her coat wasn't made for winter anywhere outside the Sunshine State. She was shivering uncontrollably and barely able to stand by the time they collapsed inside the shack to cries of "Mom!" from the kids.

Anna rushed to the door and, seeing Raelynn leaning on Wayne, asked, "Are you okay?"

"Why don't you help her get into some dry clothes, honey?" Wayne said, closing the door behind them. He stamped the snow off his boots. More clumps fell from the folds of his coat, turning to water on the wooden floor. They'd soak away soon enough. He grabbed one of the mismatched chairs pushed under the tiny breakfast table and moved it closer to the door, trying to think defensively. He was determined to sit in that chair, shotgun across his lap, watching the door until Mike returned.

Or someone else arrived.

Time passed.

Each minute seemed to last an hour.

He let the kids fuss over Raelynn. He ignored her as she warmed herself by the stove. He didn't turn away from his vigil as she wrapped a blanket around her shoulders, or as she sat down beside the stove, as close as she could get without leaning against it. She still looked absolutely frozen, dry clothes or not.

Anna bustled through to the kitchen and stretched up to reach for a can of soup from the groceries he'd given to Mike the night before. It seemed like such a long time ago. She worked the opener with practiced skill and filled the pan with the gloop, warming it through slowly on the hotplate. He gratefully accepted a mug once he was sure there was enough for everyone, and sipped the contents, warming his hands on the mug while he watched the door.

The whole place was eerily quiet save for the occasional creak and groan of the timber frame and the rush of snow sliding off the sloped roof.

As he finished the final mouthful Wayne heard movement outside. He tensed, reaching for the shotgun as someone stamped their feet on the stoop.

The sound of the latch being lifted seemed like the single loudest noise he'd ever heard. He had the gun raised ready, finger on the trigger. From this distance the buck spray would open a hundred holes in the intruder, putting them down. He was calm as the door swung open, not least as he recognized the man on the doorstep doing his best to shake off the snow before stepping inside. Intruders didn't worry about stuff like that.

"Mike," Wayne said, still pointing the gun at him, despite knowing full well who he was.

Mike reached out, hand on the barrel, and eased it aside before moving any closer. "You guys okay?"

"Thawing out," Wayne said. "We lost them in the snow. I figure they headed back down the mountain to my place."

Mike nodded. "I doubt we've seen the last of them, though."

"That's for damned sure," Wayne said. "Now I figure it's about time Raelynn started telling us the truth, no matter how ugly it is. What say you?" He swung on his chair and turned his gaze on his daughter. She still cradled her mug, but the soup had gone. "You going to tell us what this is all about?"

"Me? How should I know?"

"Save your breath if you're thinking about lying, Raelynn," Mike said. "I don't have the energy or the inclination to deal with bullshit. I'm cold. I'm tired of being shot at. And right now, Jim Lowry's dead because of whatever you brought to town. And you brought it. They rolled up asking for you at Maeve's. One of the guys following you drew his gun and shot Jim in the chest just for being there. So, what do they want with you?'

"I don't know. You've got to believe me. I don't know why they're here." She clutched Chase close to her with one arm, reaching out to put the mug down. The boy didn't resist. "We came here to get away from people like that. Maybe they've come here looking for *him*." She pointed an accusing finger at Mike. "How much do you *really* know about him?"

Mike said nothing.

"Mike's a good man. That's all I need to know. He saved your life. You're just trying to shift the blame. He's right, they came asking for you. I can play you Maeve's message if you like. So, do me a favor, just tell the goddamned truth for once in your miserable life, girl."

But she was right about one thing: he didn't know much about Mike, apart from the fact he was very handy with a gun. And that was new information.

"I'm serious. What do you know about him?"

43

"**I** know that he's hard worker and that I'd trust him with my life. Hell, I've *already* trusted him with yours. And the kids'. I think that's more than enough, don't you?"

Mike still didn't speak. Why should he bother defending himself? Wayne thought. He didn't need to. She could sling all the mud she wanted, but there was only one place those guys had come from and one thing they were after. Wayne was no fool: he knew she was dissembling. She could lie with the best of them. And, as a junkie, she had been lying for much of her life and getting away with it because he was too worried about upsetting her or losing her or making her just like her mother.

No, Mike could keep his secrets. He had earned the right to them.

Raelynn stared at him, a hardness in her eyes he didn't like. It spoke of a second life he knew nothing about, but which had haunted him for years, the seedy underside of the faraway cities, the survival instinct of the cornered creature. But, like all things, it passed. She grew glassy-eyed, falling back on her second instinct, to turn on the tears. Wayne resisted the urge to wrap her in his arms and tell her that everything would be fine. She was playing him and it wasn't going to be fine. It was never going to be fine again. She'd brought death to town.

No, the time for the arm around the shoulders and the platitudes was over. They needed to cut right to the matter of the heart: what she was running from.

So, he waited, stone-faced, and eventually she wiped away the tears and began to talk.

She sniffed through a bubble of snot, and said, "I was with this guy, Eddie. He was good to us—he took us in and looked after us after Glen walked out."

She was lying.

Again.

Or was she just so lost to the truth she'd fabricated an entirely different passage of events from reality to retreat into? Glen hadn't walked out on her and the kids, he had been sent down. Wayne was hazy on the details, but knew enough. Eddie had been caught bang to rights holding up a drugstore. He looked at Chase. Maybe she'd made up a different version of events to protect the kids. That was the kind alternative. After all, they were Glen's kids.

He let her fill the silence.

Glen's fate was irrelevant, and if he never heard from or saw the waste of space again in this lifetime it would be too soon for Wayne's liking.

"Anyway," she sighed heavily, like it hurt to remember, "Glen got involved with these guys." She waited for him to ask involved how. He didn't. "But once he was in, there was no way out of their circle. They owned him. They wanted him to do some stuff for them or they'd hurt us ... He only did it for us ... I swear ... He promised to help them get rid of a shipment." Wayne took that to mean drugs. Didn't it always? "He'd earn enough to wipe the slate clean, and with a bit of luck, there'd be enough left for us to make a fresh start."

"Let me guess," Wayne said, unable to hold his silence any longer. "It didn't work out like that." He knew where this was heading. Someone had got greedy.

"Glen did the deal," she said, an edge of defiance in her tone, "but he double-crossed everyone, me included. He took the money *and* the shipment, did a David Blaine and disappeared into thin air."

"Leaving you to carry the can?"

She nodded. "They think I know where he is."

Which was reasonable, he thought. He had to ask, "And do you?"

She shook her head, more tears. "No. You've got to believe me."

"And for some reason it felt like a good idea to run away from it all and come home, like moving a thousand miles across the country would leave all your troubles behind."

"How much?" Mike said. They were the first two words he'd uttered during the whole exchange, but they cut right to the heart of it.

"Altogether? Drugs and money?"

"How much? Give me a figure."

"Two hundred thousand," she said, then looked down, unable to meet his eye.

"Dollars?" Wayne demanded, like there could be any other currency.

"I'd say we know why they came looking," Mike said. "Two hundred grand is worth killing for when you can get a decent contract hitman for maybe five to ten per cent of that, no questions asked."

Wayne turned to his friend, lost. He had no idea what to do next. That kind of money was beyond his wildest imaginings. It was a decade's worth of earnings for a lot of people in Winter's Rage.

"Stay here," Byron said eventually. "Keep the kids safe. Do not, under any circumstances, open this door before I come back."

"What are you going to do?"

"Fix this, or die trying."

44

They didn't go straight to the diner. First, they paid the sheriff's office a visit, driving there in the dead man's car. When they were done there, Henry abandoned the cop car well out of town, somewhere it wouldn't be easily stumbled upon, switching rides back to the Caddy.

He could have tried to hide it but they'd killed the only lawman in town, so it wasn't like there was a lot of point in doing anything elaborate. They'd be long gone before the state troopers arrived. And by then the fat sheriff's car would be covered in snow, like the half-dozen other vehicles they'd passed on the drive into Winter's Rage.

The locals abandoned their vehicles happily, knowing they'd be there when the weather broke, meaning they expected the long walk to be preferable to the drive.

The diner was still open when they reached it, one of the only lights burning in town. It wasn't dark. Time, really, had lost all meaning in the storm. The sky was gray-white. There was no sun. Through the window, Henry saw at least half a dozen brave lost souls had gathered inside for warmth and shelter.

"We wait it out if we have to," Henry said. "It's warm. It's dry. And

I'm sure the old girl can cook, which makes it a marked improvement on the crap we shoveled down last night."

They went inside.

Maeve, the owner, saw them. It took half a second too long for her to plaster that fake smile on her chops. Henry really didn't like the old sow. He thought about letting Dale have some fun with her when the job was done. A bit of R and R was always good for morale.

They slid into a booth. She pushed a couple of menus across the table toward them and recited the familiar "What can I get you boys to drink?" mantra that made up sixty per cent of her life.

"Coffee, black," Henry said.

"Me too," Dale said.

"Sounds good," she said. "Coming right up." And she left them to it.

They read through the various items on the menu waiting for her to return.

Two of the folks sitting a couple of tables away were locked in animated conversation about some guy Lowry not returning. It took Henry a minute to realize they were talking about the sheriff.

"I spoke to him a while back," the woman said. She brushed her hair off her face. "He sounded weird, but he said everything was fine, that he was going to wait out the weather."

"Like he doesn't know how shitty it gets round here," the other said. "This crap's in for the winter."

"I tried him again a few minutes ago, no luck."

"He's probably holed up somewhere, got a hot toddy in his hand and is watching the game. And who'd blame him? It's not like there's a lot he can do when the weather's like this, apart from sit in that office of his and play tic-tac-toe on the old computer."

Henry and Dale exchanged a wry smile.

The locals were going to have a long wait for their token law enforcer to show his face, and when he finally did, most of it would have been eaten away by raccoons. It was hard to resist making a joke, even if they were the only two people in the diner who'd appreciate it.

Better to just sit tight, order their food, eat, and go back to finish what they'd started.

Maeve took her time in coming back for their order. She carried a silver coffee pot and filled two of the mugs on the table.

"Okay, boys, you know what you want?"

"Always," Dale said, and the way he said it, Henry knew, meant he was also thinking about his chosen way of blowing off steam after the job had gone down.

"Cheeseburger, all the fixings," Henry said, not looking her in the eyes.

"Good choice," she said.

"In which case I'll have the same," Dale said, with a predatory grin. "And how about you slap on a side order of sweet three-bean salad and creamy coleslaw? I've worked up an indecent appetite."

"You got it," Maeve said. "Be right up, long as the power don't go down in the meantime."

Henry gave her a glance and saw that she was being deadly serious. "It happens," she said, gesturing to the power plant in the distance. "Especially in inclement weather. But don't worry yourselves none, we've got plenty of candles." She left them.

"So what now?" Dale said, still examining the menu as if he was already considering dessert.

Henry knew exactly what he wanted to satisfy his sweet tooth and it wasn't an ice-cream sundae. "We wait it out."

"And what happens when this place closes?"

"Then we persuade the nice lady that she really wants to stay open, just for us. We're not going to be able to get around much, and I don't fancy driving back to the motel. I want to stay close. I want to be here when Raelynn pokes her head above ground so I can whack it off. So, other than wait, there ain't a lot we can do."

They fell silent for a moment, drinking their coffee, alone with their thoughts.

A couple of the diners paid for their meals and drifted off to wherever they thought was better than here, but there were still more than a half-dozen others still in the small restaurant. They were taking their own sweet time over their drinks. No one was in any kind of hurry, and Maeve was in no rush to usher them out through the door. This, he figured, was small-town life. Eventually Maeve returned with their meals. They looked good. Henry thanked her.

"So, it's not just me, right," Dale said, finally. "There's no way that was the old fella shooting at us back there?" He pitched his voice low so no one else in the diner would be able to hear him.

"And I can't see Raelynn handling a piece that well, can you?"

Dale chuckled at the innuendo. "So, they've got help."

"I'd put money on it. The hit that took Caleb out wasn't an easy shot, not at that distance. He's trained."

Dale nodded. "My thoughts, exactly. But not a cop. A merc, maybe. Someone paid to be good with a gun. Maybe they hired the Equalizer?" He didn't laugh at his own joke, though his lips did twitch. But, then, his lips always twitched.

"We're going to have to take him out," Henry said.

"And I don't even wanna bonus for doing it," Dale said. "Just this once I'd like to do something nice for Caleb."

45

I made my way to the road. For now, at least, Wayne and his family were safe.

At least now we were dealing in absolutes. I knew just how vengeful two hundred thousand dollars could make someone. In that context this all made sense.

As soon as the snow settled the two remaining Stooges would be out looking for Raelynn to finish what they'd started. Assuming they were on a finder's fee they were probably looking at twenty grand to kill her. Good money for men like that if they could collect on it.

There was no doubt they were motivated. The sheriff's corpse proved that well enough. Money did that to you. Money and the survival instinct. I had no idea if they knew they'd effectively turned Winter's Rage into the Old West with one shot, leaving it effectively lawless until help arrived from outside. And that wouldn't come soon enough.

I looked down the road. It was already covered with a thick layer of snow. There were no tracks breaking the monotony of white, meaning no one had come this far up the mountain recently. Or gone down it.

Which, logically, suggested that if the two men had gone back to

Wayne's to retrieve their beaten-up Cadillac, they'd driven back toward town.

That was something.

So, I walked.

And I walked.

The landscape was bleak.

I couldn't hear a sound in the world. The blizzard showed no sign of abating so, head down, I walked on.

I passed the track to the cabin we were building for Raelynn and her kids. There wasn't a single print or tire track to be seen in the virgin snow. Good. We had at least a few surprises up our sleeves, then.

I had barely turned the bend that began the labored descent into town when I spotted a vehicle abandoned at the side of the road.

Even from that distance, and despite the high-banking snow that had drifted up against it, I could see the wheels were wedged in the ditch.

It took me a moment to register that the car was pretty much opposite the long track to Wayne's place. When I did, my hopes for a quick end to things rose, even though it was unlikely I'd find one of the killers still inside. Seeing the markings, I recognized it as Jim Lowry's car. I didn't bother trying the door. The keys were still in the ignition, but there was no way I'd get it moving without the help of a tow truck. Better not to put my prints all over it.

The fact that it had been moved wasn't surprising, even if only to be dumped pretty much in plain sight. That bit was. I remembered the way Jim had parked up: the cruiser had been blocking the driveway, so they'd moved it to get the Caddy out of there, but why leave it where the first travelers on the road would be sure to see it? Why not wheel it around the back of the old place, or even take it off-road and abandon it in the trees where, once the bad weather really got a hold, it would be lost for the winter?

I saw the Cadillac's tracks, confirming my suspicion they'd driven down into Winter's Rage. There was, of course, the slimmest of chances that one had remained behind to deal with me if I returned, but that divide-and-conquer thing wasn't the best use of resources when you didn't know the full extent of what you were up against—in this case, me. Even so, I approached the house with caution, watching the windows for movement, listening to the trees for more. No one emerged. I climbed in through the driver's side door of Wayne's pick-up and started the engine. I was mobile at least. I drove slowly, wipers struggling to cope with the deluge of snow.

When I rolled into town they weren't too hard to find. Not that there were many places they *could* be.

I stood outside Maeve Cruikshank's diner, watching people come and go. I saw them through the steamed-up windows. They were easy to distinguish from the regulars. One thing the locals did was take the snow in their stride. They came for a bite, a few minutes of companionship, and moved on. None of those powerful emotions driving them. It was just everyday life. But these two were marked. Thanks to the messing that had been done with my head I could see their halos, burning bright.

There was no mistaking the color of rage.

I watched them, a few steps back from the window. With the blizzard swirling, all they would see of me was a hooded figure watching them, even if they wiped the condensation from the windows.

If they were smart they would be afraid.

And if they weren't, I would teach them.

46

"There's some weird-ass cocksucker out there," Dale said. He wiped a little of the condensation away with his palm, but still couldn't see much.

Henry leaned forward, peering out into the raging blizzard. "What kind of asshole would wait around in the snow like that and not come in?" He struggled to make out any of the man's features. In a hoodie, he was standing unmoving beside one of the curbside trees, watching the diner.

Or maybe the Caddy.

"You think it'll ever end?" Dale asked.

"What?" He might have meant the snow or the killing, it was difficult to tell with Dale sometimes.

Half an hour ago, Henry realized, he wouldn't have been able to see the hooded man. It was easing, but not enough to be an improvement, maybe just a shift in the wind. "Let's go say hello, shall we?" Henry said, dropping a couple of bills on the table; more than enough to cover the tab. Maeve would earn her tip later.

As they left their booth, a couple of old guys came in, stamping off the snow and making the usual pitiful small-talk that went with the obvious storm. They stepped aside to let Dale and Henry through. They were hardy stock. As the door opened, Henry was hit by a blast of cold air. He was building a mental picture of Wayne Cardiman from the things he saw around town. It was like an identikit the cops used for catching criminals, though in this case it pretty much came together as a picture of Daniel Boone.

The guy in the hoodie had disappeared.

He looked up and down the street, not that he could see much more than a dozen or so feet in any direction. There was no sign of anyone else crazy enough to be out there.

The snow was broken by a mess of footprints back and forth as people had come and gone. The fresh snow wasn't coming down fast enough or thick enough to obliterate them. He saw a set of prints beside the tree, proof at least that he hadn't imagined the hooded man. A few vehicles had passed through too, their tracks like black snakes along the white top. Most of the diner's customers probably lived within walking distance.

Henry took a moment to examine the prints, and even thought about following them, but dismissed it as paranoia. Instead, he hurried, head down, toward where they'd left the Caddy.

He had the keys in his hand as he approached the car, which had collected another covering of snow that was almost two inches high on the roof and hood where it had settled. The windows were white. He scraped some of the snow away and was about to open the door, when he saw there was no snow around the driver's door handle. Some asshole had tried it, he thought, looking for an easy score. Maybe a dump like Winter's Rage wasn't so different from the world he knew after all.

When he tried it himself though he was surprised to find it unlocked. He looked at his partner. "You forget to lock up?" he asked.

Dale shook his head. "Not me."

Henry very cautiously opened the door with his left hand, his right reaching for the gun at his back, ready to draw and fire in one smooth motion if he saw some smiling bastard grinning at him from the backseat. No questions asked.

It was empty.

No, he realized, not empty: there was a slip of paper balanced on the steering wheel waiting for them to find it.

Henry reached inside for the note, catching it before the displaced air could send it drifting lazily to the foot well.

"What's it say?" Dale asked, across the roof from the passenger side.

"'Leave or die. Your choice,'" Henry read. "Eloquent motherfucker."

"The fuck?"

"My thoughts exactly, my friend. My thoughts egg-fucking-zactly. You definitely locked the car?"

Dale nodded.

"Then I'd say our new player just made contact. The guy in the hoodie."

"I've had enough of this bullshit," Dale said meaningfully.

"What are you thinking?" Henry asked, despite himself.

"Time to stop dicking about. We've got a job to do and I think we need to do it. We've been acting like Girl Scouts. All nicey nice. The hell with that." He went around to the rear of the car and popped the trunk. Inside were a couple of holdalls. He reached in for them. "This loser isn't gonna know what hit him."

"For Caleb."

"No, this is for us. This motherfucker is going to die."

"One problem. We don't know who he is."

"Maybe we don't, but someone in there has got to know," Henry said, waving back at the light.

Maeve Cruikshank's diner.

47

I watched as they found the note I had left for them. Given the picture-postcard weather I felt a bit like their Secret Santa, only my gift would prove a lot costlier than a five-buck minimum. They looked confused. Angry. Not a little pissed. All in all, it couldn't have gone any better.

I wasn't about to let them into my little trick for breaking into their car: sometimes life has to have a little magic or things get real dull real fast. Let them bicker about it for a while, let them stew, blaming each other for leaving it unlocked. Let them stop trusting each other, even if just a little. Given enough time I might have been able to lock it again, which would really have messed with their heads.

But this was not a game.

It was a lot of other things, though. For Wayne it was a chance at something approaching the life he'd lost all those years ago when his wife died and his daughter fled. I'd noticed he never used his wife's name. I took that as a sign of just how deeply she'd wounded him. Maybe, just maybe, this would go some small way to giving her back to him, or at least some memories that weren't reflected in their daughter's addiction. For Raelynn it was a chance at a fresh start, even if it was a case of going back to the beginning. Sometimes that was the best place to be. For the kids, Anna and Chase, it was a shot at a normal childhood, and who wouldn't have moved mountains to give that to a couple of kids?

So, yes, I wanted this over. But I wanted it done right.

And not least for Jim Lowry, whom I didn't know, but he was an ordinary decent man and he didn't deserve to end up dead in the snow outside Wayne's place simply because he was trying to be neighborly.

The guy I'd seen kill Lowry seemed to be running the show. He had my note screwed up in his hand and was looking around for me, but was utterly oblivious to me hiding there in plain sight. The snow helped.

He looked right at me, but didn't see me. I used my burner phone to take pictures, first of him, and then his skin-and-bone partner leaning on the roof. The shots might help, they might not, but they were all part of getting to know the enemy.

I watched them take a couple of holdalls out of the trunk, which, judging by the weight and the sudden flare of joy that blazed through the snow, was them tooling up. Guns and ammo were their porn, I guess.

48

Henry locked the car again. This time he made sure to check the door before heading back inside the diner. Their booth at the window had been taken by the two old-timers who had gone inside as they had left. He wasn't in the mood to be polite. They could move.

"The booth's taken," he said.

One of the guys, with a grey handlebar moustache, looked up defiantly, "Didn't see no reserved sign," he said. "Weren't no food or drinks on the table. And, point of fact, weren't no sign of youse, either. Plenty of seats. Take another. I like this one."

Henry looked from him to the waitress. She didn't hold his eye. He really didn't like the way the old sow kept doing that, looking away like he was worth nothing. Henry had seen that often enough, and every time it was either fear or contempt that made someone do it.

The old guy wasn't afraid, though. He belligerently held his ground. His intransigence pushed Henry's buttons.

"You want me to move him, H?" Dale said.

Moustache Man's partner started to slide out of the booth, but his friend told him to stay put.

"Bad move, mister. Believe me. Of all the things you've done today that you will live to regret, this one right here, this is the one, the motherfucking payload."

"I don't like your mouth, boy. No need for that gutter language when there's ladies present."

"Oh, do fuck off and die," Henry said conversationally. It was far more menacing when you threw out the threats like they were nothing, just casual jibes.

"We have every right to sit here if we want to."

"Ask yourself this, why don't you? Do you want that seat so much you're willing to trade your testicles for it? Because if you don't move I'm going to follow you out of this place when you're done with your burger and fries, all the way to your house, where I'm going to follow you in, cut your fucking nuts off and stuff them into your wife's mouth until she chokes. You want it that bad?"

The man looked at him as though he couldn't trust his ears, or thought maybe Henry had been possessed by the devil and was speaking in tongues. But he didn't move.

Henry dropped his bag on the floor and, rattlesnake fast, reached over to grab the man by the throat, one hand squeezing hard around his neck. He could feel the old-timer's pulse fluttering against his fingers.

And still the guy resisted.

He had some balls, he'd give him that. Proper, pendulous things.

But Henry was having none of it. Too many people took liberties, these days, and that wasn't good for the soul. Sometimes you just had to make a stand, even if it was in a shit-hole of a place like Maeve's Diner. It was a matter of principle.

The man eased himself out of the seat, looking cowed.

Henry stood over him, watching.

The moment he was out of the booth, Henry slammed a hand into the middle of his chest and pushed him toward his dinner companion, who barely kept his feet.

"I don't know who you think you are," the old guy said, "but you can't go around treating people like this."

"Pretty sure no one here's gonna stop me. What do you think?" Henry reached to the back of his pants and pulled out his Desert Eagle. He pressed the muzzle to the man's cheek, right up close to his gray moustache. The old guy's skin turned white with pressure around the metal. "I didn't think so."

"We don't do things like this here. This is a good place. This is a peaceful, law-abiding place. Good people. Everyone cares," he said, somehow still finding the guts to stand up to Henry. "Just saying, a little politeness goes a long way. We ain't some big city where you need to bully folk to be heard." And all of this with the barrel of a gun pressed into his face? Henry had misjudged the old coot: he didn't have balls he had a death wish.

"I could be your genie," Henry said, confusing the man. "Just rub the barrel of my gun and I'll make your wish come true."

"There's no need for this, mister," Maeve said, moving toward them. "He's just an old man. Why don't you boys sit yourselves down and I'll bring you anything you want, on the house. Last thing any of us want is trouble. What you say?"

"Maeve, isn't it? Do you mind if I call you Maeve?" She shook her head, all fake smiles again, like he wasn't holding a gun. "You cleared our table before we'd finished with it."

"I thought—"

"And you know what? You thought wrong. All you need to worry about, Maeve, is taking orders and serving food. Leave the thinking to the important people."

"Leave her alone," the old man blustered.

"You know what?" Dale said. "If these fine folks don't like it, why don't they call the sheriff?" His grin was vile. He scratched his fingernails along the inside of his thumbs, like there was a fire beneath his skin he couldn't put out.

Henry laughed at that.

They were the only two who got the joke.

There was no support for the old guy among the other diners. Survival instinct had kicked in. They were keeping their heads down. Good for them. It paid to be smart sometimes.

"Why don't you sit over here with me, George?" Maeve said to the old guy. She gave another guy in the joint a sort of sideways glance.

Maybe she reckons I'm simple, Henry thought. She couldn't have expected him to miss it. Whatever. It didn't matter. He picked the bag up and slid it onto the bench seat beside him as he sat down in the booth. "Now, how about a cup of your mighty fine coffee, darlin'?"

Henry met the stares of each and every diner brave enough not to look away. This was getting ugly, fast.

And that was just the way he liked it.

49

Not knowing what to expect inside, I pushed open the door to the Sheriff's Department. It was a one-man show, so I figured the place would be empty if the dispatcher wasn't around.

"Anybody home?" I called, poking around the reception desk. It was nothing like a law office in a larger town. It was three rooms, essentially: Lowry's office, wood-paneled with a plate-glass window that had the sheriff's crest on the glass, a holding cell, which was basically a drunk tank where some of the locals slept it off before staggering home the worse for wear, and the reception area where the dispatcher operated the radio. "Hello?" I called. No response.

The place was deserted.

While that didn't come as much of a surprise—this was a small town, calls would be redirected to a cellphone once the office closed for the day—it didn't explain why the door was wide open.

A sense of unease combined with déjà vu had me go back to check out the door. It had been forced. In that instant everything became about situational awareness. I listened hard, eyes darting over every inch of the place, looking for anything out of place, anything that shouldn't have been there, or anything missing that should have been there.

Part of the counter lifted to allow access to the holding cell. There was little point in working out where the release was to trip it. I bumped myself up onto the counter and swung my legs over to the other side.

This side of the barrier, I saw everything I'd missed coming in: Lowry's office had been ransacked. Any other time, any other place, I'd have been on my guard, instinctively on edge, looking for the perpetrator, but I knew exactly who was behind this, and where they were right now.

The desk had been tipped over, papers spilled on the floor. They hadn't come in here looking to trash the place. They weren't petty criminals. They'd come in with a purpose, and I had a sinking feeling theirs was the same as mine.

It didn't take me long to confirm at least one of their purposes: the telephone cable had been cut and the internet router smashed beyond recognition. Again, not random violence: they were cutting lines of communication to the sheriff's office. State troopers, anyone else calling in from outside, would just get the in-box signal. I could probably fix the telephone line, it was just splicing the cable by the look of it, but the rest was beyond me. The dispatcher was in for a nasty shock when she rolled into work in the morning.

I needed to have more than just the SIG Sauer I had tucked in my jeans, especially as I'd already fired off more than half of the rounds I had in the clip.

I kicked myself that I hadn't taken Lowry's own weapon—it wasn't like the dead man needed it—or the other Stooge's weapon. I'd only seen him using the knife to torture Lowry, but there was no way he wasn't packing. It was too late to worry about it now, and there was no way I was going back up the mountain.

I was working on the theory that Lowry had a weapons cabinet. If I was going to arm myself for the coming fight, this was the place.

I'd come prepared. I dropped the crowbar I had been carrying up my sleeve. The gun safe was at the back of the office. It wasn't as secure as a lot of the ones I'd seen, but it was going to require some serious force to pry it open. Thankfully, I had an almost infinite supply.

It didn't take me long to liberate an over-and-under shotgun and another handgun, a Glock, along with a box of ammunition for each.

I stashed the weapons in my backpack along with a couple of short-wave radios. I checked they were charged.

I turned to go, then stopped. I figured I could spend a couple of minutes looking around in case there was anything else that might come in handy. Over by the door I saw a fireproof cabinet with a combination lock. Chances were it just held records that needed to be kept confidential, and hadn't been transferred to the computer system yet. A combination lock seemed like overkill over a little burg like Winter's Rage. But maybe, just maybe ...

It took longer to prise open than the gun safe. The irony of that wasn't lost on me as I strained to break the lock.

But the treasure inside was completely different.

I looked into what passed for an evidence locker in Winter's Rage. There was an array of plastic bags in there, some of which, I saw, contained small quantities of a variety of street drugs. It wasn't hard to imagine the sheriff confiscating stuff and letting someone off with a warning. Winter's Rage had always struck me as more of a meth place than a coke one, anyway. Plenty of old caravans hidden out in the wilderness around the old town, with a ribbon of dirt tracks leading everywhere and nowhere. It wasn't hard to imagine a ma and pa still out there, set up to run meth and moonshine.

There were a couple of guns, knives and other odds and ends. One very odd item, though maybe not for this part of the country. An old metal bear trap. A big one.

I took everything I might need, left what I didn't. And had one last look around. The damage I had done had been no worse than the mess the two Stooges had made before I had arrived. My prints were everywhere, but that couldn't be helped, even if it did put me in the frame for Jim Lowry's murder.

I headed back outside to find that the brief respite in the snow had given way to a full-on blizzard. It came down around me with a vengeance, cutting Winter's Rage off from the rest of the world.

50

"More coffee over here when you're ready, Maeve, there's a good girl," said Henry, sweet as pie.

She came over and filled two cups without a word.

As she was about to return to her other customers, Dale grabbed hold of her wrist. He might have looked like a weedy little runt, all skin and bone, but his body-fat ratio was way down in the low single figures. He was all muscle, and the muscles that corded around his bones were steel. She tried to pull away, but there was no way she was breaking his grip.

He squeezed tighter, fingers digging into the soft flesh of her arm. "You were in here when we were asking about a friend of ours, weren't you?"

She nodded. "Raelynn," she said, compliant. "Wayne Cardiman's daughter."

"That's the girl. Now, I've got a little question for you. Think carefully about how you answer. Have you seen her since she came back?"

Without hesitation, Maeve shook her head. She winced with pain as Dale dug his dirty fingernails in deep. "You absolutely sure about that?"

"Yes."

Henry looked into her eyes. She wasn't lying. "What about Wayne?" he asked.

"He hasn't been in for a couple of days."

"Is that so? And that's strange, is it?"

"People can come and go as they please. Nothing says they have to eat here."

"But does he normally eat here?"

She nodded. "Yes. He's a regular."

"And does he dine alone?"

She looked at him, and he could see the mental processes swirling away back there. She was considering a lie. He encouraged her not to. "Did you know when you lie your heart rate changes? You can't help it. And Dale here, he can feel the pulse hammering through your veins right now. Lie and he'll know. So I'm going to ask you again. Take your time. Does Wayne normally come in here alone?"

"No," she said. Nothing more than that.

"That's good, Maeve. That wasn't too difficult, was it? Now, how about a name? Who does he normally come in with?"

"Mike."

"That's half a name. Mike who?"

"I don't know."

"Stranger, is he?"

"He's been here a couple of months," she said. "Wayne was looking for someone to help him out. Building a cabin for Raelynn coming home."

"Good, that's really good, Maeve. So now, the big question, let's not fuck it up, where might we find this Mike?"

"He has a place up on the mountain somewhere."

Dale squeezed again.

Henry studied her. She was holding something back. He couldn't tell what. "Such a shame. You were doing so well," he said.

"I don't know. Please, you're hurting me."

Okay, so whatever it was that she knew, it wasn't where he was living. She wasn't trying to hold out on them. "Dale, let her go," he said. Dale did as he was told. Immediately Maeve rubbed the red marks his nails had left in her skin.

She waited until he nodded, dismissing her, before she moved away.

Still holding his Desert Eagle, moving it from one hand to the other, Henry eased out of the booth and swaggered over to where the other diners were sitting.

"Pop quiz, ladies and gents. Your prize, should you answer first, is the chance to walk out of that door." He indicated the street with the barrel of the gun. "So, best of luck. Your first question, where do I find Mike?"

Silence.

"Come on. Surely someone wants to get out of here alive. Really? At least one of you must know. This is a small town. You're all in each other's shit. That's just the way it is after generations of inbreeding, right?"

"There isn't a street address, not really, but some of the locals have given it a nickname," a woman said. Henry raised an eyebrow, waiting for her to explain. "He's in a shack on the mountain, maybe a mile or so from Wayne's place, same road, couple of turnings higher."

"Now, see, that wasn't too hard, was it? How about you go for a bonus round and draw us a nice map?" He plucked a paper napkin from the dispenser and flattened it out on the table in front of the woman. "I'm sure Maeve here will be able to lend you a pencil."

The waitress did as she was told, taking the stub of one from behind her ear and passing it to the woman.

Henry watched the short-order cook behind the counter. The man didn't have a heroic bone in his body. But he did make a decent burger.

A couple of seconds later the woman pushed a crude drawing over to him. He counted the turns. It ought to be easy enough to find.

Henry sauntered back to the booth where Dale sat with a grin as wide as his face.

"Looks like we've got our man," Henry said. "And how's this for priceless?" He pointed at the three words scribbled in pencil on the white paper. "They call it Dead Falls Road. That's just wonderful, if you ask me."

51

Even from outside I could see that something was off inside the diner. Every aura save two was a deep jaundiced yellow.

I was ready to take on Lowry's killers, but this wasn't the right battleground. Too many innocents, too much potential for collateral damage.

Only a psychopath thinks stuff like this is fun. As though I was crossing the road, I looked left and right, then pushed open the door to Maeve's place, letting the cold and the snow in with me as I went inside.

All heads in the diner turned my way.

The room fell silent.

"Mike!" Maeve said. All color had drained from her face. She rubbed at a red welt in her wrist.

"Maeve. Everybody okay in here?"

There was a babble of voices, everyone talking at once as though the pressure cap had come off the cooker and they were all desperate to be heard. I only heard two words, and they were Maeve's. "I'm sorry," she said.

"Nothing for you to be sorry about, ever. Are you okay?"

"I told them about you. I told them your name and where you lived."

"I gave them a map," Laney Daker said, getting to her feet like they were playing out that scene in *Spartacus*.

"And you didn't have to do that," someone else said, obvious disdain in their voice.

"They won't find his place using it," she said, proud of herself. "It led to the old coal mine."

I smiled.

"I can't pretend Raelynn's my favorite person, but it ain't right going after her and those little kids." I couldn't argue with that. "We need to get hold of Sheriff Lowry," the mapmaker said.

"The sheriff's dead." I didn't bother to sugar-coat it.

"Dead?" more than one person asked, the word becoming a question becoming a desperate hope for a different answer.

"I saw them shoot him. I couldn't stop it. Not from where I was. He didn't deserve to die like that," I said. It felt like I was trying to explain myself, to justify doing nothing, and absolve myself of guilt when I didn't need to.

"What about the third man?" Maeve asked. "There were three."

"Now there's two," I said, and left it at that.

"What do we do?" one of the old-timers said.

He had a red welt on his cheek beside his thick moustache. I assumed he'd been hit by one of the remaining Stooges. "You want my best advice? Stay safe," I said. "That's all anyone can do. Look, I don't blame any of you for telling those guys about me. You should have. Your priority, at every turn, is to stay safe and that means not antagonizing people like them. They're not normal."

"Who are they?"

"Bad men," I said, again not going into it. They didn't need the whole sordid tale. It wouldn't help.

I had a choice to make. I could either get to Wayne and his family, move them to safety, or I could go after the killers following them down that dead-end track to the old coal-mine shaft and finish this once and for all.

I took another look at the crude map, and saw they'd sent the killers two turns off the main drag too far. I could use that to my advantage. I knew where they were heading and I knew the terrain. They didn't. And they didn't know I was coming for them.

52

"I hate this place!" Dale growled, as the Cadillac came to a halt. A snowdrift more than three feet high had completely blocked the track that had been marked on the map. They stared out through the windshield as the wipers struggled and failed to cope with the snow. "So, what now?"

"Do I have to do *all* the thinking?" Henry said.

"You keep telling me it's your gig, so yeah," Dale said.

"You want to know what we do? We walk."

"We walk? That's it?"

"You need inspiration? Raelynn and her kids are on the other side of this snow. They're dollars and cents, dead. If her father's there, all the better. Maybe we'll even catch a break and get to finish that piece of shit who killed Caleb. It's only

snow. And, on the bright side, they probably think with the road blocked they're nice and safe up here on the mountain as long as they keep themselves tucked away. It's all good, man. All good. We put one foot in front of the other and we walk right on up to the ATM."

Henry killed the engine, pocketing the ignition key. The wipers fell silent against the glass. It took less than a minute for the snow to coat it so thoroughly it was impossible to see outside. "The longer we piss and moan in here, the worse it is out there. Let's just get this done so we can go back to civilization. I've had enough of this place to last me a lifetime."

"Amen to that," Dale said.

Heads down against the swirling snow, they had both retrieved their bags from the back and were ready to strike out.

The drift ahead of them looked fine and powdery. Too fine to support their weight, too high to wade through. It had been banked up by the snowplow driving through, which didn't make sense if there was a house at the end of the track they'd blocked off.

Henry shielded his eyes, trying to work out a path they could follow.

The trees on either side of the track offered precious little shelter from the worsening storm, nowhere near enough to shield the forest floor. It was covered with the same endless white as everywhere else.

This place was his definition of Hell. Not for him the rising flames. No, Hell was endless snow, ice and cold. Anyone who thought different didn't understand how bone-numbing cold was.

And here the pair of them were, again woefully ill-equipped to face the elements, in their new jeans and flannel work shirts. The snow got into their already wet clothing. The material clung to their bodies, exacerbating the chill factor.

"What are we waiting for?" Dale asked, itching to get moving. "I'm sure dear old Raelynn is dying to see us." The wind whipped away his words. He slung his pack over one shoulder, his thumb looped under the strap to hold it in place so that he could shrug it off in half a second, ready to fight. His other hand hung loosely at his side, his Glock already in his grip.

Henry led the way around the drift and through the margins of the woodland. With each step they took the snowfall seemed to ease a little. Perhaps they were just becoming inured to it. After all, there was only so much cold a man could take before it all became the same.

53

The wipers on Wayne's truck sluiced away snow and more snow, but there was no way they could swish back and forth fast enough to keep the screen clear. The weight on the blades slowed them down so much that even more gathered around them. The glass was never clear. It was like driving into a wall of white. Every sound was muffled. Dense. Distant. I couldn't hear anything beyond the *slump slump slump* of the wipers. Give it another few minutes and it would be impossible to see out.

I stopped the pick-up to clear the snow and give the wipers the chance to be more effective, at least for a minute or two before more gathered in its place. I was fighting a losing battle. I couldn't keep stopping to clear the blades. The only positive was that the two men I was hunting were suffering in the same way.

I couldn't imagine their Cadillac was much use in these conditions. The pick-up was four-wheel drive, and had a high wheelbase so it could plow through the worst the storm had to offer. The Caddy was front-wheel drive. It made a massive difference in the conditions. I figured they couldn't be far ahead of me. Not that I could see much of the road: I felt it rise ahead of me, but everything was so white it was impossible to see the incline.

I wound down the side windows in both doors so I had at least *some* visibility, even if it meant letting in the freezing cold and the churning eddies of snow. I craned my neck to get a better view outside, but the snow stung my face, making it impossible to focus as the icy cold brought tears from my eyes.

I knew the road like the back of my hand, which helped. There was a bend coming up: it was tight and, given the icy surface, the potential for losing control was great, but I couldn't afford to let my speed drop. It was all about momentum. Right now my wheels had traction—there was some weird physics going on: if I slowed, they'd lose what little grip they had.

I turned the wheel too late, too hard. The back end continued in the same direction it had been going. The pick-up started to slide. I had absolutely no control of the direction, but fought the wheel to try to reestablish any sort of influence over the spin, but physics again meant my frantic efforts were having little effect. The treads on the tires were choked with hard-packed snow. There was no way they could offer any grip as the road surface slid away beneath me. The world spun away viciously, end over end over end, forwards becoming backwards, backwards becoming forwards, and round again, as I wrenched at the wheel.

Then, with a sudden *thump*, the truck hit the bank at the side of the road and lifted onto two wheels, threatening to tip.

It was all instinct now. I leaned across, reacting faster than I had any right to, and used all of my weight to drop the pick-up back onto four wheels. That did not arrest the slide.

The truck hit the bank on the other side of the road with a bone-crunching impact, crumpling the wing and crunching the frame around the door, and this time there was nothing I could do to stop it. A moment later the world turned upside down as the pick-up rolled.

I gripped the wheel as fiercely as I could, glad for the belt cutting into my neck because it was keeping me pinned to the seat. Without it I'd have been thrown through the window, and out there anything could have happened.

My bag of tricks was flung around the cab. The stock of one of the weapons slammed against the side of my head then fell to lie on the roof of the cab. The pick-up stopped sliding and spinning.

I heard a strange noise, ticking like a time bomb, that my brain had trouble making sense of. The engine was still turning over. The wheels were turning uselessly in the air.

And there was the smell of gasoline.

My head was inches from the roof of the cab. The world through the window was inverted. I turned off the engine. The ensuing silence was almost deafening.

The gasoline reek grew stronger.

There was no way I was hanging about while the pick-up went up in flames. I fumbled around to release the belt, but the mechanism was jammed. Three tries and it still wouldn't come free. I didn't waste time with a fourth. I tangled my hand around the anchor in the steel wall of the cab, and tore it free, using every ounce of strength I possessed, enhanced and all.

Released, I slid down the seat to the roof.

The driver's door was jammed and no amount of kicking it would shift it. The passenger side was wedged tight against the bank, and the sheer weight of snow that had built up on it had come tumbling in. I reached back to grab my kitbag, then braced my back as I kicked out the glass of the windshield and crawled outside, wriggling beneath the hood until I was clear. I scrambled back up to the road.

I glanced back just once. The truck was a wreck. If Wayne had been pissed at a few scratches on the bodywork he'd be beside himself now. Well, I figured I was about to earn his forgiveness.

I was still a half-mile from the track the woman had marked on her hand-drawn map. All I could do was put my head down and walk into the fury of the storm.

54

"Is that it?" Dale asked, gesticulating through the endless snow with his gun to point vaguely in the direction of a smudge through the trees. It was more or less where the map had directed them, even though they'd been forced to hike further from the road than Henry had expected. The crude map obviously wasn't to scale. "Don't look like much to me," Dale added. "Don't know what I was expecting, but something ... bigger?"

Henry agreed. He had a bad feeling about this, nagging away at the back of his head. He trusted his instincts—they kept him alive more often than not—and right now they were screaming at him that something about this whole set-up stank. And with every step they moved closer to the shack the scream grew until it was howling.

No one lived in this godforsaken hole. The roof, or what was left of it, was covered with a thick layer of snow. A huge drift had built up along one side, like a lean-to shelter. The only window he could see was shattered, meaning it would be ice cold in there. This wasn't somewhere a guy could play house for winter, especially not with a couple of kids in tow. The snow covered any trace of footsteps leading to or from the doorway. If their intel was right, if Raelynn and her kids were inside the shack, they'd been there a long time.

"How do you want to play this?"

"Why play? We walk through the front door, all guns blazing. Let's just get it done. They can't see out—the only window's on the other side. So," Henry raised his Desert Eagle to his cheek, the muzzle pointing at the sky, "let's go make some noise." He dropped his bag beside a tree and led the way with a determined stride. Each step left him ankle deep in snow, but there was no way something so ordinary was going to slow him down now. He shivered against the cold, thinking wryly that it'd be the death of him. A dozen strides and he was at the door, Dale a couple of steps behind him.

Scorched earth. Shock and awe. That was what happened next. No messing about.

He took the briefest of breaths, holding it as he leaned back a fraction, then releasing it in an explosive exhalation as he planted the sole of his boot against the lock plate on the wooden door with as much force as he could muster. It gave way more easily than he had expected, splintering inwards. Rotten. His boot got caught up in a tangle of splintered wood as it fell away. Several splinters dug deep into his calf as he stumbled, spinning, flapping his arms like a fool as he tried not to fall.

Inside there was only darkness.

He saw a few shapes that looked like boxes.

There was no Raelynn. No kids, no old man, no fucking Mike. The boxes were stamped by some old mining company. Even in the gloom it was clear that not only were they not there but they had never been there.

"That bitch in the diner lied to us," he said.

"She's going on the list," Dale said. "One more killing. Let me have some fun with her first, mind."

"Whatever you want, dude."

There was a sudden groan and a creak that broke the otherwise silent air.

Henry didn't realize right away what was happening, but he backed off, moving quickly and just in time. Without the door in place, offering at least an element of support to the structure, the weight of snow on the roof became too great and the rundown shack collapsed in a flurry of splinters, filling the air with dust. It was almost comic.

Dale turned away coughing, one hand covering his mouth.

That was it. Henry couldn't help but laugh—it was all just so ridiculous. The anger inside subsided, but only for a moment. Then he remembered the smug look on the bitch back in the diner, thinking she'd gotten one over on them. "Looks like we might have to head back to town and nail her head to the table, make an example of her. You game?"

Dale nodded. "Oh, yeah. Can I nail something else to the table, too? Like maybe her ass?"

"Have at it. Who knows? Maybe then someone will tell us where Raelynn really is. You just know they're laughing at us. They all know where she's hiding with her damned kids, you just watch. Well, if they think they're getting away with dicking us about, they're in for one rude awakening." Henry grabbed his bag from the ground and slung it over his shoulder. He turned and headed back.

Dale didn't follow him immediately.

"What you waiting for?"

"Leaving him a message," the other man said, taking his dick out to piss in the snow.

Henry left him to it.

By the time he could see the Cadillac again he was way past starting to wish they had never taken this job on. Dale was a dozen strides behind, head down, rubbing his hands together to get the blood flowing. He looked like a drowned rat as he plowed through the snow. Henry waited for a moment to give him the chance to catch up.

There were no other signs of human habitation on the whole miserable mountain, as far as he could tell, but he couldn't see much beyond the end of his own nose. There was no sign of any paths or tracks leading away from the one he was on. Snow had reclaimed everything for Nature.

The sky wasn't as gray as it had been, and with the constant eddying, churning snow caught on the wind, it was possible to imagine that the world out there beyond them had simply ceased to be. A Florida devotee, Henry had never seen anything like it in his life. And, frankly, would be quite happy to never see another snowflake.

There was something in the air.

Its presence there was wrong.

He could taste it.

He couldn't see anything worth a damn, but his other senses were working just fine. He knew what it was on the tip of his tongue: smoke. He tried desperately to see through the falling snow, looking for the thicker gray.

And then he saw it; coming from somewhere beneath him on the mountain, the wind bullying it upwards and whipping it away. "You smell that?"

"Smell what?" Dale asked, nonplussed.

"Smoke. And where there's smoke there's fire."

"And where there's fire there's a junkie whore waiting to meet her maker," Dale said, grinning.

"You read my mind."

Henry started to walk down the hill, following the smoke.

"Aren't we going to take the car?" Dale asked.

He shook his head. "No. We don't want those fuckers to hear us coming."

55

Wayne stood by the window, watching the mountain for any sign of movement. He hadn't moved in hours. A deer had wandered past a little while ago, but apart from that he hadn't seen another sign of life out there. It was bleak. The bitterly cold wind blew across the land, churning up wave-like ripples in the snow. Visibility, looking into the heart of the snowstorm, was down to nothing. Less than nothing. The world was reduced to these four walls. And somehow he was supposed to protect his family, even when he couldn't see where the threats might come from. Despite protests from Raelynn about the cold, he had opened the window enough to slide the barrel of the shotgun through in case he needed to use it.

Raelynn huddled with the kids around the stove. She'd put a couple of extra logs in, and now it was roaring away, pushing out so much heat it almost kept the cold at bay. Almost. Wayne, still wearing his heavy coat, ignored the cold. He needed his hands free and unencumbered, so left his gloves stuffed in his pockets and relied upon his frostbitten hands to wield the gun.

He was ready.

He knew there was a good chance it would be the two strangers he saw striding through the snow, not Mike returning. He would pull the trigger without a moment's hesitation. He would do anything to protect his family. It was a lesson he'd learned the hard way, having failed to protect them twice when they'd needed him. The first time had cost him his wife. The second he'd lost his daughter—or thought he had. Second chances were hard to come by in this life. He wasn't about to miss the one he'd been given. He'd grab it with both hands. Or die trying.

The windowsill took the weight of the shotgun.

He watched.

He waited.

He watched some more, eyes never resting, searching out shapes in the snow, any sign of possible movement, any hint that they were coming.

And eventually he was rewarded by a dark shape moving toward the shack.

He felt his heart quicken and tightened his grip on the shotgun.

Only one figure.

It was carrying a shotgun.

Hurrying through the snow.

One figure. Not two.

Wayne's finger felt for the pressure of the trigger, ready to squeeze.

But he had to let him come closer first, or the shot would scatter harmlessly.

So, he waited.

His heart hammered in his chest.

He was conscious of every sound around him: the snap and crackle of the logs in the stove, the sniffles of the kids and the susurrus of falling snow. All of it.

The man didn't break stride.

He was coming fast.

Wayne counted down the yards, trying to judge the shot.

And started to squeeze down on the trigger, only to realize that it was Mike. He froze. This was the second time he had almost shot the man who was most likely to save them. Wayne was shaking as he withdrew the gun through the window and closed it, just as Mike walked in.

Mike dropped the bag he was carrying and leaned his gun against the wall. He didn't say a word. The first thing he did was snatch up the bucket of water that lay inside the door, kick open the stove door and toss the contents of the bucket onto the flames, dousing them.

The room filled with smoke and steam.

"What did you do that for?" Raelynn demanded, as she pulled the children away.

Water pooled on the floor beneath the stove.

"Because you can see the smoke that thing is belching out from miles away. It's like a giant finger pointing down at the shack from the sky, going, 'This is where they're hiding.' That's why."

"They know where we are?" Wayne asked.

Mike shook his head. "Not exactly, but they're close by, up by the old strip mine. But you can see the smoke from up there."

"Then we have to be ready to blow their brains all across the yard if that's what it takes," Wayne said, raising his shotgun. Realizing what he'd just said, he glanced at the kids. They didn't seem surprised or shocked at the idea of blowing someone's brains out. He didn't know what that said about their lives.

56

Henry saw the cabin through the trees. There was a moment when he thought he'd been mistaken about the smoke, that it was just an olfactory illusion brought on by the cold. That happened, didn't it? Hypothermic shock. You were meant to have hallucinations. And eventually feel warm instead of bone cold. Then you died. So, yeah, there'd been a moment when he'd looked up and the snow had somehow parted, blown this way and that to reveal a channel all the way down the mountain and there'd been no smoke.

And in that moment he'd been sure it had never been there, and that over the next few minutes he would stumble, then fall and lie in the snow slowly dying.

But it wasn't in his mind.

He saw a storm lamp burning through one of the windows, a single point of light that drew them down the hill faster and faster until they were running toward it.

There was no mistake this time.

This was the place.

They needed to work under the assumption someone had found the sheriff and tried to call in the state troopers. That meant moving with precision and haste, focus on getting out and far, far away before the snow cleared. He was motivated.

"Still want to go straight in through the front door?" Dale asked.

Henry nodded. "You stay in the trees. When I get to the door, shoot out that window." He pointed. "Just do me a favor and don't fucking miss, because my head is going to be alarmingly close to that and I'm fond of it right where it is." Dale smirked. "If anyone manages to get out past me, finish them. This goes without saying, don't fuck up."

"I got your back. Give me the nod, I'll take the window out. Anyone gets out, dead. Easy."

Henry tucked his Desert Eagle into the back of his jeans and delved into the holdall he'd lugged up and down the mountain. He pulled out a sawn-off shotgun and felt its weight in his hands. It was a beauty. He loved that piece. He studied the shack, still a little way off down the hill. The smoke was gone, snuffed out. He saw footprints leading up to the door. The lamp was still burning. He strained to see into the window, but it was too dark inside, and too far away to be certain, but he didn't think anyone was watching as he stepped out of the trees.

He started walking toward the door, keeping his stride long, slow and steady. He raised his hand.

The window shattered.

There was no time between the gesture and the explosion of glass.

Henry surged forward and kicked the door with the full force of his weight, momentum and anger, tearing it off the hasp and driving it inwards.

He fired into the darkness within without looking.

It didn't matter who was in the way of his bullets, everyone inside that shack was dead, or as good as, anyway.

Shock and awe.

He went in hot, that opening salvo buying him the precious seconds to get through the door and lay down some serious spray with the shotgun. He loosed both barrels into the cramped living room.

There was no return fire, no movement.

He couldn't believe his eyes.

"You have to be shittin' me," Henry said to the empty room.

But this place wasn't like the rundown old mining shack up the hill. There were signs of life everywhere, kids' toys on the floor, blankets, even a puddle of water beside the still-warm stove.

They were here.

They'd run.

But they couldn't be far away.

He needed to focus on that, on the positive, but he couldn't. This was all that Mike guy's fault. Rage swelled inside him. Uncontrollable. A black anger that consumed every thought, turning it destructive.

He snatched up the storm lamp that had drawn him and Dale to the shack, like a couple of moths, and hurled it at the sofa. Paraffin leaked out onto the cushions and seat covers. The flame held, burning bright. The smell was overpowering.

There was a soft *crump*, a noise unlike any other, and a moment later the whole thing was engulfed in flame. Henry didn't move. He stood there, basking in the heat, savoring it against his frozen skin, content to let the world burn if it just meant for one fucking minute he could feel warm again.

57

W
e were running for our lives. I'd bought us precious seconds, bullying everyone out of the shack less than sixty seconds before the window shattered and the door exploded inwards.

Sixty seconds. No time at all. Sixty seconds. All the time in the world.

The whole map ruse had been completely undone by the smoke, which had acted like a beacon, drawing the two men right where they needed to be. I cursed Wayne silently. It was stupid. People didn't think. None of them were making life—or clinging to it—any easier for me. I could have punched a wall, I was so frustrated with the idiocy of it.

Now we were on the run. Again. The difference this time, we'd run out of places to run to.

Wayne carried the boy, Chase, in his arms. He was wrapped in my blanket. The kid wasn't as much of a burden as his mother had been when I'd carted her through the snow, but he was slowing Wayne down just the same. Still, Wayne was making better ground than he would have trying to get the boy to wade through knee-deep snow. The kid had breathed in the steam and smoke when the water had been thrown on the fire to extinguish it, which left him coughing and hacking as Wayne carried him.

I ran with my bag of tricks slung over my shoulder and the police-issue shotgun in one hand, while Raelynn had grabbed Wayne's gun and held onto Anna with her free hand.

We'd skirted around the side of the shack first, sticking as close to the building as we could, so the overhanging roof provided shelter. The snow wasn't as deep there. Then once we were around the back, we struck out, heading in a beeline for the woodland, and into the trees once more. Not stopping, not looking back. Not for anything.

I heard the shot and the shattering of glass. It rang out across the mountain, echoing back to us with the promise of pain. They'd arrived much sooner than I'd anticipated.

We didn't have the luxury of time to think. I pointed in a direction, and we ran. It was as simple as that. And every step of the way I looked down at our trail, which might as well have been a mile wide, yelling, 'They went thataway …'

"Are the bad men here, Mommy?" Chase asked, from his blanket, but Raelynn was running too hard to be able to speak properly through her ragged breathing.

"It's just a game," Wayne said, trying to reassure the lad, but I could tell Chase didn't believe him.

"Then why are we running? When are we going back?" he said. "We left so quickly I couldn't get my hero."

I knew the figure he meant, a fake Superman clone kind of thing. He never let the little guy out of his sight.

"Soon," Wayne promised.

"This is as far as I go," I said, when we were well inside the trees.

Ahead of us the woodland grew denser. The blessing was that there was almost no snow on the ground. The light barely made it through the canopy of branches to the forest floor. An experienced tracker might be able to follow a trail through there, but we were being chased by a couple of city boys. They were anything but kings of the wild frontier. They'd follow the easiest track they could find, I was sure of that. And I intended to use it to my advantage.

I held out my hand and Wayne offered his in return. "Keep them safe," I said.

He nodded. "Break a leg," he said.

"I intend to do more than that."

"You're not coming with us?" Raelynn asked. I saw the fear in her eyes, the realization that they were going to be alone, and what it meant. "We can't do this without you."

"You won't be doing it without me," I promised her. "Trust me, the best thing I can do for you is stop Tweedledumb and Tweedledumber before they find you. And that means leading them a merry dance."

She shook her head. "We're better off together. If we separate we're on our own ... We can't help each other. If they find you they'll kill you," she said. The words came out in a tumble. Even in the dim light I could see the glint of a tear in her eye.

"Then I'll have to make sure they don't find me," I said, doing my best to sound reassuring. "Don't worry. I can take care of myself. I promise. Now get out of here."

I pointed them in the direction I needed them to go. It would lead them back to the road. They'd still have quite a hike to get back to Wayne's place, or all the way into town, and my job was to buy them enough time to do it.

I stood and watched them go.

Chase gazed at me over his grandfather's shoulder. He didn't take his eyes off me until they'd disappeared into the tress.

Once they were out of sight I reached into my bag and retrieved a hunting knife that I'd taken from the evidence locker of the sheriff's office.

I held the edge of the blade against my palm and felt its razor-sharp bite as I applied the lightest of pressure. It was enough to cut into my flesh. A bead of blood formed along the cut until it began to drip. I made a fist and squeezed. I needed to lay a trail they couldn't miss.

58

"That's one way to keep the home fires burning," Dale said. The cabin was a mass of flame and smoke, much clearer than the smoke that had billowed from its chimney earlier.

It wasn't exactly smoke signals, but if Raelynn and the others were lurking in the woods, watching in the hope they'd go away, maybe they'd get the message.

They were saying it loud enough.

Henry and Dale stood a dozen paces away from the fire. They could feel its heat, glorious on their skin, banishing the cold. The snow surrounding the shack had already started to melt, shriveling back from the burning timbers. It sizzled and fizzed as sparks flew from the rising pyre.

"I like fire," Henry said. "There's something cathartic about it. It purges. Cleanses. That life they had, gone. Up in smoke. Now it's only a matter of time before the flames catch and consume them. We are the fire, my friend, and we're going to hunt those fuckers down," Henry said. "They will burn."

"That they will," Dale agreed. "But don't forget about the bleeding. Bleeding is good, too." He rubbed his hands against the warmth, like a kid at a bonfire playing with sparklers, but as with all good things, the heat and their enjoyment of it had to end.

It didn't take long to find the trail leading away from the burning building. There were so many footsteps that it was impossible to count how many of them there had been, which meant all of them, even if he could see only one set of kids' tracks. He assumed they were carrying one of the brats.

The trail of footsteps was easy enough to follow even as they disappeared into the cover of the trees. Even where the lying snow became thin and patchy there were plenty of half-prints to steer them the right way. But the deeper they followed, the dimmer the light grew, and the thinner the dusting of snow on the ground became, making it harder and harder to find the next step and the one after that.

They were out of their element. This wasn't like hunting a tweaker through disused docks or abandoned warehouses or smoking out a crackhouse.

"Here," Dale said.

Henry looked where he was pointing.

In a patch of snow there was a splatter of red. It wasn't much, but it looked like blood. And it was fresh. Henry squatted down to get a better look, using the flashlight on his cellphone to illuminate it. His grin was feral as he looked up at Dale. "One of them's hurt."

"It's beginning to look a lot like Christmas," the skinny man said.

Just a yard or so away there was another drop, and beyond that another, teased out in a line, so small it would have been easy to overlook them. They were accompanied by only one set of prints that he could see. Adult. Male. Bigger than his own.

He tried to think what it meant, and the most obvious explanation was: "They've split up. I'll bet my life these tracks belong to that bastard Mike."

"Then we should look around for another set of tracks. He's not the target."

Henry shook his head. "No. We get that fucker first, for Caleb. Right? We end him, then there's nothing to stop us having some fun with Raelynn before we put her in the ground."

59

The old hunting stand had seen better days. I'd stumbled across it a while back when I was out exploring the woodland. Old habits die hard. I found it easily enough, despite the snow. The ladder that led up to the blind was missing a couple of treads, but it was still climbable.

When I'd asked Wayne about the hunting stand, he hadn't known what I was talking about and, given his familiarity with the mountain, I figured that meant it was rarely, if ever, used. Judging by the growth, I figured a lot of the trees around it had been much smaller when it was built, but now they blocked any view out into the open land beyond. I knew from memory there was a lake not far from where I was. Geese came in to land on it.

There was movement in the trees behind me. I stood stock still. I wasn't ready for them. I snatched up the shotgun and turned to face the trees where I had emerged only moments ago, barely managing to stop myself firing. It was that close a thing. Had my trigger finger squeezed even a little harder, any hope of my plan working would have been discharged right along with the shot because it wasn't either of the Stooges.

It was my friendly neighborhood deer, the one that regularly dropped by my shack at night. It looked at me with its big doe eyes before turning tail and disappearing into the woodland once more.

I was glad she was gone. I didn't want to think of her getting caught up in this, not once the bullets started flying. She was a creature of beauty. Majesty.

I squeezed at the cut in my hand, dripping out a few more platelets beneath the stand.

As long as the two men had fallen for the bait it wouldn't be long before they appeared.

I needed to work fast. We were talking minutes at best, seconds at worst. I had no time to spare. I started to dig at the bank of snow with my bare hands. I was maybe a dozen yards or so from the platform.

I worked fast, faster than I had ever done before, using all of my physical enhancements to push my body beyond the limits of normal men because, bluntly, so many lives depended on it. The snow had built up in layers and already crusted and frozen in places, but my fingers cut through it, shoveling great handfuls aside. I didn't feel the cold, didn't need to pause for breath.

Even when the hole was large enough, I didn't feel the burn of fatigue. I hadn't even broken sweat.

I stepped back and took a look at my handiwork. I had to be sure that the hole was large enough for what I had in mind. It would have to do. I turned my attention to my bag and the last of the things I'd liberated from the sheriff's office.

60

They emerged from the trees. Henry led the way, following the faint trail of blood into the clearing.

"What the fuck is that?" Dale asked, looking up at the platform in the tree. "A kid's treehouse? Weirdoes."

"It's not important," Henry said. "Focus. He's here. I can smell him."

"There's more blood." Dale pointed at the foot of the tree. He was right. There was another smear on the ladder, like the guy had forgotten he was bleeding and climbed it anyway. "You think he's up there?"

Henry shook his head. Too obvious. The platform would be an easy place to defend, and once they moved out from beneath its shadow, Mike would be able to pick them off if he was up there. But if they started to climb and he wasn't up there, they might as well paint targets on their backs because they'd be absolutely exposed, nowhere to run, impossible to hide, no chance of returning fire. Climbing that thing needed both hands. That blood trail was just too obvious. A step up. And a piss-poor one at that.

He scanned the vicinity, gaze moving from tree to tree, and across the drifts of snow, catching an anomaly in the ripples of white.

"There," he said, pointing to a discolored patch within a larger drift of snow. It was no more than a dozen yards from the tree, and had obviously been disturbed. What was doubly interesting about it was its size: it was big enough for a man to be hiding within.

He smiled. Got you.

It had the perfect line of sight to the ladder. Mike must have thought he was being really fucking clever. Well, he wasn't clever enough. This was what they did. And they were better than good at it. That was why they got paid the big bucks.

He raised a finger to his lips.

Dale went deathly still.

Henry raised his Desert Eagle. He couldn't stop the grin spreading across his face. He took a couple of steps closer. Dale mirrored him, his own gun at the ready. Henry nodded, once, twice, three times, and on the third the air filled with the sound of gunfire. Both men pumped shot after shot into the bank of snow.

A flurry of black feathers exploded into the sky as startled birds took flight from the treetops, the sound of their caws lost in the volley of shots.

And they didn't stop shooting until they'd emptied their weapons.

Henry stared at the snowdrift.

"Well, he's not walking away from that," Dale said.

"I want to see the corpse." Henry slammed a fresh clip into his gun. Not that he expected to need it, but it was habit.

He liked to stay prepared. Preparation was the key to a long and healthy life. Besides, he'd really hate to do the hard stuff, then turn around to face Raelynn's old man aiming a shotgun his way when he himself had no bullets in the clip. That kind of thing was amateur shit. It got you killed. Always expect the old lady in her rolled-down pop socks pushing the shopping cart filled with the detritus of a life badly lived to have a weapon stashed ready to put a hole in you. That kind of thinking kept you alive a lot longer than feeling sorry for the old bag ladies of the world.

Dale tucked his piece away and started to claw at the snow, eager to get at Mike's corpse. Henry was happy to let him do it. He kept his gun in his hand and slowly circled, looking around the clearing at the stand of dark trees and the shadows in between, making sure that no one was about to take them by surprise.

He had his back turned to Dale when the other man let out a scream, a deep belly-torn blood-curdling scream that dwarfed all of the gunshots they'd fired. He couldn't form words. He screamed. He pulled and pulled and pulled but couldn't get his arm out of the snow. The bank of white around him slowly turned red.

"What the fuck?" Henry ran to his partner, in that moment forgetting that Mike was out there, watching, or that he had a gun trained on them.

There was so much blood.

He couldn't understand what he was looking at until Dale's desperate struggles shook away enough snow to expose the bear trap buried in the snow.

61

I watched from astride a branch, high up overhead, my back pressed against the tree trunk. It was the perfect position to watch as the trap was quite literally sprung. It was also the perfect vantage point to make short work of the threat posed by the remaining Stooge. I held the pump-action sawn-off shotgun I'd liberated. It was the right weapon for the job. The trap had been a lucky find. I had no interest in knowing how it had ended up in evidence, but without it I'd have been in trouble. With it, well, there was blood.

He suffered. That was good. They'd rolled into town full of braggadocio, intent on causing pain to people I cared about. Now they were screaming. It was a fair turnaround. I hadn't heard a man scream like that since Afghanistan—an IED had taken his leg off at the knee among the dirt and dust. I'd fixed a tourniquet to stem the blood loss, but it hadn't stopped the screams. I had no intention of tying off the Stooge's wounds. I wasn't that forgiving.

The trap had almost completely severed his arm. There were a few tendons clinging to the bone. He wasn't going to be a problem for anyone ever again. His partner wasn't doing much to help him. I figured he had limited time before the body went into shock and all the processes of death kicked in if they didn't stop the blood loss. I lowered the truncated barrel, pausing for a moment before I pulled the trigger. It was a mercy killing.

But I almost didn't want to be merciful. Part of me would have delighted in prolonging his agony, in making sure he understood the depth of pain he had brought to the lives of others, and given him a chance to repent his sins before he met his maker.

But it was a really small part of me.

The man's chest exploded. It was brutal. It was ugly. It was fatal. His partner's face was splattered with blood. He staggered back in shock, not understanding where the threat was, or how the world had inverted on him so completely and utterly, turning him from predator into prey.

I pumped the gun and trained both barrels on him.

I could have ended it then, it would have been easy, but it wouldn't have been the end.

These guys were tools: someone else wielded them. It wouldn't end until I took the fight all the way back to the source.

"Throw the gun away," I called. "Make any other move and you'll be dead before you hit the ground. I know what you're thinking. You're thinking you've got that Desert Eagle of yours, you're fast, you're a trained killer, you can make the shot. And you know what? You just might. You just might get lucky, but even if you do, the spray from this shotgun, from this range, is going to shred you. Even if I'm dead, the muscle spasm will change the pressure on the trigger, and I can't possibly miss. So you're dead either way."

62

The man gave up his gun too easily for my liking. He dropped it. He didn't look around. Didn't look up.

"Kick it away," I said. "There's a good boy." I kept the truncated barrel of the shotgun trained on him. He wasn't going anywhere without a not-so-tender kiss. "Now, not that I don't trust you or anything, but same again with the piece you've got hidden. Finger and thumb. Nice and slow. Same goes for whatever ammo you've got on you. All of it on the dirt."

This time the compliance was more reluctant, which I was happy about. A second gun fell to the ground. A snub-nosed piece. "Now strip."

"Take my clothes off? In this weather? You've got to be kidding me," the man said. "I'll freeze to death. Just shoot me and get it over with."

"Don't be so eager to wish your life away. Take them off and throw them behind you."

The man did as he was told, shivering as he slipped off his blood-spattered shirt and threw it on the ground. He stood there topless, well defined muscles in a powerful upper body, waiting for me to tell him to ditch the jeans.

"Naked," I said.

"You're a real gent," he said. But he did as he was told.

I watched as he stripped down to his shorts, then pushed the bands of the boxers down over his hips.

"I would say there are no hidden weapons," I said, "But I guess it must be pretty cold. Turn around."

Again, he did as he was told.

I made him wait, hands cupped around his cock, as the cold ate into him.

He did his damnedest to defy the cold, but not in any way that could ever be meaningful. His entire body shivered as little tremors racked him. He was in a world robbed of heat. Even if he got his hands on one of the two guns in the dirt he'd be in no condition to level it, let alone fire an accurate shot, no matter how determined he was. The muscles were betraying him one cord at a time.

And still I made him wait, until the little tremors had become proper shakes. Uncontrollable muscle spasms.

"You're a bastard," he said.

I wasn't about to argue. "You want to put your clothes back on?" I asked.

He said nothing. He was nodding, but that could just have been the shakes gripping him.

"Knock yourself out," I said. "They're wet. The wet will do just as much harm. This isn't going to end well for you, you know that, right?" I said.

He looked down at the one-armed corpse. "Hard not to work it out," he said.

He wasn't yellow. There was plenty of light around his aura, his halo suffused still with the bile-filled red of rage. I was impressed. I'd expected him to be frightened by now.

Fear would come.

He hurried toward the pile of discarded clothes.

I took the opportunity to jump down from the tree.

The drop was even further than from the roof of the cabin Wayne and I had spent most of the autumn building. I landed just as lightly.

The hitman had his back to me and didn't see it. That only increased his surprise as he turned, holding his jeans, to see me standing there. His freezing fingers refused to obey him and couldn't manage the zipper. He looked at me as though he'd forgotten how the deadly laser beams in his eyes worked and he couldn't get them to burn me to a cinder no matter how fiercely he willed it.

"You're going to talk to me now," I said, the tone conversational, the threat lurking beneath the words anything but.

"Why the fuck would I do that?"

"Maybe I should just shoot you then," I said.

"Maybe you should." He gave up on the zipper and and shrugged into his wet shirt, pulling it tight around him. He didn't seem much of a big man now.

"Think about it for a minute. All you have to do is help me out here, then you're free to go home, leave all this behind you."

"Just get this over with."

"I understand," I said. "You're more afraid of what will happen to you if you go back to Florida without finishing the job, right? It's not professional pride, it's survival instinct. I can respect that. I also means that it doesn't matter what I threaten you with. In your mind what's waiting for you back there is much worse. So, I'm the prize behind door number three."

"Prize every time," he said.

"Well, then, how about you tell me who sent you for Raelynn?"

"Not a chance," he said.

"Not even if I say pretty please?"

"Look, man, no offense. You beat me. You're obviously good at this shit. But you aren't the kind of guy who'd pay someone else to kill a couple of kids. And that's what you're up against, and that's why you can't win this. Kill me, more will come. And keep coming."

"The kids?"

The man laughed. "Right, you didn't know. You thought all this was just to take down a junkie. Nah, man, they've decided they're going to make an example out of her and the kids. Make sure no one steps out of line again. We were meant to take pictures to prove the job was done. Take out the entire family tree. No survivors."

"I need a name," I said.

The man shook his head. "Not from me."

"Yes, from you."

63

"How the fuck am I supposed to climb up there with my hands tied?"

"Don't worry about that," I said. "Leave the practicalities to me. All you need to decide is if you'd rather go up the ladder, or trussed up, by the wrists, as I haul you."

"Are you nuts?"

"Hey, I'm just presenting the choice. I'd rather you climbed up, but I'm more than happy to help you out."

"Psycho," he said, shaking his head. The length of rope I had found in the back of Wayne's truck and added to my bag was more than enough for me to reach the platform before he had to start climbing behind me. His progress was slow and clumsy. It would have been quicker to pull him up, or knock him out and carry him up over my shoulder, but I didn't think the ladder would support the added weight.

He reached the top and dropped to the platform floor.

"You afraid of heights?"

"Not me," he said. "But you know the deal, not too keen on falling from them."

I nodded. "I'm going to have to leave you here for a while."

"I don't need a fucking commentary. You talk too much. Anyone ever told you that? Just do what you're going to do. Put a bullet in me now. Blow my kneecap out. Cut my balls off. Whatever it is you've got in mind, just get on with it. I don't get out of this," he said. "We both know that. Even if you turn all merciful and decide you have to let me go, I'm a dead man walking. Raelynn and the kids have to die for any other outcome."

"And you know I can't let you kill them."

"So, like I said, I don't get out of this. Everything else is just the spider playing with his food. And, frankly, it sucks."

I hadn't expected him to cooperate. And I could pretty much depend on him trying to escape. So, I did the only thing a reasonable man could do. I punched him. Hard.

He fell to the deck, all sense knocked out of him.

For all the bravado, I was reasonably sure he wouldn't be able to resist what I had in mind. I'd never met anyone who could.

64

I found the Cadillac abandoned beside a snowdrift blocking the track to the old strip mine. The keys were in the ignition. I took it and drove to Wayne's place.

There was no sign of any smoke coming from the chimney as I pulled off the road onto the narrower track that led down to his house. After the amount of crap I'd given them back at the shack, I figured they were just being cautious.

I walked toward the house slowly, making sure that Wayne had plenty of time to see me. Twice he'd come close to firing a nervous shot. I didn't fancy it being third time unlucky.

He came to the door. He wasn't holding the shotgun. "You okay?" he asked, relief obvious in his heavily lined face. He looked like he'd aged another decade in the last couple of days.

"I'm good. You guys?"

"Fine. The kids are wiped out. Rae's pissing and moaning about the cold. You know, all good stuff."

"Why don't you get some heat going then?" I said, with a soft smile.

He looked at me like he couldn't understand what I was saying. Maybe it was Swahili or something. Then it dawned on him, and it went from couldn't understand to couldn't believe. "It's over?"

I nodded. "It is." Which wasn't quite true.

"So, what happens now?"

"I'll be leaving soon," I told him.

"Leaving? Are you coming back?"

"I don't know. Maybe. But it's going to be easier if I'm not around when the authorities finally come to sort this stuff out. My prints are in Jim Lowry's office. I'll have killed three people. There have to be consequences, even when you're being a good guy. Don't worry, you can tell the truth. All of it. They won't be the only ones looking for me, and I'll have a decent head start."

"I'll tell them you saved us. They'll know. That will have to make a difference."

"You'd be surprised," I said. "But for now, it'll just be simpler if I'm not here. For everyone. If word gets out, other people will come looking, even though they know I'll be long gone. You don't want to cross these people, Wayne. Believe me. Just tell them what they want to know, with my blessing. You're a good man. And it's a damned shame we didn't get that cabin finished."

"Where will you go?"

"Better you don't know. Saves you having to lie."

I held out the bag for him. I wasn't going to need it and it would be better if I wasn't caught with it, all things considered.

"What's this?"

"The stuff I liberated from the sheriff's office."

Wayne raised an eyebrow, but then shrugged. "I'll find a way of getting it back where it belongs."

"Appreciate it. Look, I've got some bad news, too ..."

"Spit it out," he said, expecting the sky to fall.

"Your truck."

"What about it?"

"Pretty much a write-off," I said.

"It's insured," he said, not even a flicker of red around him. "You coming in?"

I shook my head. "Better not. I've got one last thing to take before I hit the road. Do me a favor, say goodbye to Raelynn and the kids for me. And tell them not to worry. They won't have to spend the rest of their lives looking over their shoulders. It's sorted."

"You got it."

We shook hands. I turned my back on him and started to walk away.

I was barely halfway back to the battered old Cadillac when I heard Raelynn calling my name.

I pretended I hadn't heard.

I could hear her running toward me.

I stopped and turned.

"You were going to leave without saying goodbye." It wasn't a question.

"I was," I said.

"Why? Why would you do such a thing?"

"I thought it was better that way."

"Better for who? For me? Or for you?"

"For all of us."

She shook her head, like she couldn't quite believe I could be so dense. "All I wanted to do was thank you," she said, and slipped one of her hands into mine. Her skin was soft and warm against the cold of my own. "I owe you that much."

"You don't owe me anything," I said.

"I owe you everything," she said. "I was hoping we'd find time for me to show my appreciation." She reached up and placed her other hand on my cheek. It felt good. She stood on her toes and leaned closer, our lips almost touching.

It was a bad idea.

It was always a bad idea.

But for once I didn't care. I closed the last few inches and our lips touched for a heartbeat. I felt her heat. And part of me really wanted to give in to it, just for a while. I'd forgotten what human contact felt like. Wasn't that the very definition of loneliness?

I pulled away.

"Is there something wrong with me?" she asked. "I'm clean. I swear. And this—"

I cut her off. "It's not you," I started to say, knowing I couldn't insult her with the next two words that always seemed to go with that brush-off. "Honestly," I said instead. "But right now you'd be best served giving your love to those kids. They need you, and they need you clean. Think about them and get yourself sorted out. You don't need a guy like me to validate you. You're beautiful, and I suspect there's a great person in there." I put my hand on her heart. "All you need to know is it's safe to let her come out. No one is going to be coming for you. Not now. Not ever again. I'm going to make the problem go away altogether. Just be strong for those kids." It was probably the most words I'd said to her. It was almost eloquent. It certainly wasn't the kind of speech you expected from a jarhead.

"You're right," she said. "I need to get off that shit, properly off it, go into a program, and maybe this is the place to do it. There's history, with Mom and everything. But I've also got friends here. So maybe I can turn it around."

"Only you can."

"Will you be coming back?"

I shrugged. "No promises."

"But you'll try?"

I didn't say no.

She waited, and in the end took my silence as the answer I meant it to be.

"That's good enough for me," she said.

She was still standing there when I drove away.

65

The clearing was absolutely still when I returned.

Not that I'd expected it to be a hive of activity, but I did think he'd have put up some sort of struggle. Not that he'd have been able to escape from his bonds anyway, and in these conditions no one was going to stumble upon him. Not that anyone would have been looking for him. A more reasonable fear was that the cold had finished him. Like the old saying went, dead men could tell no tales.

I clambered up the ladder, relieved to see that he was still there and that he was awake.

"You took your time," he said. There was still no fear, no anger in his flesh. He was resigned to his fate.

"Didn't realize I was working to a timetable."

"I heard a car engine."

"Did you think someone was coming to save you?"

"No."

"You're a smart man. I borrowed your Cadillac, hope you don't mind."

"Fuck you."

"Raelynn has told me the name of the man they ripped off."

"Bullshit she did."

"Now all I have to do is track him down and work my way up the chain. I'll find someone willing to talk. I understand you can't. Professionalism and all that."

"You're so full of shit." He laughed. Despite the futility of his position the man was still able to laugh. You almost had to admire him. "We took care of him before we even came here. As Dale would have said, 'I'm Obi-Wan to your Princess.'" I looked at him, not following. "I'm your only hope."

I shrugged. I had no reason to disbelieve him. "And you're not going to tell me without a fight?"

"I'm not going to tell you at all."

"Fair enough."

I slipped off my coat to show that I meant business, but not before I had removed a pair of pliers from my pocket; another treasure from Wayne's truck.

"What are you going to do with those?"

"Well," I said, like I was considering my options, "I've got a few choices. I *could* pull a couple of your teeth and expose the nerves. That tends to work wonders. It hurts. I mean really hurts. And the cold weather will only make it worse. I figure twenty minutes and you'll be crying like a baby, begging me to make it stop."

"You can't do that, man. That's not right."

"Not right? I think I like you. Despite everything, it's almost as if you imagine there's some code of honor at play here. Let me tell it to you straight, you've done worse. Live by the sword, die by the sword."

He shook his head violently, his lips squeezed tightly together.

"*Or*," I said, like it had just occurred to me, "I could pull out a few of your toenails. I've seen that done. It's surprisingly painful, and effective when you need to get the truth out of someone. There are a lot of things I can do. And, like you said, you won't talk, so I get to do them until your heart gives in."

I was starting to get to him. I could tell. There was a tinge of yellow to his hue now.

I was getting inside his head.

I wanted to make him remember all of the things he'd done to other people. I wanted him to realize that I was capable of all of them and more.

"You can't do that!"

"Why would you even think that? Seriously. There's you, there's me, but what I'm not seeing is someone here to stop me. You're not going to claim the protection of the Geneva Convention, are you? That'd be priceless." I drew the hunting knife from my belt. "Or, you know, come to think of it maybe you're right. Maybe I should just cut your balls off."

"You're crazy."

"No, definitely not that. But I am damaged. My old employers did that to me. So maybe we're not so different in a lot of ways. I'm just better." I held the edge of the blade to his cheek. I knew just how sharp it was: I could still feel the wound across the palm of my hand. I allowed the blade to make a cut on his cheekbone. Just once. Not deep, but deep enough to sting. He wouldn't be able to tell how superficial the cut was, only that he was cut and that he was bleeding into his ear. I did the same on the other cheek and paused as if to admire my handiwork. "You can tell people they're badges of honor when you're inside."

"Inside? What the fuck are you talking about now?"

"Well, I've been thinking about it, and I appreciate the bind you're in. You're just doing a job. It's not personal. And right now you really wish you hadn't taken your boss's money. So, there's a little piece of me that thinks, But for the grace of God, and all that. But there's another part of me that frankly thinks it'd be pretty fucking apt if the guys you failed got to pay you a visit in Supermax. Maybe they'll think you've cut a deal, sold them out, set the sniffer dogs on their trail. Maybe they'll decide to cut their losses with you, or think you'll make somebody just the perfect bitch. So many possibilities."

"Just kill me now!"

I made another couple of cuts, deeper this time. "Tell me what I want to know. I'll make it fast. Not only that. I'll make it painless. You're dead already, if it's me or them. We're both men of the world, we know this to be true. So what does it matter if you cough up the name? There's no point torturing yourself to die in an hour or two or even a day or a week. Sometimes the only thing you can do is face the grim truth. You fucked up. I'm the reaper. That's my pitch. You buying?"

He fell silent, contemplating his options, as if he hadn't already spent enough time stewing over them. I didn't figure he was playing for time: it wasn't as though an extra minute was worth holding out for in his position. I drew the knife across one ankle, then the other, deep enough to sever the tendons. He wasn't walking away from here, literally or metaphorically.

He gritted his teeth, biting down against the wave of agony that came with the first cut. On the second he screamed, and as he tried to fight back against the scream, bit deep into his tongue. It was so much worse than it might have been if he'd just spilled his guts when I asked nicely.

I looked at him dispassionately. "I am very good at this," I promised. "Better than you. Are you ready to really scream?"

He shook his head. Blood smeared his lips and dribbled down his chin.

"Viktor Krip," he said.

"That's better. Why on earth couldn't you have just come out with this earlier and saved yourself a lot of suffering? Now, where might I find him?"

"Miami," he said. "That's it. That's all I know. There is no more. I don't know where he is. I don't know who's next in the chain. None of it. He was my point of contact. A voice on the phone. That's it."

I believed him.

He'd given me everything he knew.

"Thank you." I drew the knife across his arm, cutting up, from wrist to inner elbow, and the blood began to flow.

He was done.

It would take time, but not long, and with the storm coming in, he'd be food for the woodland fauna.

"Bastard. You said you'd kill me."

"And I have. You won't survive this. It'll stop hurting soon enough. You'll even start to warm up as you slip into unconsciousness."

I stood up, fished out my burner phone and took a photograph of him to join the macabre gallery I'd already assembled in the phone's memory.

66

The executive suite of the Four Seasons Hotel, Miami, was the height of decadent luxury with its jaw-dropping view out over Biscayne Bay. It was winter still, but winter here was nothing like winter back where I'd come from. The temperature outside was still close to eighty degrees. Thankfully the air-conditioning kept that at bay by providing a welcome chill.

It was the kind of place where the guests didn't have to ask how much something cost. They could afford it or their expense accounts could.

A thick-set man in a dark suit read the sports section of the morning edition. There was a knock at the door. He folded the paper and put it down on the coffee-table. He moved easily, but not quickly. He was a big man. Ex-football player. Some folk down in the lobby might even have recognized him. Whoever stood on the other side of that door could wait for him. This might not be his room, but he remembered the days when it had been, and so much more, when he had the world in his hands and all he had to do was run with it.

"Room service," the voice on the other side of the door called.

He hadn't ordered anything.

He used the security peephole in the door. He saw a man in a hotel uniform. His features were distorted by the fish-eye lens. He didn't recognize the guy, but that was hardly surprising—the hotel had so many staff he couldn't possibly keep track.

He opened the door and stepped aside to let him in.

He faced down the business end of a SIG Sauer P230. He was in no doubt that the man holding it was prepared to use it. He'd met men with desperation in their eyes, men whose fingers were as likely to pull the trigger by accident as they were intentionally. The man in front of him was not one of those. The man in front of him was in control of the situation, of himself. He was used to handling a weapon.

"Why don't you turn around, find yourself a seat, take a load off?" Byron Tibor said. "I'd like a quiet word with your boss."

Instead of turning, the man went for the gun. He was fast. That had been part of his appeal as a player. He was just quicker than the rest. He had better reflexes.

But Byron was faster.

In the instant that the man lunged, Byron pulled the gun aside and swung his other hand, slapping him hard on the ear. It was a brutal hit, hard enough to deafen him. The bodyguard staggered a step back, head reeling, then fell to his knees as the butt of the SIG Sauer slammed into the other side of his head. He pitched face forward into the expensive carpet.

Byron stood over him. He eased his legs apart with his boot, and drove a savage kick up into the bodyguard's testicles to make sure he wouldn't be getting up any time soon.

67

I t had taken me longer than I'd have liked to track him down, longer still to get into the suite, but I hadn't expected his fancy football-player henchman to be quite such a soft touch. A case of reputation rather than ability.

I grabbed the guy by his jacket collar and hauled him onto the sofa with one hand. In almost the same motion, I slipped the tiny bugging device I'd brought with me from my pocket and fixed it to the wooden surface underneath the coffee-table.

"Do you want to tell me what you're doing to him?" a man asked, emerging from one of the suite's three bedrooms. He took my presence in his stride, glancing down at his insensate bodyguard who still clutched at his groin. He did not speak to him. "And for that matter, just who do you think you are?"

"Doesn't matter who I think I am," I said. I shook my head. "I've come to give you this," I said, and fished a small envelope from inside the jacket pocket of my borrowed uniform. I dropped it onto the coffee-table in front of him.

"What is it?"

"A present. Don't worry. It won't bite. Why don't you open it and take a look inside?"

He lifted the flap and tipped the contents out onto the table.

"Sorry about the quality," I said, "I had to take them on my phone. And it's a cheap piece of crap."

"Why are you showing me these?" he asked, as he spread the three photographs on the glass top. There was no emotion on his face, none to his halo, either: no anger, no fear, not even disgust.

"Caleb Jacobs," I said, pointing at the first of the pictures. The head of a man whose face had been blown away. "Sadly for him, I was only able to identify him from the contents of his billfold. If that was stolen and I've given him the wrong name, I apologize. He wasn't a good man. Jacobs served time for robbery with violence and was wanted on several counts of aggravated assault. It would seem he enjoyed the violence more than the robbery."

"I still don't understand."

"The second man is Dale Pasternak, wanted in three states that I know of for murder and crimes of a sexual nature. This guy was a piece of work."

"I'm really not following. What have any of these men got to do with me?"

"If you take a look at his arm, you'll see he had a bit of a problem with a bear trap," I said, ignoring his question.

He looked up from the picture and, for the first time, showed a flicker of emotion: surprise.

"Now, the third man is more interesting. That's Henry Dalhousie. Henry's the real pro in the group. The other two were just psychos he picked up along the way, but he was the real deal. He once killed three fifteen-year-old girls because they cut up his car on the road."

"More than a little excessive," he agreed. "But I'm not sure that makes him any worse than the other two, does it?"

"He cut their feet off and watched them bleed to death while they tried to crawl away from him. That's just one thing in his jacket. There's a lot of other stuff in there, and it makes for pretty grim reading."

"Judging by the fact you keep using the word 'was', I'm going to assume you killed them and that these are your trophy shots. But here's the thing. I'm still not clear as to why you're here. Care to enlighten me?"

"That's easy. I'm here to give you a message."

He inclined his head, making a show of listening.

"You hired these men to kill someone. A woman by the name of Raelynn Cardiman."

"I think you're mistaken."

"I'm not. It took almost two hours of pain before that man gave up your name. You might have known her by a different name." I jabbed a finger at the last photograph, which revealed the injuries I had inflicted on him.

He shrugged. It was the smallest thing, but in that moment I knew he was no better than the three men I had left dead on the mountain in Winter's Rage. "Have you come here looking for a job? Is that it?"

"No, I've come to tell you to leave Raelynn and her family alone."

"You come into my home to threaten me?" He laughed "Now that's rich."

"You've got me wrong. I haven't come to threaten anyone. What I'm proposing is we draw a line under it."

"Elspeth, Raelynn as you call her, owes me money. A lot of money. Are you here to pay off her debt?"

"Chalk it off as an expense," I suggested. "The cost of doing business with a junkie."

"It's not my call."

"Then make the call up the chain. That you can do. Sell the idea of peace, hard, to your boss. Because if I hear that Raelynn or her family or anyone else in Winter's Rage has been killed, I will come looking for you. I know that you're answerable to other people. I get that. It's business. That's the way the world works. But I'll hold you personally responsible. And you don't want that. So convince the next man in the chain she's not worth it."

He drummed his well-manicured fingernails on the arm of the leather chair he'd sat in and looked me in the eye. I still held the gun, but was no longer pointing it at anyone. His ex-footballer was in no shape to make a move.

He sighed. "Are you sure you don't want a job?"

"I'm sure."

"Shame."

"Do we have a deal?"

"Do I have a choice?"

"No," I said.

"Then we have an arrangement," he said.

That was all I had come to hear.

68

"**W**hat the *hell* were you thinking?" His voice carried. The man was incandescent. "How could you let someone like *that* get in here?" Viktor wasn't in the habit of being submissive. This was his temple. Within these walls he was used to being worshipped. He was a god.

Let the useless son of a whore feel his wrath.

The man tried to mumble an apology, but the words could never be enough against his fury. There was nothing he could say that Viktor wanted to hear. He hated incompetence. His world was built upon a foundation of strength. Concrete and steel. It should have been a simple job. Elspeth White was nothing. Less than nothing. She was inconsequential. And she was a thieving cunt. But that was by the by.

"Make yourself useful, pack my bag," he snarled. "Everything. We're leaving. Let's see if you can get *that* right."

He watched the man get unsteadily to his feet, then head through to the ludicrously expensive bedroom. Viktor found no comfort in the place now. It wasn't a refuge or a place of release. It was reduced to four walls. He looked around. He would miss the view, if nothing else. But there were other places. He would find a new home.

The man who'd just walked out on him was more capable than any of the fools he'd wasted his money on. Well, that ended now.

Viktor needed to make a call. He had to reach over the fan of macabre photographs for his cell. He had no interest in looking at the images of the dead. They were where they deserved to be. But there had to be a reckoning. No one got away with slapping their cock across his face. The man, whoever he was, was going to have to pay for this. That was just the way it worked.

He made the call. "It's me. I've just had an uninvited guest. The men we sent to sort out our Elspeth White problem let us down. Badly."

He listened while the voice at the other end reflected his own anger. "That won't be necessary," he assured him. "They are already dead."

In a way that was a disappointment.

It was always good to look into the eyes of the dying in that last moment: it was said you could steal a little of their soul for your own. Not that he believed the hoodoo voodoo bullshit. He just liked watching men die.

"Yes. He managed to get in here dressed as a bellhop. It was ... unfortunate," he said, looking at his bodyguard as he delivered that damning indictment. He told the voice on the phone about the man's threat, and assured him that there was no way he was going to take that lying down. "Whoever he is, I'll take care of it," he promised. "I just thought that in the spirit of our arrangement you should know exactly what was happening. I know how you hate surprises . . . Yes. You too. See you soon, Uncle."

He ended the call and put the cell down on top of Henry Dalhousie's tortured corpse.

There would be a reckoning.

When he got hold of the photographer he'd regret getting some skin in the game. And when he'd dealt with him, he'd make the drive to Winter's Rage himself and put an end to Elspeth, Raelynn or whatever the fuck the junkie called herself now. He'd look her in the eye and steal her soul.

This was his home. He'd liked it here. And now he was going to have to start all over again.

69

The parking garage beneath the hotel was virtually silent. One car was just leaving but, apart from the fading noise of its engine echoing in the concrete confines of this underworld, the only other sounds were the *click-clack* of the man's heels and the squeak of his suitcase wheels as it rumbled along.

I'd guessed right: Viktor didn't trust the concierge driver who was available to park and collect his Mercedes S Class.

The sounds stopped suddenly. I heard the click of the lock disengaging as the bodyguard popped the trunk.

Even before it was open far enough for him to see inside I fired two shots into his chest, the suppressor on my SIG Sauer reducing the sound to a *phut-phut* that was ludicrously tame considering it had snuffed out the man's life. Even so, the double-tap sound still seemed to echo around the garage.

I saw the look of surprise on his face change to shock, then understanding, but none of it mattered as far as his body was concerned. He fell.

I saw the man behind him.

He understood what was happening.

His cool, calm exterior melted away as he started to run, his steps echoing impossibly loudly in the concrete hell he suddenly found himself in.

I took my time, climbed out of the trunk, and raised my gun. I didn't say anything. There was no need. No words could ever have been adequate, anyway.

I was disappointed he didn't turn and fight. I'd expected more from him. I walked calmly in his wake, my footsteps deliberately measured, echoing so much more loudly than his.

And he ran faster. He cried out as he turned his ankle, a sickening snap accompanying the sudden break as the heel of his shoe came off. It didn't stop him. He kicked the expensive shoes off and sprinted barefoot for the stairwell and the promise of air, light and Heaven up above.

He was never going to make it.

Not to the light.

His kind had no place in Heaven.

I took a breath and squeezed down on the trigger once.

His arms raised in surprise. Or surrender. Or both.

It didn't matter.

By the time the second bullet took him between the shoulder blades he was already falling.

His wallet lay open at my feet where he'd dropped it.

I stuffed the SIG Sauer down the back of my jeans and untucked my shirt to cover it, then stooped to retrieve the wallet while he lay bleeding out.

Inside I found his cell-phone.

He hadn't set up a pin code or fancy fingerprint lock. I pressed the home key and the screen lit up. It was hubris. He couldn't imagine something as personal as his phone—which contained all of his life—falling into the hands of an opponent. And yet here we were.

I thumbed through the call log, tapped on the most recent one.

"What do you want now, Viktor?" the voice on the other end said.

"I'm sorry, Viktor can't come to the phone," I said.

"Who the fuck is this? Where's Viktor?"

"Uncle, Uncle, is that any way to talk to the man he warned you about?"

"I asked who you were."

"I've always wanted to say this," I said.

"Say what?"

"Names are not important."

"Bullshit. I want to know your name so I know what to put on your tombstone. Now put Viktor on the phone."

"I told you. He can't."

"What have you done to him?"

"I can send you a picture if you like? A picture's worth a thousand words. Isn't that what they say?"

"If you've hurt him, I'm going to make you wish you'd never been born."

"You're way behind the curve on that, Uncle. There's a line a mile long with the same idea. But here's the thing, I'm nothing if not a man of my word. We had an agreement, or at least I *thought* we had. That was good enough for me. I'm traditional like that. My word is my bond. I'm nothing without my word. I thought he'd be the same way, given your line of business. But then he had to go and make it obvious he had no intention of honoring our agreement the second I walked out the door."

"He wouldn't do that."

"Cut the bullshit. He's a better liar than you."

There was silence for a moment as the man considered this. "You bugged the room." It wasn't a question. A man thinking out loud when he had worked out the only possible answer to a problem. "What do you want?"

"You already know what I want. It's the same thing I've wanted from day one. I want you to leave Raelynn Cardiman—Elspeth White to you—and her family alone. I want you to stay away from them."

I didn't bother waiting for the response.

I had delivered the message.

I took a photo of the man where he lay, a pool of blood slowly turning into a halo around his body that had nothing to do with anger and sent it to the same number.

Even before I had slipped it back into his wallet, the cell-phone rang.

I didn't bother to answer it.

We were done here.

70

Winter's Rage was on the verge of another storm, worse by far than the last. This one would continue all winter long. The locals called it The Rage. It came every year, like clockwork.

Higher up the mountain the snow had been lying for a couple of months. It wouldn't melt until the spring thaw. The roads were passable with caution, mainly thanks to Jim Burges's snowplow, which was in action every day without fail. Most of the narrower and rarely used lanes off the main drag needed to be excavated before anyone would be able to use them.

A new sheriff had been appointed from out of town. Life went on. It was what happened in small towns like Winter's Rage. There was an investigation into Jim Lowry's murder. Or there had been. It was closed from on high.

There were a couple of strangers still unaccounted for, and Mike Roberts. He'd run. Never a good sign, yet, weirdly, most of the towns-folk hoped he'd be back one day because, no matter what the lawman said, Wayne Cardiman and Raelynn insisted he'd saved their lives, and those precious little kids', and that was good enough for everyone who was anyone in Winter's Rage, where they took people at face value. The other two would turn up, one day. When the mountain surrendered them.No one was in any sort of hurry to find them.

The door to Maeve Cruikshank's diner opened. A man shuffled in. He unbuttoned his coat, allowing snow to fall from it onto the "Welcome" mat, revealing a gun at his hip. He kept his hat pulled low, obscuring his face as he slid into one of the booths.

"Coffee?" Raelynn asked, moving up beside him. She looked like she was born to the job. She smiled at all the customers, even those who gave little more than a grunt her way. But, best of all, she was clean and she was happy.

The newcomer tipped his hat back further on his head and raised a finger to his lips, smiling a smile that could have brought all the snow down from the highest peaks.

"Mike," she whispered, barely able to hide her happiness at seeing him. "I knew you'd come back. I told Dad. I just knew." She put the coffee pot down and slid onto the bench seat opposite him.

"I'm not staying," he said, taking all the joy out of her in three little words.

She shook her head, not understanding. "Then why are you here? People are looking for you."

"People are always looking for me," he said. "But I said I would try to come back and here I am. Call it unfinished business, if you like."

She reached out and placed her hand over his. "I knew you'd come back," she said again.

He didn't pull away from her, even though he knew he should. There was no point in giving false hope now any more than there had been when he'd left a few months ago. "How's Wayne?"

"He's good. He's loving being Grandpa. It's given him a whole new lease of life."

"You seen the cabin? There's still plenty to be done on it, but hopefully he'll be able handle most of it now the heavy lifting's been done. Who knows, maybe you'll be in there for spring?"

She nodded, genuine tears in her eyes this time, not the crocodile ones she'd shed for him the last time. "It's going to be great."

"I know it is. You deserve it. Look at you. You look good, Rae."

"It's great to see you," she said.

He smiled at that. "You too."

"So why did you come back? Not just because you said you'd try."

"To tell you that it's finished. No one else is going to come looking for you."

"I don't know what to say."

"Believe me, you don't have to say anything. Just promise me this. Promise me that from here on out you'll live your life properly."

"I can do that," she said. "Thank you." She squeezed his hand, but there was a sadness in her smile now. She knew this was goodbye. Once and for always.

He rose from the bench seat, touched a finger to his lips and rested it on her cheek, a small moment of tenderness that broke her heart into a million tiny pieces. The good thing though, she knew, was that it would heal stronger for having broken because that was what hearts did.

He pulled his hat down again and headed for the door, raising a hand in farewell.

She watched him go.

Outside the snow began to fall, thick and fast. There was hardly any traffic in the street. It wouldn't be long before the town of Winter's Rage was cut off, but he would be long gone by then.

ALSO BY SEAN BLACK

The Ryan Lock Series in Order

Lockdown (US/Canada)

Lockdown (UK/ Commonwealth)

Deadlock (US/Canada)

Deadlock (UK/Commonwealth)

Lock & Load (Short)

Gridlock (US/Canada)

Gridlock (UK/Commonwealth)

The Devil's Bounty (US/Canada)

The Devil's Bounty (UK/Commonwealth)

The Innocent

Fire Point

Budapest/48 (Short)

The Edge of Alone

Second Chance

4 Action-Packed Ryan Lock Thrillers: Lockdown; Deadlock; Gridlock (Ryan Lock Series Boxset Book 1) - (US & Canada only)

3 Action-Packed Ryan Lock Thrillers: The Devil's Bounty; The Innocent; Fire Point (Ryan Lock Series Boxset Book 2)

The Byron Tibor Series

Post

Blood Country

Sign up to Sean Black's VIP mailing list for a free e-book and updates about new releases

Your email will be kept confidential. You will not be spammed. You can unsubscribe at any time.

Click the link below to sign up:

http://seanblackauthor.com/subscribe/

9 781909 062597